Advance Praise for *Chasing Rhinos*:

"*The award-winning book, the Accidental Audience, began the adventure of an ex-police officer's journey of self-discovery while solving criminal cases. Second in the series, Chasing Rhinos, is even better as readers delve deeper into the main character, her relationship issues, and new mysteries to solve on an international scale. Well worth the read—kudos to the author!*"

—BRIAN MCCULLOUGH, AUTHOR,
On the Edge of Now science fiction series

"*This story will take you around the world with anticipation and adventure! Wood's writing style made it difficult to put down the book until I reached the back cover, and drooling for the next book has already begun! I used to think James Patterson was my favorite author—however, he may have to move over, and get out of Wood's way!*"

—ROBIN HAVLICEK

"*Truly, a must read! Compelling and insightful, Faith Wood's Chasing Rhinos provides an in-depth understanding of the human psyche in her latest Colbie Colleen mystery. Suspense builds quickly, drawing the reader in as the end of each chapter piques curiosity for the next. If you like Sue Grafton, you're gonna love Faith Wood!*"

—JOAN BELL
Entrepreneur

Chasing Rhinos

Layne I'm so grateful to know you in my life :) With Love & Friendship Faith

Chasing Rhinos

a Colbie Colleen suspense novel

Faith Wood

Double Your Faith Productions
Vernon, British Columbia, Canada

ISBN: 978-1523349029

ISBN: 1523349026

Printed in the United States of America

DEDICATION

From time to time, our travels may leave us speechless—but only until we magically weave those experiences into wonderful stories, polished and honed, so we can share them time and again.

I'm grateful for the opportunities contributing to the stories I share with you. For me, travel isn't about escaping life, but rather about preventing life from escaping me.

I hope you will feel the same.

.

CHAPTER ONE

Recovery is always a crapshoot no matter what the doctors say. Colbie learned that lesson the hard way, and Brian was in the throes of learning the same thing, albeit slowly. Three years faded to memory since his kidnapping and subsequent freedom—but, if she were honest, he wasn't bouncing back like she thought he would. She expected him to be strong, admirable, unwavering—all the things she knew and hoped he could be. Perhaps her expectations were unreasonable as she watched him go through the motions of living a normal life—but he didn't fool her. He was different. His spirit was different. His soul, empty.

Yet, helping him was a sensitive and complex matter involving cognitive, emotional, and social implications. Expecting anything other than a roller coaster recovery was wishful thinking and, as much as she hoped for something more promising, it wasn't to be. His memory and concentration faltered frequently—as did his ability to deal with flashbacks—although he refused to admit he was different. Venomous denials entered into most conversations and Colbie feared his retreat into a chasm so deep would render him unable to return.

She didn't blame him—all of her training in victim psychology and therapy told her he may never recover from his ordeal. There were days when he switched off emotionally, exhibiting a lingering hopelessness unlike his personality before the kidnapping. Throughout the last three years, his personality morphed from loving and kind to disengaged and aloof. Of course, he scheduled appointments with a therapist as soon as he was strong enough, but progress was slow. Always irritable, his weight gained ground, but he was fragile in body and mind, and he no longer wanted to meet friends for dinner, or hang out with her to cozy up and watch a movie on a rainy Friday night.

In what she could only consider a desperate move, Colbie considered reaching out to his parents even though she was fully aware doing so was a futile attempt. According to Brian, they were on an Alaskan hut trip lasting at least three months. From there? Who knows? Colbie wasn't exactly sure what the hut trip was, but she was pretty sure it would be difficult to get in touch with them. Brian's parents were 'finding' themselves in an attempt to renew their love for each other, reliving their early years by traipsing across myriad continents. *Well,* she thought, *at least they're getting off their asses and doing something—it's a hell of a lot more than we do!* Perhaps an ugly thought, she had to admit Brian's lackluster existence was beginning to get on her nerves.

She thought about contacting Ryan to discuss Brian's recovery, but, since he moved to the East Coast just after the kidnapping thing, he wasn't in their lives anymore. It was a sting Brian refused to discuss, but Colbie knew Brian's best friend's non-communication was a deep-rooted hurt her boyfriend had trouble accepting. He couldn't make sense of it—a friendship of more than two decades simply disintegrating for no apparent reason? He could understand it if something happened to fracture their relationship but, as far as he could tell, there was nothing.

"Want some coffee?" Colbie pushed her file folders to one side of the diminutive table, making room for Brian's cup as he pulled out a chair.

"Sure—sounds good."

She watched as he tasted his coffee, then added just the right amount of sugar. "So, what do you have planned for today? I have to do some research at the library, then I'll be free . . ."

"I don't have anything planned, so whatever you want to do is fine with me."

And that's the way it was for the last eleven months— zero interest in doing anything. "Okay—I'll be back around two so, if you think of anything, just let me know."

"Check . . ." He opened the paper to the funnies, intent on shutting her out.

Fine, she thought, grabbing her coat from the hook by the back door. *If that's the way you're going to act, take it somewhere else . . .*

Frost laced the window panes of the door, but not enough to compromise her view of Brian as she glanced back.

He never looked up.

Chapter Two

Nearly six months in the making, her office space was exactly as she pictured it—comfortable with just the perfect amount of professionalism. When Colbie first entertained the idea of setting up her own psychological and behavioral profiling practice, she envisioned a tiny, hole-in-the-wall office, its walls a professional library lined with resource books. Nothing expensive. Never did she consider a sleek office sporting all the latest technological accoutrements—back then, she considered a working laptop her best friend. Now? She had everything a professional needed, including an assistant, thanks to a couple of successful high profile cases within the last two years. And, the move to the East Coast was exactly what she and Brian needed. After Brian's kidnapping, her subsequent investigation, and the apprehension of high-ranking police officials, she and Brian needed a change of scenery.

She hoped.

Without looking up, she felt her assistant standing in

her office doorway. "Tammy—do you remember that case a couple of years ago—in Europe, I think—that had to do with stolen art?"

"I think so—in Rome. Why?"

"I don't know—but, for the last couple of weeks, I keep thinking about art."

"What type of art?"

"You know—the expensive stuff."

"You? Expensive art?" Tammy laughed as she raised one eyebrow in a dramatic arch.

"I know, I know! What I know about art is next to nothing!"

Tammy smiled as she watched her boss scribble notes on a yellow legal pad. From the time Tammy and Colbie met during the investigation of Brian's kidnapping, she respected her boss's intuitive senses. She would never forget the day Colbie suspected something was wrong with her and, rather than sit on her butt wondering about it, Colbie arrived on her doorstep, knocked, and waited. Her face swollen and bruised, Tammy answered the door holding an icepack to her jaw. Without missing a beat, Colbie urged Tammy back into the small foyer, the ex-cop in her compelling her to glance around the room to make certain no one was there. Once inside, she examined and treated the young mother's injuries while vowing to get the S.O.B. who did it. Of course, she knew exactly who it was, but she never got the chance to make good on her promise—two hikers found Vinnie Alberico at the bottom of a deep ravine outside of town, ravaged by critters and decayed by scorching sun. One could only guess how long he'd been there, but when Tammy and Colbie heard about it, they figured it wasn't long enough.

Neither shed a tear and, as Brian's kidnapping case drew to a close, they promised to keep in touch. A year later, Tammy stood at the threshold of her new life, thanks to Colbie.

"Well, I have faith," she continued. "You'll figure it out. Let me know if there's anything I can do to help. Remember— unleash your power of faith, and you can do anything!"

Colbie laughed at her assistant's optimism. "Thanks—I will. Any calls?"

"Only one—someone named Ryan. He said you'd know who he is . . ."

"Ryan? Are you sure?"

"Yes—why? Don't you want to talk to him?"

"I just can't believe it, that's all—I haven't spoken with him for three years. He suddenly moved to the East Coast somewhere, and we lost touch. It was too bad—he was Brian's best friend, and he never let me down when I was searching for him." Colbie hesitated, recalling how important Ryan was to her investigation. "I know it hurts Brian to lose their friendship."

"But, that doesn't make sense—if he were Brian's best friend, then why did he suddenly pick up and move?"

"I have no idea—he left the day after he told us he was moving."

Tammy crossed her arms, and leaned against the door jamb. "That doesn't make sense . . ."

"That's what I thought, but it wasn't any of my business. He already made his decision to move by the time he told us, so what we thought really didn't matter—done deal."

"Well—he said he would be available after nine o'clock

tonight. He asked me to tell you it won't be too late if you decide to call."

"Thanks—we'll see. Will you please close the door on your way out? I have some thinking to do, and I need it quiet."

"Yep—buzz me when you're ready to receive visitors!" Tammy gently closed the door, as Colbie leaned back in her chair, closing her eyes.

Since she was young, Colbie perfected tapping into her intuitive mind whenever and wherever she felt like it. Some times were a bit more difficult than others, but, for the most part, she could summon needed information instantly. That day, however, she could tell something prevented her from gaining insight about the art impressions—something was jamming her frequencies.

Relaxing deeper into her body and mind, she snatched pieces of visions, trying to expand them into something clearer. Something she could hold on to. Something concrete. But, nothing made sense—vast expanses of swaying grass, small medicine droppers, and an empty picture frame. She knew not to inject interpretation when receiving information, but the snippets weren't cohesive, each seeming to represent something disparate from the other. She dug deeper, requesting clarification, but nothing—thirty minutes later, she returned to her reality none the wiser.

By the time Colbie was ready to call it a day, Tammy was already gone. When she and Colbie hashed out a deal for her getting on board, Tammy asked for flexible hours so she could be a 'real' mom—all she wanted was to be home when her son got home from school, so being at her post after three o'clock each afternoon was rare. Depending on Colbie's case load, weekends were often consumed with work, but not so much as to interfere with her time with him. To some, such a deal may not sound like much— but, to her, it was worth a fortune in gold.

As Colbie gathered the files she wanted to review at home, lights from adjacent office buildings flickered on, lending a warmth to an otherwise indifferent city. Colbie stood at the massive window, watching offices blink to life, thinking about the past three years. Brian. Her life. Ryan.

"Excuse me, Miss—should I come back?" Colbie turned as the cleaning woman began to close the door. "I'm sorry—I didn't know you were here."

Colbie smiled, motioning her in. "Don't be silly! I was just day dreaming . . ." She gathered the files from her desk, jamming them into her worn messenger bag. "I'll get out of your hair!"

****

The commuter train belched to a stop, brakes squealing against the metal of the tracks. *Right on time*, she thought, as she took her seat in the third car. In forty-five minutes, she would be home, the grime of the city left behind. The commute didn't bother her, and it was something she had to consider when making the move to open her practice. Living in a bedroom community seemed the best answer for she believed its quiet surroundings would be a relaxing environment for Brian. When she asked him what he preferred, he refused to state his preference telling her whatever she wanted to do was fine with him. So, she chose a quiet three bedroom in a small community by the water, hoping it would be just what Brian needed.

It wasn't.

Commuters jockeyed for position as the conductor announced upcoming stops. Hers was second to last, so she had a while to go—more than enough time to consider Ryan's phone call. *Why is he calling me now?* She glanced at her watch—eight forty-five. He told Tammy he would be available after nine, and as the train rolled into her destination, she considered whether she should return the call. There really wasn't a reason to ignore him—he had no idea how she felt when he left so suddenly. No time to say goodbye. In fact, if she were honest with herself, she was crushed when she realized he thought so little of her by not giving a heads up about his impending move.

By the time Colbie made it to her car, a light snow dusted the streets, swirling in different directions as she blew it from the driver's side window. It reminded her of the weather when Brian went missing—too early for flowers, too late for winter. It was the time of year that felt like no man's land, waiting for something to happen to tell it which way to go. She fired up the engine, adjusting the heat even though Brian told her a million times it wouldn't be warm inside until the engine warmed—but she never felt like waiting.

Patience wasn't her strong suit.

For the past three months she waited—well, procrastinated was more like it. Colbie had an important decision to make—really important. And, again, if she were honest with herself, separating from Brian was likely in the cards. *If that truly is my final conclusion, then why wait?* It was the same question she asked herself time and again since Christmas, her answer always the same—she loved him.

She thought.

But, for the last three months she wasn't so sure—the truth was she was entertaining the idea of chucking the whole relationship thing. Brian's refusal to take responsibility for his recovery was pissing her off, and she flat out wasn't sure if she wanted to deal with it anymore. Well, maybe she was sure, but it wasn't until the moment she arrived at her car, brushing the snow away with her hands, she made her decision.

It was time.

Five minutes later, blocks from home, she played the conversation with Brian in her mind. There really wasn't a good time for what she needed to discuss with him, and she vowed to speak calmly as she explained her reasons for needing a break from their relationship. Altogether? She wasn't sure. All she really knew was she needed a positive, loving environment, and she wasn't getting it at home.

By the time she reached the door, second thoughts were taking root. *What if he doesn't handle it well? Am I responsible for his happiness? Shit—if he refuses to take a break, then what am I going to do?* She sat on the garage step leading to the kitchen, considering the ramifications—none good. She figured Brian would do one of two things—be non-committal, or he'd go off the deep end. If he chose the former, it would be easier for her to handle it because she'd still be pissed off. Yes, emotional honesty would be shrouded with anger, but she'd deal with that later. But—if he chose to go off the deep end—she'd have to decide if he needed mental help, or if his response were nothing more than deluded machination. Just as it was with his recovery, his response was a crapshoot.

There was a part of her wishing Brian would already be in bed, but as she opened the door, there he was—right where she left him. Same position. Same clothes. Same vacuous look on his face. Had he moved at all? She doubted it, yet, at the same time, she knew that was impossible—she left him nearly fourteen hours earlier.

"Hey—how are you? Sorry I'm so late . . ." Considering the conversation she needed to initiate, she was disgusted she resorted to apology. She had nothing to apologize for—but, she wondered, *does Brian see it the same way?*

"What time is it?"

"Almost nine—did you eat?"

"Yeah—I made a bologna sandwich."

"That's it?"

"I wasn't hungry . . ."

"Okay." She looked at him, then pulled out a chair, draping her coat over the back. "Brian, I think we need to . . ." He looked at her, barely registering her lead-in to a conversation that would change his life. But, just as she felt strong enough to launch her case, her cell chirped, indicating a personal call. *Damn it! What now?* Colbie checked the number, not recognizing the area code. If she answered, chances were good she wouldn't feel like talking to Brian after hanging up. It was late, and her conversation with him really could wait until morning. If she didn't answer, she may miss something important.

She opted for importance.

"Colbie Colleen . . ."

"Colbie? It's been a long time! It's Ryan . . ." He waited, anticipating a positive response. He knew her well enough to know she wouldn't turn down a conversation with him.

"Ryan? Tammy told me you called—how did you get this number?"

"Really, Colbie? You know I have my ways . . ." He laughed as he thought about the investigation to reclaim Brian's freedom.

Colbie smiled. Indeed—he had his ways, and they always seemed to work. Boyish charm helped. "What's up? Why are you calling?"

"I know it's late, but I have a profiling gig for you. My clients . . ."

Colbie interrupted. "What clients? What do you do? When you left, you didn't tell us anything . . ."

An uncomfortable silence lasted a little too long. "Yeah, well . . ." Ryan wasn't sure where to start, so he decided to answer her second question. "I . . ." He hesitated, unsure of how Colbie would respond to his new vocation. "I'm a private investigator."

"What?" Colbie was certain she sounded like a seventh-grade girl when her voice increased several notes in pitch. "What do you mean, a 'private investigator?'"

"I know, right? It's a long story—but the short version is after I moved out here for my new job, it was okay for the first year or so. But, something wasn't working, and I found myself thinking about Brian's case. Then, it clicked—I realized I was never so alive as I was while working with you on the investigation."

"Seriously?"

"Yep—so, after I came to that conclusion, I decided to do something about it. I opened up my own private detective firm."

"I can't believe that! Well, I can, and I guess I have to admit there's a part of me that's a little jealous—lately, I haven't been able to make any decisions about my life! Good for you!"

"What do you mean?"

"Nothing. Nothing . . ."

The resignation in her voice told him everything he needed to know. He heard it a couple of times throughout Brian's investigation, and he knew she was working through something monumental.

"You know you can trust me . . ."

That she did know. "It's really not important—now, tell me about your client. Or, is there more than one?"

"Plural. Clients. Their needs coincide, and they do business together on occasion . . ."

"Okay—shoot. I'm all ears . . ."

"First I need to know one thing—how do you feel about accepting a case that will take you to South Africa?"

****

"South Africa? What's in South Africa?" Tammy couldn't believe what she was hearing.

"Remember when Ryan called a couple of days ago? Well, that's what it was about—a case in South Africa. At least, I think it will wind up there—if my feelings are correct, it's the final destination—not the first stop."

"Holy crap—how long will you be gone?"

"That's the thing—I'm not sure. But one thing I do know is I have to count on you to hold down the fort."

"Of course—that goes without saying."

"Good—I knew you'd say that!"

"When are you leaving?" Tammy wasn't exactly pleased her boss was about the embark on international travel, but when Colbie made up her mind about something, there was no changing it.

"On Friday—that means we have a lot to accomplish between now and then. You'll need to advise our clients I'll be out of the country for an extended time, so refer them to one of the professionals on our preferred list. Provide client files, if necessary . . ."

"Check . . . what else? And, if I'm not being too nosy, what does Brian say about this?"

And there was the stickler. Brian didn't know—at least, not yet. Colbie thought it prudent to have everything in motion before breaking the news. She paid the mortgage for six months, and arranged for someone to do the shopping and cleaning—she wanted to make it easy for him to get on without her being there. Her greatest fear was he would experience a crippling, crushing desire to keep her firmly rooted in place. With him. The truth was Colbie thought of the South African gig as the perfect solution to put some distance between them—enough distance that would allow her to think. Reassess. Decide. Ryan was clear the case could take several months, but he didn't think it would be longer than six—probably less.

More than enough time.

"He doesn't know yet . . ." Colbie shuffled through files as she admitted the worst. "I didn't tell him because I think it's a good thing, and it gives the perfect reason to experience a brief separation."

"A brief separation? Six months isn't a 'brief separation.'"

Colbie met Tammy's incredulous stare. "It is to me . . ."

CHAPTER THREE

Making decisions can be a tricky thing. As much as Colbie wanted—needed—to get away, her stomach was in knots knowing Brian was in such a fragile state. Even though no one uttered the words, everything about Brian's condition screamed PTSD, and it was clear he was insecure about his relationship with Colbie.

Most days, he put on the fear of losing her like he put on his socks. Before his kidnapping, he scoffed at her idea of being a profiler—but, by the end of his ordeal, he understood and admired her abilities. Still, he didn't think she could make a living at it, and her success over the past couple of years made him look foolish for thinking it was an impossible career. He didn't like looking foolish. Worse, as far as he could see, she really didn't need him anymore. She could make it on her own, and he was becoming convinced she would leave him—then what would he do?

Colbie sat at her desk, staring at towering high rises

across the street. *What a lousy view*, she thought as she chewed on the dilemma of what to do about Brian. In fact, the view of nothing but concrete was one of the reasons she decided to live outside the city. It was peaceful. Calm. And, no matter how much she convinced herself buying the house in the country was best for Brian, it was really best for her. Cities made her feel—soiled—and when the commuter train entered the soft air of the country each evening, she felt as if she were where she needed to be. It allowed her the freedom to be herself—not that she couldn't do the same on the streets of the city—but it was different. In the country, her soul felt nourished somehow, and it was that feeling of freedom that made Ryan's offer appealing—the thought of it sparked visions of expansive savannas meeting the horizon with no one else in sight. No honking horns. No blaring sirens. No sound, except nature's.

She knew she had to tell Brian about South Africa, but she pulled back when the time came. Yes, she told Ryan she would take the gig, but the last few days didn't present the best opportunity to discuss it with her so-called better half. Brian was sullen and unresponsive, and when she brought up the possibility of his getting a job at breakfast that morning, he snapped.

"Work? Are you out of your freakin' mind? Who's going to hire me?" His words tinged with anger, he stared at Colbie as if she were from another planet.

"Oh, c'mon—you had a great career! There's nothing saying you can't reactivate it . . ."

"Doing what? Go back to engineering? I don't think so."

She stared at him, uncertain of who was in front of her. "For God's sake, Brian—your boss loved you, and I can think of a couple of awards you received from the ASME. It wouldn't be that hard to get things going again!" Brian's total lack of enthusiasm was starting to annoy her, and it was beginning to make the decision to join Ryan in South Africa more appealing.

"You and I both know there's always someone younger and better just waiting to kick me to the curb. Why should I open myself up to that? Admit it, Colbie—I don't have anything to offer anymore and, if I did decide to work again, it would be nothing but a lie. I'm a fake. I don't measure up to someone younger and smarter . . ."

Really? Imposter Syndrome? It was odd—he was exhibiting defining symptoms of the psychological disorder, but that morning was the first time she labeled it as such. It made sense, however—ever since he returned home, he couldn't recognize any of his former accomplishments as positive. He felt unworthy of praise or recognition and, for the first time, she recognized the seriousness of his teetering on a narrow precipice of psychological demise. Coupled with the PTSD? It was a dangerous cocktail. *Maybe,* she considered, *I recognize it now because I felt the same way throughout my life . . . maybe that's why we clicked in the first place.* She knew she was good at what she did—her intuitive skills—but her natural tendency was to poo-poo any accolades, especially those coming from colleagues or superiors. Regular bouts of insecurity burrowed into her life, and she still had trouble overcoming it even though—due to her training—she had the tools to do so.

"Fine. Then what are you planning on doing?"

"About what?"

"Work, Brian! What are you going to do about work? You just can't sit around here all day doing nothing! It's not healthy for you . . ."

No answer. Brian stared at his coffee cup, refusing to

acknowledge her question.

"Well, all I know is something has to change . . ." With that, she grabbed her coat, slammed the back door, and headed for her car.

So there Colbie sat, thinking about what to do. As she watched sunlight breath life into the icy morning, she recalled her meditation from days earlier—swaying grasses. An empty picture frame. Medicine droppers. In that moment, she understood.

Decision made.

****

Navigating Heathrow was daunting, and not being a seasoned traveler made it that much more difficult. Colbie had to admit she was nervous, and she reverted into the comfort of her shadow world, moving from concourse to concourse trying to find baggage claim. She recalled the words of her father when she was about to embark on a trip by herself for the first time at age sixteen. "Just remember, he said, "don't speak to anyone—and, if the numbers of the gates are going down, you're nearing the center of the airport. You can always find someone there to help you . . ." *Funny I should remember that so many years later,* she thought, as she glanced at the gate numbers stretching down the long corridor.

Making her way toward baggage, she felt the full effect of being alone in a city she knew nothing about. Of course,

Colbie learned a few thing on the Internet, but it wasn't the same as experiencing it for herself. Ryan couldn't meet her in London because his part of the investigation took him directly to South Africa. She was to ferret out information about recent art thefts in Europe—London in particular. When and where were the easy parts because they were documented with local authorities—at least, some of them were. Others were shrouded in mystery with few facts known—they were Ryan's clients.

Before she left the States, Ryan sent her a comprehensive portfolio and dossier for each victim. The thefts appeared to be quick and stealthy, private collectors the intended targets. No museums. No news stories. Ryan promised to bring her up to speed the second she landed in Cape Town but, until then, she had to go with what she knew—millions in art were missing, some showing up on the black market originating in South Africa. Owners wanted the thefts and recovery to be hush-hush, intent on not calling attention to themselves. Colbie understood their not wanting to be in the limelight, but there were millions at stake—that alone warranted bringing in the authorities. No, something wasn't right, and on the way to her hotel she laid out plans for the following day. The collectors individually agreed to meet with her, the first scheduled for early afternoon. Until then, research, maybe a bite to eat, then to bed so she would be fresh for the first leg of her investigation.

As the cab pulled up to her hotel, Colbie gasped at its grandeur—the art collectors were footing the bill for the entire investigation, and they spared no expense. A valet greeted her, unloaded her luggage, and guided her to the front desk for check in, then waited patiently. Colbie figured she must have looked panicked for he seemed to take a liking to her, making certain she had everything she needed. Within fifteen minutes, a bellman unlocked the door to her room, holding it open so she could enter first. London in the waning months of winter was damp and cold, and the last thing Colbie expected was a fireplace casting a soft glow around the room. From the doorway she noticed a leather couch flanked by two easy chairs in front of the fireplace, a beautifully appointed queen bed, and the pleasing mix of modern and traditional.

"Thank you." Colbie handed the bellman his tip, gracefully dismissing him. After endless hours of travel, she was eager to be alone.

As soon as the door closed behind him, she slipped off her shoes, hung up her coat, and plopped onto the plush couch. The fireplace performed its intended effect, and Colbie felt her body begin to melt into the soft cushions. Her thoughts became more fluid as she relaxed, thinking about the money paying for such swanky digs. *To shell out this kind of loot,* she thought, *the stakes must be high* . . . Her eyelids fluttered as new visions flitted in and out. A savanna. Ryan. A broken white gate hanging from its hinges. Sinking deeper into a relaxed state, visions streaked into her mind, then vanished as if being crumpled up and thrown away. A bamboo hut. Dark vials. There was one more, but she couldn't quite make it out—requesting its return, the vision lingered, but all Colbie could see was a large clump of . . . something. She had no idea of what it was.

Normally, her meditative states lasted about an hour. That afternoon, however, her energy felt too depleted to continue after only twenty minutes. It was a signal—she had to replenish.

A quick shower and a bit of makeup later, Colbie headed to the bistro downstairs. She planned a quick bite to eat, then back to her suite to dive into Internet research. Her first task was to conduct an in-depth session on the art collectors whose canvases were kyped right under their collective noses. And, that's what bugged her—what about the security cameras? *Surely, each collector would have sophisticated security systems . . . cameras should monitor each piece.* She made a mental note to focus on the security issues when reviewing the collectors' individual files.

A perky hostess showed her to a small table tucked into an intimate back corner, away from prying eyes. Her cop training surfaced, and she chose the booth side facing the entrance of the restaurant. It also gave her the best vantage point for people watching—her experience in profiling was the direct result of her ability to size up individuals based solely on how they carried themselves. When she was young, it was a game—now it was the basis of her life as well as how she made her living.

She ordered a stunning, deconstructed meat pie, a small salad, and a glass of the house Cabernet. She planned on tucking into her room for the rest of the day and evening, so one small glass wouldn't hurt. As she sipped, she observed patrons as they spoke to the hostess at her stand, some pointing in the direction of a particular booth or table. The hostess's ponytail swung slightly as she seated them, more so when she hurried back to the stand to answer the phone. Colbie watched as she listened to the voice on the other end, then glanced at Colbie. Moments later, she stood at Colbie's booth.

"You have a visitor at the front desk—would you like me to inform the chef you may be delayed?"

"A visitor? Do you know who it is?" No one other than Tammy and Ryan knew where she was staying.

"No, Ma'am."

Colbie thought for a moment before answering. "Okay—please let the chef know, but I'll be back in a couple of minutes." She slid from the booth, the hostess right behind as she headed for the front desk.

"I'm Colbie Colleen—I have a guest?"

"Yes, Ma'am—he's waiting right over there . . ." The concierge pointed to a seating area by the front window.

Colbie looked in the direction of his pointing finger. "Where? I don't see anyone . . ."

"Right . . there . . ." No one was there—standing or seated. "I'm sorry, Ma'am—he must have left." The concierge scanned the lobby to be sure.

"What did he look like?"

"He was tall—blond hair."

"Thank you. If he comes back, will you please ask him to wait for me?"

"Yes, Ma'am . . ."

Colbie took her time returning to the restaurant in case her mystery visitor returned. She nodded to the hostess and thanked her, hoping her meal wasn't too long in coming— she was famished! As she neared her booth, she noticed someone—a man—sitting opposite of her place setting, and she recognized him immediately.

"Ryan! You're supposed to be in South Africa! What are you doing here?"

Ryan stood, wrapping her in a warm hug.

"I'll get to that later." He spun her around, eying her from top to bottom. "You look fantastic—success agrees with you!"

Colbie laughed, and it occurred to her she hadn't laughed with such delight for quite some time. "You phoned the hostess?"

"How else was I going to get you away from the table?"

"Ryan Fitzpatrick! I should have known something was up!"

Ryan let go of her hand, motioning toward the booth. "Did you order? I'm starving . . ."

"I did, but the chef is holding it—I imagine he can hold it a little longer until yours is done." She motioned to the waitress, and requested a menu.

A few minutes later, Cab in hand, he joined Colbie in a toast. "To renewing old friendships—a new beginning!" Colbie grinned as they clinked glasses, thinking how lovely it was to enjoy his company.

"So—what are you doing here? I thought you were in South Africa . . ."

"I was supposed to arrive there last week—but, at the last minute I changed plans. We'll go together . . ."

"Are you in the hotel?"

"Yep—I thought it would be easier. We really have quite a bit of work to do before we're off to Cape Town. Our reservations are open-ended, so we can take as much time as we need to prepare the investigation."

"These guys have deep pockets, and they're clearly not afraid to provide us with the best they have to offer."

"True—there's a lot at stake, but I have the feeling we're not getting the whole story." He set his glass down, tracing its rim with his index finger. "That why I called you—I can't figure it out, and I know you can."

"What do you mean? What's missing?"

"If I knew that, I wouldn't be here sitting with you, would I?" He grinned as he delivered the slight admonition.

"Funny. You know what I mean . . ."

"You know what? Let's finish eating, then head to your room to brainstorm—I'll fill you in on everything I know."

"Sounds like a plan . . ." She glanced up from her salad.

He hadn't changed, at all.

CHAPTER FOUR

❝ My clients—as you probably guessed—are the richest of the rich, and they function completely off grid. Trying to track their moves or locate them is next to impossible—they live their lives behind the veil of dummy companies and aliases, refusing to call in the authorities for anything that may go wrong."

"I figured that—what about security systems?"

"Sophisticated—top of the line." Ryan propped his feet up on the sleek glass coffee table, making himself right at home.

"I assume you already viewed the videos—any luck?"

"Well, to be honest, I haven't looked at them—and, that's why I'm here. We have appointments set up for the next several days to meet with the victims, and you and I are going to view the vids together."

"What's the possibility of the big guns not showing? Do

you think they'll send a representative instead?"

"It's always a possibility, but I don't think so . . ."

Colbie kicked off her shoes, and joined Ryan on the couch. "I'm still a little confused, so I need to have you start at the beginning—tell me everything you know!"

"Get comfortable, then—it's a long story, and I'm pretty sure I don't know the half of it. But, before I launch into that, I want to know one thing . . ."

"What's that?"

Ryan grinned. "Did you miss me?"

****

Nigel Blackwell polished off the last swig of scotch, swiping at the bottom of the glass to make sure no moisture collected on the bottom before placing it on the handcrafted, black ironwood desk. He was always careful—the desk was his pride and joy. Not so much for its worth, but for its sentimental value because it represented his first major deal. Growing up in Cape Town had its challenges, and he vowed at an early age he would rise above the repression created by international sanctions imposed in the early '80s. And, that's exactly what he did—by the time he turned eighteen in 1996, an economic shift was in full swing, and Cape Town—as well as other major cities—experienced exponential growth. It was the perfect time to insert his business expertise—street business expertise—into the local economy by founding his own import-export business a few years before the end of the decade. As money continued to infuse Cape Town, so did his business as demand for African folk art increased—something he anticipated when he opened his doors.

The handcrafted table took three years to perfect and, due to the density of the wood, the artisan craftsman made ponderous progress simply because of the size of the project. Most artisans carved small animals representing indigenous species of South Africa from the ironwood—but to carve a table weighing about the same as a Mack truck? He knew it didn't make sense, but he wanted something to honor his hard work, sweat, and knowledge of how to play the system. He wanted it to represent him.

He wanted it to be indestructible.

By the time the first decade of the new millennium ticked over to the second, Nigel's business was prosperous enough to allow him a posh lifestyle in any city, not just Cape Town. Always on the A-list, he filled his life with meals at swanky restaurants, a few turns on the golf course each week and, of course, travel—anywhere he wanted to go. Anytime. Still, in spite of his gallivanting, he made certain to keep a tight rein when it came to his company. His clients always felt welcomed, turning to him when compelled to purchase or sell an item that may otherwise be—difficult—to obtain. Everyone who was anyone knew Nigel Blackwell never disappointed, and his reputation among collectors was stellar—the go-to guy.

"Boss—I'm heading out. Anything else before I go?" Akhona Addington poked his head around Nigel's office door, straw hat in hand. He knew just about as much about the business as Blackwell did, always making certain incoming and outgoing products were protected by state-of-the-art security. He checked video surveillance three times a day, and it was his final task before leaving for the evening. That evening, everything checked out.

"I'm good—I'll see you in the morning. We have a new piece coming in, and I'll be here early. You'll be here, as well, I suppose . . ." Blackwell counted on his right-hand man to take care of business, but he insisted on being present when a new product arrived. Clients appreciated his personal touch, and it provided them a modicum of comfort knowing he was overseeing the transfer.

"Indeed—I'll be here." Addington flashed him a toothy smile, and closed the door.

Nigel sorted through the day's mail, flipping items of no consequence into the wastebasket. Most of his legit business was conducted via the Internet, but, once in a while, he received something via snail mail, mostly by charity organizations. That evening, a large envelope protruded from the rest of the mail as if to call particular attention to its importance. Just by touching the envelope, Nigel knew it was something worth a glance—the paper was an elegant ivory with an embossed logo in the upper left corner, an ornate scroll pressed into gold sealing wax its only form of secure closure. *What have we here*, he wondered, breaking the seal. As he opened the invitation, a small piece of vellum slipped from the card, fluttering to the floor by his feet. Normally, he would have wadded it up, and pitched it in the trash—the vellum, however, contained fluid script writing in fountain pen—*meet me*.

Burnett? Why does he need to meet me? The invitation turned out to be from Samuel Burnett—multi-millionaire. Philanthropist. Art collector. Turns out the old boy was sponsoring a soirée for the upper crust—of which Nigel was one—three weeks out. The handwriting on the invitation was clearly that of a woman—the penmanship on the small, square piece of vellum was not. *Interesting*, Nigel thought as he marked the day and time in his planner. *What's he up to now . . .*

****

Halfway through their evening, a plan was in place. Colbie had to admit she enjoyed her time with Ryan—he was fun, but she found his serious side intriguing, as well. As he did when working on Brian's kidnapping case, he thought things through carefully, weighing the anticipated consequences of each action. Working through the particulars of the art theft case, they picked apart what they could, but, until they gained traction, they didn't have a lot to go on. They needed to meet with each victim before they really knew what was on their plates.

"First up, Samuel Burnett—theft victim number one. He acquired a modern piece called *Girl Among the Petals* for a cool seven hundred and fifty grand five years ago, and it's gone. No trace. Nothing on security—so he says."

"Holy crap! Are there pictures of it?"

"That's what we'll soon find out—he's our first appointment tomorrow afternoon."

"I assume he's here in London . . ."

"Yep—about an hour out." Brian checked the map to be sure.

"What's your plan? Will we orchestrate the meeting, or will he?"

"We will—from the first time he called, I told him he needed to comply with what we need for the investigation. Hell, he's paying us enough for our expertise, so he should be okay with it . . ."

"Did he concur?"

"He did—he'll send a car for us tomorrow at one o'clock. We should arrive at his estate by two—before we do anything, though, I want to walk the grounds to get a good feel for what we're dealing with. Then, after speaking with him, I think we should view the security camera files first thing. What do you think?"

"I think you're starting to sound like a die-hard investigator! How did you get to be so good?" Colbie winked at him for she knew it was her tutelage that got him to where he never knew he wanted to be—a top notch private investigator.

"You know I have you to thank . . ." Ryan lifted his glass in heart-felt toast. "Without you—well, I think it's safe to say I'd still be stuck in the same old crap job, doing the same old crap thing."

It was a long time since Colbie felt appreciated by someone other than her mother. Ryan wasn't a serious guy by nature, but her senses told her he was deeply touched by her contribution to his new career. "Well, I couldn't have found Brian without you—and, I couldn't be more thrilled to work with you again."

They sat for a moment, each lost in memories of the challenges and successes during the past three years. Colbie yearned for the love she once felt for Brian, but she knew it was fading. *Will things ever be the same?* She doubted it. All she had now was her career . . .

Ryan felt as if his memories were just beginning.

They couldn't be more opposite.

****

At one o'clock, a polished, black Cadillac Escalade pulled up to the entrance of the hotel, its driver in his finest dress uniform. Wool, perhaps. Colbie couldn't quite tell, but he was clearly dressed for inclement weather. As he greeted them, he confirmed their identities, then opened the door to spacious seating. A small, stocked bar was tucked inconspicuously behind the driver, and he invited them to make themselves comfortable as he pulled into congested traffic. Twenty minutes later they were on the fringe of the smothering cloak of the city.

As they made their way out of London, bustling streets turned to quiet country lanes serving as thoroughfares for bicycles, a few cars, and the occasional farm tractor. Very Agatha Christie-ish. The English countryside was more bleak than Colbie imagined—leafless trees shivered in the cold as unrelenting rain pelted their barren trunks, nothing appearing inviting. As they drove through each village, Colbie half expected to see Miss Marple riding her bike to a local meeting. *God, I'd hate living here,* she thought as she considered a life of dreariness.

"Get a load of that place!" Ryan pointed to a country estate just ahead. "I wonder how much it costs to maintain it . . ."

"It would cost enough—I can't imagine living in such a place! It looks like a mausoleum—no thanks!"

"Oh, c'mon—you mean you wouldn't like having conversations with ghosts of English past?" Ryan glanced at her, hoping she caught the dig.

"Really? If I recall correctly, you didn't believe in my conversations with the other side . . ."

"True—I didn't. But, that doesn't mean I don't now. Why do you think I called you to partner with me on this case?"

"That's the only reason?"

Ryan didn't have time to answer. The driver turned onto the cobbled lane leading to the mausoleum mansion, announcing their arrival. Massive English oaks lined the drive, and Colbie imagined how regal they must look during the spring and summer. *An unbroken shade*, she thought as they turned left into a circular drive.

As they pulled to a rolling stop, a man—mid-forties— stood on brick steps the color of sand, flanked by a young woman. *Daughter?* Colbie scanned the grounds as she stepped from the limo, and it wasn't until she stood in front of the mansion that she fully grasped its size. Towering, stately columns dwarfed anyone standing next to them, their structure and design speaking of centuries passed.

Their host extended his hand as he approached.

"I gather you must be Ryan and Colbie! Welcome to my humble abode . . ."

Humble abode, my ass! There's nothing humble about this place! Colbie smiled and accepted his hand, searching his face for a flicker of humor. "Colbie Colleen . . ."

He winked. "I know, humble it's not—but, it's home!" His grin was infectious, and Colbie couldn't help a genuine grin herself.

"You must be Samuel Burnett—Ryan Fitzpatrick!" Burnett's handshake was strong, and confident. Ryan took particular notice of their host's grip, then slowly turned to view the grounds. "Nice—do you mind if we look around before going inside? I'd like to get an idea of access points . . ."

"Help yourself—by the way, this is Maggie." Burnett slipped his arm around the young woman's shoulder, giving her a quick squeeze. "My youngest . . ."

She gave her dad a peck on the cheek, then turned to Ryan and Colbie. "I can show you around, or you can set off on your own. We have fifteen acres, but most of that is landscape. Other than what you see here, there's only one other building—it houses the art collection."

"It's a separate building from the house?"

"Yes—it's the only way Daddy can showcase his collection with the respect it deserves." Ryan couldn't be sure, but he thought he caught a moment of hesitation in her voice. "So—by yourself, or with a guide?"

Colbie stepped in. "Well, if you're game, a guided tour will be great!"

"I'll leave you to it, then—take your time. We'll discuss the particulars inside when you're ready." With that, Samuel Burnett disappeared through the front entrance.

"Shall we?" Maggie gestured to her right, guiding them

along the cobbled walkway. "The art building is in the back garden—I'm afraid today's weather isn't presenting the best first impression, but it's really quite beautiful when everything is in bloom."

Colbie walked behind Ryan and Maggie, trying to get a sense of who lived there. So far, so good. From first impressions, the grounds appeared manicured and simple. Nothing ornate. Strategically located inconspicuous cameras captured images of anything and everything passing by, and Colbie made a mental note to inquire about other cameras which may not be so visible. Maggie chattered a mile a minute about inconsequential things, carefully avoiding the real reason for her guided tour.

Colbie dutifully listened, then jumped in. "What do you know about the theft?" She knew instinctively Maggie knew more than she was saying—no time like the present to get things on the table. Gently, of course.

"I really don't know much . . ."

"Were you here when the theft occurred?" Colbie stopped to have a face to face with the young Burnett. Maggie quickly glanced away from Colbie, as if trying to recall the event. It was a poor attempt at acting, and Maggie's body language told Colbie everything she needed to know. Yep. The lovely Miss Burnett knew more than she let on—much more.

"I was—I mean, I was staying here, but I was out with friends the night it happened."

"Do you remember anything—special—about that night?"

"What do you mean, 'special?'"

"Well, do you remember anything unusual happening such as the lights going out, a storm of any kind—anything different than the usual routine." Colbie wasn't sure, but she was fairly certain Maggie Burnett was playing the dumb blonde—and, it didn't suit her well.

"No—not that I remember."

"What time did you leave to meet your friends?" Colbie needed to get Maggie off her self-perceived hot seat—she was beginning to shut down, and Colbie couldn't risk her not wanting to talk. She flashed Maggie a best-friend grin. "I gotta tell you—this place isn't bad! Where do you hang out to have fun?"

"There's a pub in the village—and, I often meet friends in London. If I had to stay here all the time, I'd lose my mind!"

Ah. There it was. Honesty with a sprinkling of discontent. "Well, London's not far—maybe you can show me around, if you don't mind. I promise not to cramp your style!"

"Oh, you wouldn't cramp my style—my friends are weirdos, and they'd be the first ones to tell you that!"

It worked. Maggie's posture relaxed as she thought about spending time with them.

"My friends are a little bit different, too—and, I wouldn't have it any other way! Since this is my first time here, I'd love to see some of the sights . . . maybe we can meet up with some of your 'weirdo' friends—they sound fun! Of course, I won't have a ton of extra time, but maybe we can get together before we leave . . ."

Ryan shot Colbie a glance. He knew exactly what she was doing, and he admired how adroitly his partner maneuvered her target to the desired result. She was a pro, and being with her again made him realize how much he didn't know.

Maggie tapped her phone, shading her eyes with one

hand so she could see the screen. "There! I'll let you know tomorrow—okay?"

"Perfect! It will be fun—for now, though, we need to get back to work!"

CHAPTER FIVE

"Nightcap?" Ryan shook the rain from his coat, then slipped into the booth. It was a long day, and by the time they pulled up to their hotel, the clock had long since seen the hour of ten. Burnett, of course, treated them like royalty—tea and biscuits were served promptly at three o'clock, but it wasn't enough to hold them until breakfast. Besides, neither Colbie nor Ryan wanted to burn time by eating—they had enough to do without that.

Colbie nodded. "Please! I can use it!"

"Gimlet?" His eyes twinkled as he let her know he hadn't forgotten.

"I'm surprised you remember . . . rocks, please." Colbie settled into the booth, looking him squarely in the eye. "We didn't have much occasion to have drinks together three years ago . . ."

"True—but you taught me to watch and listen

everywhere I go. I guess that makes me a quick learner, huh?"
He lifted his water glass in a toast. "We'll toast properly when
the good stuff comes . . . but, for now, this will have to do. To
you, Colbie Colleen . . ."

"Me? What did I do?"

"Oh, more than you know . . ." Ryan took a sip, then
placed the goblet on the table, recalling the first time he laid
eyes on his partner. Right away he knew she was a spitfire—
not from what Brian told him about her, but from her spunk
when she spoke to him. The first time she opened her mouth,
he could see the sense of humor in her eyes. They didn't
sparkle, really—but, they were different. He recognized a
kind of knowing he hadn't encountered before—she touched
his soul in a manner completely unfamiliar to him.

"You're being silly . . ." Emotion tugged at her as she
raised her glass—spending time with Ryan was so easy. So
natural. *Why can't I have that with Brian,* she wondered,
thinking about why she left him behind.

"Maybe, but, you have to admit . . . Ah! Our drinks!"
The waitress slipped white cocktail napkins in front of them,
careful to position the glasses just so before leaving them to
their conversation. "So—should we recap before we order?"
Ryan clicked the tip of his pen as he snatched the cocktail
napkin from under his glass, rousing her from private
thoughts.

"Good idea . . ." Colbie fished for a small piece of paper
and a pen in her purse. "I recorded our conversations with
Maggie and Burnett, but on the off chance they're squirreled,
we need to make sure we're seeing and hearing the same
things."

Ryan nodded, shifting his weight to a more comfortable
position. "Agreed—let's take Maggie first. What do you

think? Aboveboard?"

"For the most part, yes—but I get the distinct feeling she's not telling us everything she knows."

"I picked up on the same thing." Ryan smiled. "Maybe I've been hanging around you too long!"

"You should be so lucky . . ."

"Seriously—did you pick up on anything when you were talking about meeting her friends?"

"I did, but I can't quite pinpoint it yet—I want to meet with them to see if my intuition amplifies. I may be picking up on her, but I think it's a friend—an important friend. Male."

"A boyfriend?"

"Not really—but when I was with her, I had visions of bamboo and thatched huts. It didn't make any sense, so I tucked it away. The weird thing was when I shook hands with her as we left, I heard—in my mind—a gunshot. I have no idea what that's about . . ."

"A gunshot? You're sure?"

"Really? Ten years on the force, and you're asking me if I recognize a gunshot?"

"Point taken . . . I know you recognize a gunshot when you hear it—but what do you think it means?"

"I have no idea—I'll think about it." By thinking about it, Colbie meant accessing her intuitive mind for clarification.

"Okay. Next. Her father—what do you think about him?"

"A genuinely nice guy, I think—he's clearly distressed

about the theft, and he's willing to pay to apprehend the bastards who ripped him off. He strikes me as an affable, but silent type—however, no matter how nice and welcoming he was to us, I wouldn't want to get on his bad side."

"Bastards? Plural?"

"Oh, there are definitely more than one involved . . ."

"That's my gut, too. And, I know what you mean about Burnett—when we were checking out the surveillance tapes, he was intent on watching every little thing. In fact, he was so focused, he didn't notice my watching him. There was a definite change in his demeanor, and he transformed from the nicest guy in the world to someone filled with hatred. Or, anger. Not sure which . . ."

"Agreed. Did you catch anything from the camera?"

"No—but when the security guard took a phone call while we were looking at the recordings, I noticed he didn't want to talk in front of me."

"That's natural, don't you think?"

"Yes, but he didn't seem natural—know what I mean?"

"Uncomfortable?"

"Exactly—it was an 'I can't talk now' thing . . ."

"We can't read too much into that—it could have been anyone. Maybe he and his better half had an argument—who knows?"

"I know. Still . . ."

"Gut feeling it was something else?" It had been a long time since Colbie and Ryan spent time together, and she admired his motivation to use his intuitive mind. They used to discuss Colbie's belief that everyone can learn to invoke and use intuitive information, but Ryan never expressed interest in learning how to develop the skill.

"Gut." He fiddled with the corner of the napkin—a tell for Colbie. Ryan subconsciously exhibited a nervousness about something.

"Can you pinpoint it?"

He glanced up, meeting her question head on. "I think he's on the inside—sweat beaded instantaneously above his brow, and he shot me a glance to make sure I wasn't listening."

"Who do you think he was talking to?"

"That's just it—I have no idea. None. That's why you're here!"

Colbie leaned forward, taking Ryan's hand gently in hers. "You have to trust in your ability—the answers will come. Sometimes when you don't want them to . . ." Her fingertips lingered as she tapped into him. "Why do you feel guilty?"

"Guilty? I don't feel guilty about anything . . ."

His denial was a bit too strong. "Well, you're dealing with something, so if you need to talk about it, I'm always here for you." She pulled back, straightening the napkin on her lap.

"Thanks—if I come up with anything, I'll let you know! Now, how about that real toast?" He lifted his glass.

"To us . . ."

****

The plan was to meet Burnett at his estate one more time before splintering off from Ryan to investigate individual leads. They needed time to interview those who were on the grounds the day of or the weeks leading up to the art theft. Thankfully, Burnett wasn't so arrogant as to have a staff the size of a football team—five was plenty, three of whom were groundskeepers. The other two were the security guard, and a domestic named Annie. Colbie was particularly interested in speaking with her—any housekeeper worth her salt knows the inner workings of her employer's family. The only problem was they're usually pretty tight-lipped when it comes to offering information. *Fierce loyalty is overrated,* Colbie thought as the driver pulled onto the lane and through the estate gates.

Unlike the previous day, no one other than Annie greeted them at the entrance to the estate mansion. She was a tall, stately young woman, probably no more than thirty, and Colbie immediately picked up on her willingness to follow rather than lead. She stood submissively, eyes cast down, until she knew the precise moment she must greet her guests. No handshake. Simply a brief welcome, and an order to follow her.

"Regrettably," she offered as they stepped into the massive foyer, "Mr. Burnett is on a phone call—he asks you to make yourselves comfortable, and he'll be with you as soon as he can." Annie gestured to a sitting room beautifully appointed with handcrafted art pieces and furniture—not enough to look cluttered, but just enough to lend an element of creative class to an otherwise austere room.

Colbie took the lead. "That's not a problem, at all—in fact, Mr. Burnett asks that we interview anyone who was on the premises when the heist took place—I assume you were here?"

Annie's expression flitted from timid to fear. "Yes, Ma'am."

Based on her initial impressions of the servant, Colbie knew a gentle, girl-to-girl approach would work best. "Ryan—if you want to touch base with the security guard, I can handle everything here." Colbie smiled at Annie as she gave Ryan his cue to get out of there.

She didn't have to hint twice. "Good idea . . ." He nodded to Annie, and headed for the art gallery studio in the back garden.

"Okay—why don't we have a chat?" Colbie patted the spot next to her on the couch. "I need to hear anything and everything leading up to, the day of, and the weeks after the theft." She grinned, as Annie sat beside her. "That ought to take us a while, don't you think?"

Annie relaxed as Colbie's infectious laugh filled the room. "Yes, Ma'am . . ."

"Good heavens—you don't need to call me 'Ma'am.' I feel old enough! Call me Colbie . . ."

"Right. I'm not sure if I can tell you anything you don't already know . . ."

"That's a good thing—since we're just beginning our investigation, I don't know much. That's why I'm counting on you to help me get this thing jump-started—so, let's start at the beginning . . ."

"I'll try . . ."

"How long have you been employed by Mr. Burnett?"

"Three years."

"Where did you work before coming here?"

"I spent two years working for a family in Waterford, Ireland, and before that I worked at the World's End Pub."

"A pub? I've never been to England before, and one of the things I want to do is go to a pub for a pint!" Colbie needed to whittle away at Annie's apprehension, and coming across as someone who was just like her was a good way to do it.

"That's what everyone says when they come to England— but, they're not that great. It's hard work, and long hours."

"Not unlike here, I suppose—how many hours a week do you work?"

"I have weekends off, unless there is something going on."

"Going on?"

"Yes—like a party. We have one coming up in three weeks, and I have to be here almost every day. There is much to do . . ."

"I can imagine—what's the occasion?"

"All I know is Mr. Burnett asked me to mail invitations last week, and that's what I did."

"Do you have a guest list?"

"Yes—shall I fetch it for you?" Annie was up in a second, returning moments later with a small, spiral-bound notepad. "It's not a big party . . ."

Colbie glanced at the names on the list, none of which she recognized. "Have all of these people been here before?" She handed the list back to Annie, watching her carefully.

"Not all—several have, however."

"Who?"

Annie glanced again at the list. "Alison Winthrop—she's been here several times. Margaret Van Hulett—once or twice, I think. Oh—Nigel Blackwell. He's been here many times—he and Mr. Burnett are good friends."

"What does he do?"

"I don't have any idea . . ."

By the end of an hour, Colbie didn't have much more than when she started. Clearly, Annie didn't have as good a handle on the goings on of the mansion as Colbie hoped—or, if she did, acting should have been her chosen profession.

"Colbie! Please forgive me—my call took longer than I thought." Samuel Burnett blew through the door, shooting a look at Annie, noticing there were none of the usual niceties associated with a guest's arrival. "Annie—please bring our guest some tea and biscuits." Relieved to be off the hot seat, Annie leapt up and headed for the kitchen.

"So," Burnett commented as he made himself comfortable in a wing-backed chair across from Colbie. "What did you learn from Annie? She's such a sweet girl, but sometimes I think she's not so bright. But, as long as she does what she's asked to do, she'll get along well here."

His comment reminded Colbie of her first impression when she met Tammy—she thought Tammy wasn't the sharpest knife in the drawer, but she was mistaken. "I think she's a lovely girl—and, she really didn't have much to offer in the way of usable information. She did mention, however, you're throwing a party within the next few weeks. Correct?"

"Yes—not a big affair. Perhaps twenty or thirty—a get together, really." He paused for effect. "Would you like to attend?"

CHAPTER SIX

N ick Cummings belched as he motioned to the barkeep.
"Keep 'em comin' . . ." he ordered, drawing a smoke
from its wrinkled pack.

"Drowning sorrows, mate?"

"Sorrows? Hardly—just thinking about work . . ."

"I'll leave ya to your thoughts, then . . ." The barkeep
knew better than to interrupt when heavy thinking was
involved. He placed a pint of stout in front of the young man,
then quietly went about his business.

Cummings didn't have much time—he arranged to
meet Maggie that evening, and it was already four o'clock.
It left little time for his meeting—who was, by the way, late.
As always. For some reason, Conrad James thought he could
show up whenever without consequence—they agreed on
three-thirty and, if he didn't show up within the next fifteen
minutes, Cummings was out of there. He didn't have to wait

around for someone like James—he had other things to do, and if James couldn't make time to hear what he had to tell him . . . well, then, he could cram it.

He took a long draw just as a hand clapped him hard on his shoulder.

"Sorry I'm late—I got tied up at the office. You know how it is . . ." Conrad James straddled the stool next to Cummings. "Let's get to it, then—what's so damned important?"

"I was about to get the hell out of here . . ."

"Well, you didn't—so, cut the crap. Why am I here?"

Cummings took another drink, taking his time placing the pint carefully on the bar.

"Someone's snooping around . . ."

"What does that mean—snooping around? About what? Where?"

"Burnett's. I think it has something to do with the art theft . . ."

"Who? How many? Have you seen them before?"

"Oh, so now you're interested, eh?" Cummings smashed the last of his cigarette in a chipped ashtray that hadn't been wiped for a week—as far as he was concerned, James could damned well wait for the information.

"Don't screw with me, Cummings—I hold all the cards, so, get to it. What do you know?" James could never be considered a patient man, and that day was no different.

"That's pretty much it—other than Burnett called in big-gun investigators from the States to investigate."

"How do you know? Who?"

"None of your damned business—if you don't believe me, check it out for yourself." With that, Nick Cummings snatched his jacket, and strode out the door.

****

Colbie clicked off her cell just as Ryan showed up. She opened the door, all smiles.

"I just got off the phone with Maggie—I'm meeting her at a pub on the outskirts, but I'm not sure where it is. Seven o'clock . . ."

Ryan held up his hand for a high five. "Nice—do you want me to go with you?"

"No, probably not—if both of us show up, it may put her friends on edge."

"We could always go as a couple—then we'd fit right in."

Colbie eyed Ryan with a raised brow. "Not a bad idea, but we can't count on Maggie's not mentioning we're investigating the art theft—if both of us go, it may be intimidating." She had to admit, however, it would be more fun with Ryan at her side.

"Good point—I'll go anyway, but I'll hang back. I'm not comfortable with your going alone—you may as well get used to it!"

Colbie smiled at his protective nature. "I'm pretty sure I can take care of myself. I was a cop, remember?"

"Cop or not, I'll still feel better if I'm keeping an eye on things from the fringe."

"Okay—I'm not going to argue. I'll order up a snack, and we can come up with a plan . . ."

****

Even though Colbie was well into her thirties, she could still pull together a hip vibe when needed. Maggie's friends, she was certain, would be wearing the latest designer fashions, and showing up in less wouldn't play well. She chose jeans, a designer sweater, and knee high, full grain leather boots. A cashmere scarf completed the ensemble, and Ryan did more than raise an eye when she met him in the lobby of the hotel.

"Look at you!" He grabbed her hand, twirling her in a circle. "You clean up real good . . ."

Colbie laughed, delighted at his approval. "Well, Ryan— you clean up real well . . ." she corrected, winking as she did so.

"Who cares about grammar?" He gave her another approving up and down. "Maybe we should hit the town after you meet with Maggie . . ."

"Let's see how everything goes first . . ." With Colbie, business always came before anything else, and the results of her self-discipline were evident.

"You're right—let's hit it. Maybe we can get you out of there before nine." He glanced at Colbie, hoping for a reaction.

"We'll see . . ."

Their cab was waiting as they pushed through the lobby doors, its driver a far cry from Burnett's chauffeur. Dreadlocks skimming the middle of his back, he looked as if he hadn't bathed in a month, a jagged smile revealing cigarette-stained teeth.

"Welcome to London—where can I take ya?"

"McGuiness Pub—do you know where it is?" Just by looking at him, Colbie wasn't sure of his ability to get them where they needed to be.

"I'll have you there in fifteen minutes—less, depending on traffic!" He grinned, and punched the gas pedal.

True to his word, they pulled up to the pub two minutes earlier than anticipated. Its façade was unassuming except for the gargantuan bouncer protecting the front doors. A line of hopefuls snaked around the corner as he checked I.D.s, rejecting those who didn't have proper credentials, or their names didn't appear on the list. As Colbie and Ryan approached, he clearly looked twice—Ryan suspected it was because Colbie looked hot, but Colbie knew it was because he didn't recognize them. Maggie assured them, however, Colbie's name would be on the list—but that didn't mean Ryan would be on it. If he were sent packing, their plan was to meet at the coffee shop around the corner at nine o'clock.

The bouncer checked the list, and welcomed both of them by unfastening the red rope much like those in old-time theaters. Once inside, the unassuming building morphed into a hip, crowded bar and dance club, bodies cramming the dance floor, jostling cocktail waitresses winding through the crowd as dancers ground on their partners. Colbie didn't see the allure of such moves—*crude*, she thought—and she briefly questioned if she were getting old. The scene before her was unappealing and, after only five minutes, she couldn't wait to get out of there.

The good news was it would be easy for Ryan to get lost in the crowd. He separated from Colbie as soon as they entered, and headed for a spot where he could keep an eye on her as she tried to find Maggie and her friends.

"Cameron! Over here!" Using their agreed-upon pseudonym, Maggie waved, motioning for Colbie to join them. As she weaved her way to Maggie's table, Colbie noticed five girls and a guy sitting with her, drinks in hand, laughing. The girls were draped in money, but the guy seemed more to Colbie's liking—jeans, boots, and leather jacket. "Maggie! I found you! I had no idea this place would be so crowded!"

Maggie jumped up, giving Colbie a quick hug as well as the obligatory peck on the cheek. "Believe it or not, it's always like this!" She stepped aside and pointed to a curly-haired blonde. "This is Silvie, and the one next to her is Andie . . ." Maggie proceeded to introduce all of her friends, ending with the young man in the leather jacket. "And, that's Nick Cummings . . ." She pointed as Nick raised his glass at the introduction, flashing an engaging grin.

"I hope I remember your names . . ." Colbie took a seat next to Nick. "But, since you're the only guy here, I'm pretty sure I won't have any trouble remembering your name!" She extended her hand. "I'm Cameron . . ."

Nick accepted, officially introducing himself. "Maggie tells me you're visiting her father . . ."

Colbie gently pulled her hand from his, her intuitive antennae on the rise. "I'm only here for a couple of days, then I head to Paris. I'm trying to cram in as much as possible in forty-eight hours!" By Nick's comment, Colbie assumed Maggie hadn't spilled the beans about the investigation, but she couldn't be sure. He seemed genuine enough, but when Colbie grasped his hand, visions of question marks appeared. That's all. Question marks. *Oh, great,* she thought. *What the hell does that mean?* But, figuring it out would have to wait until later—her immediate task was to ascertain whether any of Maggie's friends may have information about the theft.

"So, Nick—do you like living in London?"

"Yeah—it's alright . . ."

"Are you from here?" Colbie believed in learning from what some might consider insignificant information. During her years of interrogating suspects and interviewing victims, she learned to listen for nuggets of info that may come into play later. Her ability to remove blinders to consider everything instead of only one or two things provided opportunities to access the truth, and she had to take advantage whenever possible.

"Originally? Nope—South Africa." Bingo.

"No kidding—I thought I heard a different accent! What made you come here?"

"Work—isn't that what always makes someone move?"

Colbie detected a change in Nick's posture. She took her time shifting her position, allowing a few extra moments to tune in on the young man sitting beside her. "I suppose—I moved for the same reason. Twice!" She took a sip from the glass just placed in front of her—a gesture from Maggie.

"I hope you don't mind my ordering for you," Maggie

called from across the table. "You seemed to be having a heart to heart with Nick, and I didn't want to interrupt!" Maggie lifted her glass in a toast. "To new friends!"

Colbie returned the gesture. "Heart to heart? No—I was just asking him where he was from . . ."

"Have you ever been to South Africa?" Maggie seemed to be enjoying her drink a little too much. "Did he tell you what he did there for a living?" Another swig.

"No . . ." Colbie turned to Nick. "But that sounds intriguing—what did you do?"

Maggie couldn't wait for his answer. "He worked on a game reserve!"

Nick shifted uncomfortably, and hailed the cocktail waitress for another drink. "It sounds cooler than it really was—Maggie seems to be quite enthralled, however. Not sure why . . ."

"Well, you have to admit," Colbie countered, "it's not everyone who gets to work on a game reserve. I think it sounds interesting, too . . ." Coincidence? Nick's time in South Africa piqued her interest, and it was worth focusing her attention on him. "What did you do at the reserve?"

Nick suddenly jumped up, offering his hand to Colbie. "I don't mean to be rude, but I'm late for another engagement. It was a pleasure to meet you . . ." He gulped his drink, and was gone in an instant after a peck on Maggie's cheek. Colbie suspected he whispered something to her for Maggie's face fell for a brief moment, but she quickly recovered, turning her attention to Colbie. "So, what do you think of Nick?"

"Very nice—he seems the type to work on a game reserve!"

"I know—kind of sexy, huh?" She turned in her chair to watch Nick disappear through the door.

There was no mistaking it, and Colbie recognized the symptoms—Maggie Burnett was in love with Nick Cummings. "Indeed! What did he do on the reserve?"

"I don't really know, but I think it had something to do with big game. Elephants. Rhinos. Something like that . . ." Maggie returned her attention to the new drink in front of her.

"Really? Sounds interesting . . ." Colbie purposefully sounded disinterested, but the truth was she didn't want to maintain her focus on Nick at the risk of snubbing the others at the table. She couldn't risk undue attention, and she needed to make the most of her time at the club—chances of meeting up with Maggie's friends again in such a relaxed atmosphere were nil, and it wouldn't be too long before they were so gassed that information may be easily skewed.

Colbie scooted over to an empty chair. "Silvie—I'm Colbie! It's nice to meet you . . ." Silvie seemed quiet, but that could be because Andie monopolized conversation with anyone within ten feet. She chattered a mile a minute, and Colbie wondered if the constant stream of verbal consciousness were booze induced, or if she were simply a motormouth. Either way, listening to Andie non-stop would be enough to drive anyone over the edge.

It was tricky to assess Silvie's age–there was something about her that made Colbie consider Silvie's being an old soul—deeply set eyes added a slightly haunting look to her pale skin, and Colbie picked up on a feeling of sorrow. Silvie's chair was pushed back from the table as if she didn't enjoy being in the middle of conversation, and she gave an impression of living on the fringe—not in an edgy way. It seemed as if she had trouble fitting in, and Silvie clearly didn't exhibit interest in speaking with her—she unwittingly crossed her arms over her chest as if protecting herself from impending verbal onslaught.

"Thanks—you, too." Her tone bordered on dismissive.

"So—how long have you known Maggie?" Colbie kept her voice light and friendly.

"About ten years . . ." Nothing more. Silvie had no interest in providing unsolicited information, and her attitude made Colbie think the sallow-looking string bean had something to hide.

"That's a long time! You're lucky—my close friends splintered to different states soon after college . . ."

"That sucks." Silvie reached for her watered-down drink, refusing to make eye contact, her attention focused on the front door as if she were waiting for someone to arrive. There was no mistake—Silvie snubbed Colbie like a pro. "Please excuse me . . ." She stood, revealing a statuesque body that could rival the best of models. Nodding briefly at Colbie, she grabbed her clutch, and headed for the ladies' room.

Great, Colbie thought, so *much for that!* She checked her watch, and returned to Maggie's conversation, hoping she could get the hell out of there. Her host was engrossed in conversation with someone whom Colbie didn't know or recognize, and it was the perfect cue—a few minutes later, Colbie was out the door, Ryan in close, unnoticed pursuit.

****

"Other than the fact they were smashed ten minutes after I arrived, it went okay . . ."

"Just okay?" Ryan pulled out a chair for Colbie at an inconspicuous table for two in the corner. "You were with them for well over an hour . . ."

"I know—but, after Nick Cummings decided to beat feet, there wasn't much to learn. I tried to stir up a conversation with Silvie, and the only thing I can say about her is she's an ice queen."

"Was she the tall one?"

"Yes, and she made it clear she had no intention of lowering herself to my level by engaging in conversation." Colbie pulled off her gloves and lay them on the table, smoothing the leather with her palms. "I don't know—my gut says she's a bitch, but I don't have any sense of her being involved with the thefts—or that she knows anything about it—in any way. Maybe she's just a mean girl . . ."

"Mean girl? That's a rather millennial comment, isn't it? I didn't know you're so . . . hip!" He laughed, knowing Colbie appreciated his sense of humor.

"Oh, yeah—hip. That's me!"

They settled in, and a pretty, young barista greeted them then took their order. A perfect refuge from the damp, biting cold, the shadowed and intimate coffee shop was perfect for quiet conversations and clandestine meetings. Tucked away on a cobbled side street, they had the place to themselves except for a couple of stragglers—just the way they liked it. Colbie and Ryan spent hours in a neighborhood café while they hammered out their plan to find Brian, and the familiarity didn't go unnoticed.

"This place reminds me of where we used to brainstorm

during our investigation . . ." Ryan's eyes met Colbie's, both recalling their intense search. "And, speaking of Brian—have you heard from him?"

"If you can call it 'speaking,' then yes . . ."

"Meaning?"

Colbie straightened and stiffened in her chair as if preparing for verbal battle. The mention of Brian's name put her on edge, and she knew she needed to deal with her situation sooner than later. "I suppose you picked up on the fact our relationship is deteriorating—unfortunately, I don't think there's anything I can do to prevent it. I really thought our move to the East Coast would snap him out of his spiraling depression—but, it didn't work. He's worse now than ever . . ."

"In what way?"

"Everything! He doesn't communicate, react, or take any initiative to live his life. Maybe he wants me to live it for him—I don't know. You'd think my training would make it easier for me to deal with him, but it doesn't—intellectually, I know what's happening, but, on an emotional level, I can't help thinking I should be the one to help him rise from his ashes of despair. But, I don't think I can . . ."

Ryan felt Colbie's hurt from across the table. "What are you going to do?" He felt it best not to pry too much—if she needed him he would be there for her, and she knew it.

"To be honest, getting away from Brian was one of the reasons I wanted to work this case with you . . . I'm hoping it provides clarity because, right now, I'm mired in mud."

Time to lighten it up. "Gee, and here I thought you accepted the gig so you could work with me!"

Colbie grinned, and fired back. "Don't be so smug!" Just
in time, the barista arrived and placed two double lattes in
front of them as well as two cinnamon streusel muffins in
the middle of the table. "You're right, though—I thought it
would be fun working together again."

"Are you having fun, so far?"

"Well, I wish we had a little more to go on even though
we're only starting the investigation, but, yes—I'm having
fun."

"Good! Now let's go over what you learned tonight . . ."

"You're right—thinking about Brian isn't going to get us
anywhere." Colbie took a deep breath and exhaled slowly as
if cleansing her mind and soul. "Okay—as I said, it wasn't
much, but I think Nick Cummings—the guy in the leather
jacket— is a key player in some way."

"What makes you think that? He wasn't with you very
long at the club."

"I know—but he sure changed the subject when Maggie
mentioned he used to work on a game reserve in South
Africa."

"Really? That's pretty cool—what did he do?"

"I'm not sure—the second we started talking about
Africa, he was gone. But—Maggie did mention she thought
he had something to do with elephants. Or, rhinos . . ."

Colbie and Ryan finished their first round of lattes
considering a possible link between Nick and the art thefts.
On the surface, there didn't seem to be anything, but Colbie
couldn't let it go. Her gut told her he knew more than anyone
else at the party table that night, and he clearly didn't
want to talk about it. Did Maggie tell him her father hired

investigators? Perhaps so.

"Can you dream up an excuse to see him again? Maybe if you had more time with him, you can tap into what's going on . . ."

"I'll try, but, even if I can see him again, there's no guarantee I'll pick up anything."

"Well, it can't hurt to try . . ."

"True. But, you know what's funny? I have a feeling I'll see him sooner than I think." Colbie leaned forward, meeting Ryan's eyes. "In fact, I'm sure of it . . ."

CHAPTER SEVEN

Brian sat on the toilet, hands trembling as he struggled to open the childproof cap. Ever since the kidnapping, an inexplicable tremor appeared and, for the most part, he found it difficult to do the simplest things. Medication didn't help and, after exhausting all physical possibilities, Colbie assessed his tremors were most likely due to psychological stress. *Didn't she want to help me*, he wondered, turning the bottle in his hands. *Have I changed that much?*

He sat, legs tucked toward the stem of the commode, recalling what it was like before someone took command of his life—before he lost himself. When he first met Colbie at a friend's barbecue, he knew she was the one—slender and funny, she seemed the antithesis of what he pictured a cop to be. Yet, when she stood before him with a smile that instantly melted his heart, he knew she was probably the best cop to ever make it through the Academy. He also knew she would be the best thing to ever happen to him.

He was right, too. At least for the first five or six years—after that, their relationship resembled wine slowly turning to vinegar. Conversation between them diminished to nearly nothing, and he was at a point where he needed to make some decisions. That was why he went on the camping trip in the first place—to have a little time to himself. Time with his best friend was just what he needed, and Brian recalled Ryan's once telling him, "If I miss a minute, I've missed too much . . ." He was beginning to see what his friend meant.

Why me? he wondered, retreating to a time he never wanted to remember. The only problem was he couldn't help it—he thought about the gun barrel stuffed in his mouth. The beatings. The shattering of the little finger on his right hand. "You don't need it," his kidnapper taunted. "In fact, you probably don't need the other one, either . . ." He thought about the pistol butt to the back of his head.

He thought about being zip tied to a chair.

From the time he returned home and throughout the subsequent trial, he could think of nothing else. And, without realizing it, the trauma finally ate through him until he could barely remember anything before that day. Yes, for the first couple of years, Colbie was sympathetic—a dutiful sympathy, perhaps—but she lost patience as his third year of freedom took hold. She expected PTSD for he had many of the symptoms—feeling unsettled, replaying the kidnapping relentlessly in his mind, and screwed up sleep cycles. But each time she suggested a psychiatrist, Brian lost it, and he retreated to what he called his man cave—the tiny second bedroom with the shades always drawn. Still, Colbie knew to expect a strong reaction when one is ripped from normalcy. But, as she saw it, he did little to help himself. That—coupled with his inability to cope with her newfound success—was the proverbial recipe for disaster. Their relationship faltered to the brink of break up, neither willing to go there unless it were the final option.

But what rankled Brian more than Colbie's inability to deal with his affliction? Ryan. His best friend. The guy he could talk to about anything. Brian never could figure out why Ryan split so suddenly after everything returned to so-called normal and, after he left, Ryan only got in touch a couple of times. It were as if their fifteen-year friendship didn't mean a damned thing! So, between the declining relationship with the love of his life and the desertion of his best friend, there seemed little reason to carry on.

****

Tammy pulled off her right glove with her teeth, fumbling for Colbie's house key in her purse. The truth was she wasn't sure why she was there—but she had a feeling something wasn't right. *I promised her,* Tammy argued with herself. *But, what if I'm wrong? What if everything is just fine? Then I'm going to look like an idiot . . .*

She tried again. "I know you're in there—if you don't answer, I'm using my key!" Still, nothing.

Tammy slipped the key into the lock, gently turning it as if she were going to wake someone by entering. The door opened easily, and she slipped inside, quickly closing it with the hope of no one seeing her.

"Brian? You here? It's me—Tammy!" The house felt unusually cold. *Why's it so freezing in here?* She peered into each room on the first floor, searching for signs of something.

Anything. But as she continued her search, her boss's home felt lifeless and uninviting.

She tried again. "Brian!" This time her voice was commanding as if scolding a child. "If you don't answer, I'm coming upstairs . . ." Tammy heard the words come out of her mouth, slightly stunned at how silly she sounded. It could very well be Brian was out and about—and he certainly didn't need to check in with her. Still . . .

The banister on the stairs was cold to her touch as she made her way to the upper floor. "Brian?" Gingerly, she opened doors to each bedroom, finally turning the knob to the master. "Brian? You here?" Nothing. She entered, noticing a sliver of light from underneath the door of the master bath, and relief flooded through her. "Brian?" Her hand rested lightly on the latch, then she pushed without opening it completely.

His body lay slumped in front of the door.

Chapter Eight

Sleek and the color of gun metal, the limo pulled up in front of the hotel precisely at seven o'clock courtesy of Samuel Burnett. The driver was different—clearly a man of elegance and taste. Apparently, Burnett had an eye for class with the style of his driver as well as his own.

"Ma'am?" The chauffeur opened the door for Colbie and Ryan, waiting patiently until they settled in the plush leather seats. "Please—Mr. Burnett wants you to be comfortable. The bar is stocked . . ."

Within moments, they pulled into traffic which wasn't nearly as bad as during the day. Ryan mixed a vodka gimlet on the rocks for Colbie, then settled back with a scotch and soda of his own.

"You look smashing . . . that's what they say here, isn't it? Smashing?" He seldom got to see her dressed to the nines, and that evening he liked what he saw. Colbie wore a sleek cocktail dress of ivory silk, the bodice delicately laced with small pearls. Three-inch, cream-colored satin heels added to her ensemble's understated elegance, as well as her height.

"Thank you. You don't look so bad yourself—who knew you'd clean up so well?" Colbie winked at the handsome man sitting across from her. "I can't remember seeing you dressed up before . . ."

"That's because it rarely happens—I'm a cowboy boots kind of guy, in case you haven't noticed!"

Colbie flushed, and cracked the window to allow in a few puffs of fresh air. Time to change the subject. "Let's take a run at who we know is going to attend tonight—under twenty-five people, depending on who shows up. I suspect there will be a few no shows . . ."

"Why do you say that?"

"You know me—just a feeling . . ."

"Spill it . . ."

Colbie thought for a second, gazing out the window into a night filled with city lights. "Do you remember when I had a vision in which I heard a gunshot? Well, before I got dressed this evening, I took some time to dip into my intuitive mind bank—I heard the shot again, and I heard the name 'James.'"

"Do you know anyone by that name?"

"I know several men named James, but they don't have anything to do with this . . . no, I think it has to do with someone we're going to meet this evening. Do you have the guest list?"

Ryan reached into his inside breast pocket. "Of course—right . . . " He checked the other pocket. "Damn it! I left it in my room!" He looked at Colbie, silently apologizing for his rookie move.

"No problem—we'll figure out who's who when we get there." She thought she noted a sigh of relief. "Now—let's run over our cover. We're from the U.S., co-founders of an up and coming technology firm. We hire the best. The brightest. We're known for cutting edge—in fact, we insist on it. But, we're at the party as private friends of Samuel Burnett. He'll introduce us only as his good friends from the States and, if questioned about our business lives, we need to steer the conversation in a different direction. Or, change the subject—whichever the situation dictates."

Ryan thought for a second. "Agreed. And, we can never mention the name of our organization. We have to use the pseudonyms we gave Burnett, too—Cameron Carlson, and Regis Patrick. But, I'd prefer not to use last names . . ."

"Agreed."

Colbie and Ryan continued fine-tuning their plan and, just before seven-thirty, the limo pulled through the estate's gate, fourth in line behind vehicles normally associated with political dignitaries and rock stars. Samuel Burnett stood on the steps, graciously greeting his guests, shaking and kissing hands, gently guiding them in the right direction. Moments later, their limo pulled directly in front of the estate doors—the driver elegantly helped Colbie from the vehicle while Ryan played cowboy, bolting out the other side.

"Cameron! Regis! Welcome!" Burnett turned his attention to Colbie. "And, you, my dear, look stunning!" His engaging grin on full display, he played his part to the hilt. He took her hand, kissed it gently, then turned his focus to Ryan. "Please, make yourselves at home—I'll join you shortly!" Burnett guided them to the front entrance doors, then turned his attention to the next limo in line.

Game on.

***

Two servants welcomed guests in the foyer, taking
coats, and nodding to butlers who were showing attendees
to a small ballroom. Servers circulated with champagne and
canapés as guests greeted each other, while a four-string
quartet played at a level conducive for conversation in front
of magnificent French doors. The effect was stunning—even
though the room could accommodate a true ball, that night
was for congenial conversation with nothing to gain except
a good time. Business deals? Maybe one or two, but, for the
most part, the party was for friends getting together with
friends. Soft light cast enticing shadows, the overall feeling
one of warmth and familiarity.

As Colbie and Ryan crossed the threshold, Colbie paid
particular attention to who was already there. Champagne
glass in hand, Maggie gracefully moved from guest to guest,
laughing with the ease of someone in her element. Her
father's stand-in until all guests arrived, she chatted with a
British looking middle-aged man as if he were her best friend
until she noticed Colbie and Ryan entering the room.

"Cameron!" Maggie excused herself, and welcomed
Colbie with the cheek kiss. "How good of you to come!" She
turned her attention to Ryan. "And, Regis—we weren't sure
you could make it. Welcome to our home!"

Colbie glanced at Ryan with an approving look. So
far, nobody dropped the ball—Maggie and her father were

Chasing Rhinos   71

playing their agreed upon roles, and no one was the wiser.

Maggie led Colbie and Ryan to a couple standing nearest to the door—Marilyn and Charles Mansfield—and, a few introductions later, she turned her attention to arriving guests, offering gracious personal attention. Colbie and Ryan welcomed the opportunity to get to know the attendees— after all, it was the reason they were there. Nonetheless, after a socially acceptable amount of time to wrap up polite conversation and move on, Colbie and Ryan excused themselves with the intent of having a private convo.

"They're an interesting group, aren't they?" Ryan sipped his drink, doing his best to look inconspicuous.

"Indeed. What do you think of the Mansfields?"

"I don't think they have a clue—Marilyn seems the type to focus on fashion, and I doubt she knows much about art. Same with her husband . . ."

"Agreed. Check out the guy standing close to the musicians . . ."

Ryan turned as if contemplating the expensive art strategically highlighted by soft lighting. Standing closest to the cello player was a man who would catch the eye of every woman in the room—whether they admitted it, or not. He towered over the other guests—at least six four or six five—his lanky body made for wearing the most expensive clothes. And expensive they were—a deep purple cashmere sweater accented his ink-black hair, his slacks made of fine wool. *Good choice,* Ryan thought. *It's stinkin' cold here . . .*

"What do you think? Any idea of who he is?" Colbie couldn't take her eyes off of him—something that didn't go unnoticed by her partner.

"Nope—Burnett provided dossiers for everyone, pics

included, but I don't remember seeing this guy . . ."

"Same here . . ."

"Can you tune in to him?"

"Not really—there's a lot going on, but I can try to strike up a conversation."

"Unless he beats you to it. Remember I said you look smashing . . ."

"Thanks—but, I seriously doubt he's going to find his way to me."

"Don be so sure . . ."

Colbie thought she heard a bit of jealously in Ryan's voice. "Ryan . . ."

Just then, Samuel Burnett strode into the room, ready to mingle with his guests. "Good evening, everyone! Welcome! As you can tell, this isn't a large get-together—I prefer to spend a delightful evening with the truly special people in my life. Some of you already know each other—others, you will meet for the first time." He nodded to Colbie and Ryan. "Make yourselves comfortable, and please . . . enjoy!" After a quick burst of applause, Burnett began circulating, choosing Colbie and Ryan first.

"Cameron, my dear, you do that dress justice!"

"Thank you, Samuel—it's so kind of you to invite us." Both played the game, giving no indication of their ruse. "I recognize several guests from their dossiers—but, the dark-haired man standing by the musicians—who is he?"

Samuel glanced at the quartet. "Him? That's Nigel Blackwell—he lives in South Africa. Cape Town, I believe, although I know he travels the world, so I'm not certain if he's there often."

"Travels the world? Doing what?"

"Import-export—he's been at the top of that game for years."

"Really? Sounds interesting . . ."

"He's quite the ladies' man from what I hear!"

"Well, he's certainly an imposing figure . . ." That was one way of putting it. 'Greek god' may be another.

"Shall I introduce you?" He looked at Ryan. "You, as well, Regis . . ."

Colbie answered for both of them. "Not yet—I want a chance to observe for a few minutes, if you don't mind."

"I don't—besides, I suspect he'll find you." With that, Burnett moved to a small group of guests admiring one of his paintings.

Colbie glanced at Ryan as he shot her the 'I told you so' look. "Import-export? Interesting . . ." Something was beginning to click in her brain, and she suddenly thought of Nick Cummings. "Remember the guy at the club last night?"

"The one who left in a hurry? Yeah—what about him?"

"He's from South Africa—I wonder if they know each other?"

"Maybe, but Cummings doesn't really look the type to be hanging around with Blackwell—not even the same league."

"You might be right . . . but I think it's worth checking out."

"A feeling?"

Colbie turned to Ryan. "Yes, but it's opaque—I can't really make sense of it."

"Is that normal—for you, I mean . . ."

"No—I may not know right away what a particular symbol means, but it rarely comes to me as veiled."

"Alrighty then—let's go fishing!"

Colbie and Ryan's roles as rising entrepreneurs didn't raise suspicion as they introduced themselves to Burnett's guests. Their parts came easily and, within the hour, they found themselves in a pleasant chat with Nigel Blackwell. He drifted toward Colbie and Ryan, striking up a conversation with ease and, after only minutes, Colbie assessed Blackwell as smooth, and well-bred.

Ryan assessed him as a player.

****

Shortly after midnight, the limo pulled up to the hotel. "As interesting as the night was, "Colbie commented, "I'm ready to sleep in my own bed!"

"I hear ya—I'm pooped." Ryan offered Colbie a helping hand as she exited the vehicle, a courtesy usually extended by the driver. "Nightcap? Or, should we call it a night?"

Within minutes, they stood at the door to one of the

glass-lift elevators. "As lovely as a nightcap sounds, I think I'm ready to hit the sack."

"Check. I'll walk you to your door!"

****

Nigel Blackwell sat in a well-worn leather chair positioned in front of a dwindling fire, replaying the events of the evening. It was uneventful for the most part—he and Burnett had little time for conversation—business conversation—but they could chat later. The real interest of the evening was Cameron—a beauty to be sure—but there was something else about her he found intriguing, yet he couldn't put his finger on it. Most women considered him to be quite the catch—she acted as if she could care less. *Refreshing*, he thought, swirling ice gently in its glass as he recalled the charming redhead. *Perhaps she's worth looking into . . . and, what's up with that Regis fellow? Partners? Maybe. But I doubt it . . .*

By the time Blackwell called it a night, he decided. He would call Cameron the following day—he knew the hotel, so she wouldn't be difficult to track down. Besides, if he did have trouble getting in touch, Samuel Burnett would be happy to pass on her contact information. One thing Blackwell knew was women, and he was certain Cameron Carlson was interested.

Very interested.

****

By the time Colbie climbed into bed, a bitter, driving rain slashed at her hotel windows, the damp cold of London taking up residence in her body. Even so, a hot shower, and cup of hot chocolate later, she was ready to relax. But as she plumped and propped her pillows against the headboard, a sense of danger surged through her, yet not strong enough to be concerning. It wasn't an unfamiliar sensation and, as frightening as it might be to most, for Colbie it was commonplace. Her time on the force frequently placed her in dangerous situations, and she learned early on to temper her intuitive mind.

She closed her eyes, her mind's eye immediately centering on Nigel Blackwell. At first, nothing in particular— until she witnessed an argument with a man who looked like an English professor at an ivy league school. Tweed jacket. Patches. Pipe. British? She wasn't sure. The man arguing with Blackwell attended the party, but she had no idea as to his identity.

Colbie let the picture form on the screen in her mind's eye, lingering on it until it started to fade. She mentally wadded the image up like a piece of paper, tossing it aside as another took form. This time, a male lion, its mane nearly obscured by swaying grass, lying on the ground while silently surveying it's surroundings as if expecting something. He focused on Colbie as if he were in the same room with her, his eyes making direct contact with hers as the vision took shape. With intense focus, the lion rose in the tall grass and, with the same movement of a house cat stalking its prey, it crept toward her, eyes locked on hers.

Fear wrapped around her, a cold sweat enveloping her body like a wet, wool blanket. The lion crouched, then leapt toward her in one powerful, swift motion, its massive face lunging in front of hers! Colbie felt her body jerk spontaneously and, with a gasp, she commanded the vision to dismantle, watching it dissipate into shattered fragments.

Oh, God! Oh, God! Oh, God! She tried to calm her mind and body, but her heart raced frantically—never had she encountered such a strong and overpowering vision, and she wasn't quite sure what to do. She lay prone on her bed and, after a few moments, she instinctively took her pulse—elevated, but she could feel it coming down. Then a swig from the water bottle she kept on the nightstand. *Well, that scared the livin' crap out of me,* she thought as her body started to destress. *I don't know what the hell just happened, but I know it isn't good.* What bothered Colbie most was the all-encompassing fear—she'd been in dangerous situations many times while on the force, but she never felt anything so soul searing.

The image of the lion vivid in her mind, Colbie rewound Samuel Burnett's party trying to make sense of the vision. She went over each servant. Each guest. The only person she could recall who caught her attention was Nigel Blackwell, but he certainly didn't scare her.

Not at all.

CHAPTER NINE

"Tammy! Slow down! Take a deep breath, and tell me what's wrong . . ." Colbie checked the time on her cell—just before dawn. After a quick mental calculation, she figured the time in the States was about ten the previous evening.

"It's Brian . . ." Tammy paused, a sob catching in her throat.

"What about Brian—is he alright?"

"I don't know—he's on his way to the hospital!" Tammy buckled as she heard Colbie's anguish on the other end.

"What? The hospital? What happened?"

"He's alive . . . I found him in the bathroom, and called 911 right away!"

"Do you know what happened? Did he slip and fall? And, why were you at the house?" Colbie knew Tammy well enough to know she wouldn't have just dropped by—it was out of her way. She must have had a reason . . .

"I don't know—all I know is I had a feeling something was wrong, and I couldn't shake it. So, I decided to stop by to check on things . . ." Tammy waited a few seconds. "Colbie? You okay?"

Colbie couldn't answer. She was afraid something like this would happen and, in that instant, she knew she shouldn't have left Brian alone. "What did the paramedics say?"

"Not much, but I heard one of them call in, and he mentioned pills."

"Pills? He tried to kill himself?"

"I don't know! They wouldn't tell me anything!"

Colbie tried to process what she was hearing. "What hospital?"

"I'm not sure—which hospital is closest to you?"

"Probably St. Pat's—I pass it on my way to work."

"Okay—I'm heading there now. I'll call you as soon as I know something." Tammy paused. "What are you going to do? Come home?"

The thought of returning to the States before concluding their current case never occurred to her, but Tammy was right. Leaving to be at Brian's side was probably the best choice—she could carry on the case from her end, and she'd still be a help to Ryan. Still, her heart collapsed when she realized how her life just changed.

"Home? I don't know—I guess so. I can't think right now . . . call me as soon as you know something."

"I get it—call if you need me." Tammy rang off, leaving Colbie to her thoughts and heartache.

The thought of losing Brian was far different than choosing to end their relationship—attempted suicide spoke to deeper issues. Colbie curled up into a fetal position in bed, pulling the covers over her shoulders, up to her chin. Tears stained the perfect white sheets with the remains of party mascara, creating charcoal-like streaks on her pillow.

I should have stayed, she murmured. *I knew I should have stayed . . .*

****

Ryan sat on the ottoman in front of the easy chair in Colbie's room, staggered at the news. "Have you heard from Tammy? Where's Brian now?"

"She called about thirty minutes ago—she finally found out rescue took him to St. Pat's which is about fifteen minutes from our house. He's recuperating. Thank God Tammy didn't ignore her premonition—if she didn't act on her feeling that something was wrong, we'd probably be facing something completely different." Colbie straightened her bathrobe as she curled up on the couch—she didn't bother to dress. She couldn't bring herself to do anything except think about Brian. What she did wrong. What she was going to do.

"I suppose this means you're going to head back . . ."

"What choice do I have? Brian needs me, and I'm not

going to bail on him this time! I can't believe how selfish I was by agreeing to work this case with you—I knew how fragile he was, and yet I completely ignored it!" Fresh tears spilled, and she swiped at them with her fingertips. "I'll try to get a flight for this afternoon . . ."

"So soon? I mean, I know Brian needs you, but Tammy said he wasn't in any danger. And, as long as he's in the hospital, you know he's being taken care of . . ."

"I know, but I think I owe it to him to get back as quickly as I can." She looked at Ryan. He seemed broken, and she was sure he was wondering what part he played in his once best friend's breakdown.

"I understand." He joined Colbie on the couch, slipping a comforting arm around her shoulder. She melted into him, her body tiny against his.

And, there they sat. Each thinking of Brian. Each other.

Themselves.

****

Travelers crowded around flight schedule monitors, checking to see if their flights were canceled. Weather conditions deteriorated since morning and, by the time they reached the airport, a British winter storm was in full swing. It was a good thing her flight was already delayed for a few hours because traffic leading to the airport was at a standstill.

A freak storm, they called it.

Finally arriving by early evening, Ryan hopped out to grab Colbie's luggage as she paid the cab driver and, once inside, they realized there was another delay—it would be well into the night before her plane would take off. In some ways, she was content to stay with Ryan, accepting his comfort and wishing she didn't have to go. But she knew that was impossible—Tammy worked her magic by getting a reservation, and there was no turning back. Even if there were, Colbie made the decision to get to Brian as quickly as she could. She hadn't spoken with him since his arrival at the hospital, but Tammy indicated they admitted him to a regular ward. *Why not the psych ward*, Colbie wondered as Tammy filled her in earlier. She tried calling, but the nurse told her he was sleeping, and she shouldn't interrupt—not to mention the nurse didn't have any idea who Colbie was, and she wasn't about to be giving out salient information over the phone to someone who wasn't on the 'list.'

Bags checked, they made their way to the gate to wait for Colbie's plane, stranded travelers occupying every seat. They tried the air club next and, to their luck, two seats opened up as they walked in.

"Cocktail?" Ryan helped Colbie off with her coat. "I'm putting your gloves here . . ." He held up the gloves so she could see him jam them in her coat's right pocket.

"Fine—thanks." She slid into the booth, and picked up a menu. "I don't think I should drink—maybe an appetizer, though. It's going to be a long flight . . ."

"Done!" Ryan soon placed an order for two appetizers, and two Cokes. "So—how are you feeling?"

Colbie tilted her head back, closed her eyes, and sighed. "I don't know—I'm numb."

"I can imagine—I wish I could do more. But, you and I

know Brian doesn't consider me a friend anymore."

"Oh, I don't think that's true—but, for some reason, he feels you betrayed him when you left so suddenly after we found him."

"It wasn't that soon—a couple of months, maybe . . ."

"Well, to him, it was soon—and, he refused to talk about it. I asked him several times if he heard from you, but he'd always said no, brushing it off as if it were nothing."

"I did try to get in touch, you know—I emailed him several times, but never got an answer. After the fifth time or so, I figured he wanted nothing to do with me."

Colbie fidgeted in her seat. "Do you mind if I ask you something?"

By the way she looked at him, Ryan could tell she was serious. "Sure—ask away!"

"Why did you decide to . . ." Before she could finish, her cell buzzed, and she quickly checked the caller I.D. "Oh, no—it's the hospital!" Alarmed, she answered before the third buzz.

Brian.

Ryan motioned silently he would check on her flight, allowing her the privacy she needed. She nodded, listening to Brian, tears welling to the point of nearly spilling.

"Are you sure? I don't mind, Brian—I want to be with you!"

But, it wasn't to be. Fifteen minutes later, Ryan sat across from his partner as she relayed her conversation with Brian—it was over. He didn't want her to come back.

"Do you think he was just saying that?" Ryan asked.

"No—if you could have heard his voice, you'd know he meant business. He's done. With me. You. Everything. As soon as he leaves the hospital, he's going to stay with his parents for a while."

Ryan knew Colbie well enough to know she was relieved, but he could see the sadness in her eyes. "How are you? How do you feel about it?"

Colbie sighed, downing the last of her Coke. "Okay, I guess. I admit, I didn't see it coming . . ." She was about to suggest they get out of there when the cell phone she had specifically for their case vibrated. She checked the caller I.D.—a number she didn't recognize. Colbie motioned to Ryan, holding her index finger to her lips.

"This is Cameron . . ."

"Cameron? Nigel Blackwell . . ."

****

Brian sat on the edge of his hospital bed, the phone receiver dangling in his hand as he considered life without Colbie. Resolve dissipated to emptiness the second they hung up, and he wondered if he made the right decision. *Maybe life will be better without her, he thought. Maybe I don't need her. Maybe I can go on . . .*

He swung his legs back on the bed, slipping them under the covers and shifting his weight so he could sit up. Nurses scurried to patients' rooms, each looking identical in their uniform scrubs except for the occasional bobbing ponytail or shortly-cropped hair. Brian smiled at the words of his nurse. "Get some rest," she said as she left his room as quietly as she entered. *Yeah, right! As if I can get any rest in this place . . .*

He stared out the window, watching a construction crane grip large, steel girders, swiveling them precariously as its operator moved cargo from site to site. He remembered an article in the town paper indicating completion of the new hospital wing was slated for early spring, a date he questioned when he realized how much work still needed to be completed. *They'll never make it,* he thought as he watched the lengths of steel swing in the breeze.

Then he thought about Colbie. What would his life be without her? Did he have the guts to carry on? Tears fell as he thought about their life together, and her insistence that she wanted to be with him. The problem was he didn't believe her, although the panic in her voice offered the possibility of his being wrong.

As he lay alone with his thoughts, he realized the enormity of his mistake. His attempted suicide? A horrible plan. And, then, a funny thing happened—Brian felt a surge of confidence he hadn't felt for years, and he knew what he had to do to fix his life. Getting discharged from the hospital wasn't going to be that easy, however.

Unless he walked.

****

"Nigel? This is a surprise!" Colbie motioned to Ryan to keep quiet. "Did Samuel give you my number?"

Nigel Blackwell laughed, delighted at how quickly she deduced how he got her contact information. "Indeed, he did! I hope you don't mind . . ."

"Mind? No, of course not—can I help you with something?" She shot Ryan a look, her eyebrows arched in disbelief. In return, Ryan shot her the 'I told you so' look. Again.

"Nothing of import—I am hoping, however, you'll accept my invitation to dinner tomorrow night . . ."

"Dinner? Well . . ."

"Cameron—you're not going to make me beg, are you?"

Colbie smiled at his attempt to make her feel guilty if she chose to say no. "I think I can fit dinner into my schedule—what time?"

"Excellent! I'll send a car for you promptly at seven—wear your finest . . ."

"We're going fancy, are we? Fine—I'll be ready."

She rang off, looking for confirmation from Ryan that the conversation with Blackwell just took place. "That was weird . . ."

"What's weird? I told you he took an interest in you, but you said I was nuts—believe me now?"

"We're going to dinner tomorrow night . . ."

"I gathered that—where?"

"I don't know, but I have to look my best." Colbie did a

mental check of what she had hanging in her hotel closet—
her little black dress with a dove grey cashmere shrug was
perfect.

"Well, I know one thing—if we don't get the hell out of
here, we may ending up spending the night!"Ryan grabbed
her carry-on luggage, heading for the nearest check-in desk.

"I hope they haven't loaded your bags . . ."

CHAPTER TEN

C onrad James placed his pint on the bar, wiping away
a slight foam mustache with his fingertips, thinking
about the soirée at Samuel Burnett's the previous
evening. For the most part, he knew everyone there with the
exception of a few—Cameron Carlson, and her boyfriend
the most notable. For the life of him, he couldn't see what
she saw in him—she carried herself like a woman of class
and he seemed so—pedestrian. *A rather common man*, he
thought as he signaled the barkeep for another. *They're more
than business colleagues—and they're not fooling me for one
second* . . . There was something about them that didn't feel
quite right, but he couldn't put his finger on it.

It was James's nature to be an elitist. He had little time
or patience for those who held little hope or possibility of
reaching his station in life—and, he had no desire to engage
the company of those he deemed less than he. Which is
exactly why he detested his meetings with Nick Cummings.
In his opinion, Cummings was nothing more than a classless
hack who sported criminally mediocre tattoos and, if he

had his way, he and Cummings would never cross paths. Unfortunately, the overgrown street urchin was a necessity in his life—at least for a while longer.

The last time they met, Cummings alluded to someone snooping around Burnett's estate, but, in a display of annoying impudence, he stormed out before James could squeeze him for additional information—an upstart move, and one James didn't appreciate. Cummings left him at the bar knowing little more than when James got there—he provided no names. No reason for thinking someone may be snooping around the Burnett estate. Over the days following their last meeting, James called and messaged him, but Cummings decided to play a dangerous game by not picking up or answering his texts. James's last message lacked tact, threatening Cummings's health if he didn't show up at the pub at precisely six o'clock that evening. It was a tactic he knew would work—being the little worm Cummings was, James had no doubt he would arrive on time.

He checked his watch—not quite six. *That little bastard better show up*, he thought as he drained his glass. *I don't have time for this shit . . .*

Minutes later, the heavy door to the pub opened, revealing waning rays of filtered light with dust particles appearing suspended in space. Cummings paused to crush his cigarette just out side the door, then entered with the swagger of someone who mattered. It was just as James thought—Cummings showed up at two minutes past the hour. Nick knew he was late, but he could have cared less—it felt good to have control over a man for whom he had obvious distaste.

"You're late . . ." James pulled a pipe from his pocket, lighting it ceremoniously. The mere act of smoking a pipe indicated leisurely thought, and it served as a cue to

Cummings he was ready for a long conversation.

"Sorry, mate—couldn't be helped." Cummings signaled the bartender, ordering a pint of Guinness.

"Couldn't be helped, my ass—next time? Well, I'm sure you can imagine . . ."

Cummings watched the bartender scrape foam from his pint with a smooth swipe. "I'm short on time—why am I here?"

"You know damned well why you're here—the guys snooping around Burnett's . . ."

A smirk flickered across Nick's lips. "Who said they were guys?"

James paused, mid puff. "What's that supposed to mean?"

"Just what I said—I'm not so sure they're guys." Cummings flicked the tip of a new cigarette, tapping it on the bar top to pack the tobacco.

"Tell me everything you know—and don't leave out a damned thing this time."

Cummings leaned forward, resting his forearms on the bar. "Is that an order?"

James emptied his pipe into the same ashtray he used the last time he was there. "Damned right it is . . ."

Nick Cummings thought for several seconds, considering his situation. The pros and cons. If he screwed James, he was dead meat—but, he had to admit it was fun toying with him. "You were at Burnett's party—was there anyone there you didn't know?"

James instantly thought of the beautiful redhead named Cameron. "Two—a woman and her sidekick. Do you know who they are?"

"I wasn't there—what did they look like?"

"A classy woman. Red hair—Cameron—she was with her business partner, Regis . . . something. I don't remember their last names."

Cummings took a long drag on a partial cigarette. "Like I said, I wasn't there . . ."

Conrad James was beginning to lose his patience—he didn't appreciate someone so insignificant playing games with him. "Let me put it this way . . . you're out of time." He tapped the pipe on the side of the ashtray, then carefully placed it in the right pocket of his tweed topcoat.

"Alright, alright—when I was talking with Maggie, she let it slip 'a couple' was investigating the art thefts. She didn't say who . . . but, I got the distinct impression it's a man and a woman." He paused. "And . . ." Cummings's forehead furrowed as he searched his memory.

"And, what?"

"I met a friend of Maggie's—I'm pretty sure her name was Cameron . . ."

"Cameron what?"

"How the hell should I know? Maggie introduced her to all of us as Cameron. That's all . . ."

"Who's 'all of us?'"

"Just a bunch of friends—we got together at one of the clubs outside the perimeter."

James leaned closer, lowering his voice. "Listen to me, you miserable little hack—find out about this Cameron bitch. You have forty-eight hours . . ." Conrad James rose, adjusted his coat, and glared down Nick Cummings. "Got it?"

Cummings looked away. "Got it . . ."

****

"Thank you—I appreciate your help." Brian smiled at the young woman behind the desk.

"You're welcome! You better hurry, though—your flight leaves in twenty minutes!"

Brian thanked her again, and made his way toward Concourse C. The red eye wasn't crowded, but he still didn't have time to kill before boarding. He slipped away from the hospital that afternoon without notice and, by eight o'clock, he was on his way to Logan International Airport even though his flight didn't leave until nearly midnight.

Two hours later, he reached the gate, a crusty looking middle-aged man announcing the all-aboard as he checked his computer monitor. Within five, Brian took his seat, thinking about what was in front of him. Colbie had no idea he was arriving in London, and he wasn't sure if he were going to tell her. *Maybe I should lie low for a while,* he thought as the flight attendant cruised the aisle to make sure everyone was strapped in. A part of him wanted to tell Colbie of his plans—the bigger part told him to hang back.

****

Colbie and Ryan agreed to have breakfast in her room, but not before ten. By the time they reached the hotel the previous evening, it was well past one in the morning, and Colbie needed time to digest the previous twenty-four hours. In some ways, she knew Brian was right—her feelings for him spiraled in the wrong direction over the past year, and she was tired of being his babysitter. He didn't do anything to help himself, and she couldn't stand his self-indulgent behavior without giving thought as to how he was affecting her. Still, there was guilt—she knew she hadn't treated him fairly as she watched him sink further into depression, and she tired of finding ways to help. He didn't listen. He didn't try. And, it was damned clear he didn't want to.

She scheduled room service for ten-thirty—French toast, strawberries, and two cups of coffee—figuring a hearty breakfast ought to hold them until early afternoon—until then, they would map out their upcoming trip to South Africa to further investigate the art thefts. There was a definite link between the thefts in London and Cape Town, and Colbie had a gut feeling Nick Cummings had something to do with it. They also had to review the evening of Burnett's party— everything with Brian happened so fast, they had zero time to compare notes. To Colbie's thinking, there wasn't much to investigate with the exception of Nigel Blackwell, and the fact he called her set off her internal alarm.

Shortly after ten, Ryan rapped on her door. "C'mon in!" Colbie snatched her wet bath towel, chucked it onto the bathroom floor, then closed the door. "It's open . . ." She looked up as Ryan crossed the threshold with a bouquet of spring flowers in hand.

"I thought a taste of spring may help cheer you up," he commented as he looked around the room. "Too bad I didn't think of bringing a vase!" Ryan grinned, extending the bouquet.

"Good heavens!" Colbie accepted, delighted by its fragrance.

"Well, after your conversation with Brian, I thought you might need a little cheering up . . ."

"You're right about that—coffee?"

"Of course . . ."

"Room service will be here in about twenty—until then, you'll have to put up with what I brewed myself. Thank you, by the way, for the lovely flowers." She closed her eyes, drawing in a deep breath. "They're better than perfume . . ."

"You're welcome. So . . . how are you?"

"I'm fine—but the more I think about Brian, the more I rag on myself for being the worst kind of girlfriend."

"This isn't your fault, you know—I'm not saying you were a saint, but Brian has to take some responsibility, too, for the demise of your relationship."

"That may be, but the fact remains I wasn't there when he needed me most—an undisputed fact." Colbie took a sip of coffee, then settled on the couch within easy reach of her laptop. "You know what? I don't feel like talking about Brian—we need to solidify our plans for South Africa . . ."

"Agreed. What do you think of my going on ahead, and your staying here to wrap up the interviews with the other art dealers?"

Colbie was slightly stunned at his suggestion, but she refused to show it. "Really?" She searched Ryan's face for a signal of what he was thinking. "It's fine with me—when do you want to shove off?"

"Well, that depends on you—are you comfortable working here on your own?"

Of course—why wouldn't I be?" Colbie's tone had an edge Ryan hadn't heard before.

"Only because of what you just went through with Brian—you may need a shoulder. You know . . ."

Colbie softened at his response. "I'll be fine—besides, there isn't anything you can do. And, as you said, I need to stop beating myself up—it is what it is."

"Good—that's the Colbie I know and love!" Before she could respond, room service arrived. Ryan fired up his laptop as she tipped the lanky young man, immersing himself in his digital calendar.

As she plucked the cloche lids from their plates, Colbie wondered if Ryan would mention her dinner plans with Nigel Blackwell that evening. When Blackwell called to extend his invitation, Colbie sensed a tightening in Ryan indicating he wasn't wild about it—she considered his being a bit jealous, but promptly dismissed the idea as absurd.

"Dig in—it looks good!"

Ryan replaced his laptop with a plate—he hated eating from a coffee table, a habit Colbie remembered from years ago. "Too easy to dump something on the floor," he explained. "Besides, I can sit back and relax at the same time!"

Colbie followed suit. "The only problem is it winds up on you instead of the floor!" She smiled, recalling how many times she watched Ryan spill something on himself—he always joked about it, saying it gave him a good reason to wear old clothes. "Now you have me doing it," she teased as she dabbed at dribbled strawberry syrup on the front of her blouse. His easy-going personality was one of the reasons she enjoyed his company—never pressure to be something she's not.

"So—what's the plan? We only have a couple of art dealers to interview, but my gut tells me we're getting nowhere fast. I think you're right—we need to shift our focus to South Africa."

Ryan wiped a renegade drop of maple syrup from his chin. "I'm glad we're on the same page. Yes, we made some progress here—but something tells me we're only scratching the surface of something bigger."

"Much bigger," Colbie agreed. "Ever since Burnett's party, I've had a weird feeling . . ."

"About?"

"I'm not sure yet, but I know it has to do with Nick Cummings. And, there's someone else—maybe two other people are involved."

"You mean an art theft ring?" Ryan stopped chewing, and looked at her. "Are you serious?"

"Not a ring—but, there's something we definitely haven't discovered . . ."

They sat in silence for a few moments, considering the path of their investigation. "In that case," Ryan commented, "I'm not comfortable leaving you here alone. If you're right, we need to be careful . . ."

"I agree we need to be careful, but I'll be fine—I think

you're right. You need to get on the ground in South Africa."
Colbie placed her plate on the table, curling her legs under
her as she settled back into the couch.

"So—what's the plan?"

****

The flight was uneventful. Brian managed to get some
sleep, but he couldn't help reliving the events of the last few
days. He felt a modicum of remorse about surreptitiously
leaving the hospital but, as long as they got their money, he
was sure they were fine with it. Not to mention they legally
couldn't make him stay.

The jet touched down just before eight, and by nine
he was on the way to his hotel. It wasn't difficult finding
accommodations close to Colbie's—four blocks, at most—but
he needed to have enough breathing room so she wouldn't
discover he was there. He wasn't stalking her, really—it was
more like assessing the situation before he got in touch with
her.

Morning traffic didn't allow him to arrive until ten-
thirty and, by eleven, he was settled and ready to explore his
surroundings. The plan was to stay away from Colbie's hotel
—he preferred to scope it out under cover of an evening sky.

No sense being stupid, he thought. *No sense being stupid,
at all* . . .

****

"So, all in all, it went well . . ."

"Was Cameron there?" Nick Cummings tried to appear nonchalant, as if there were nothing on the line.

"Cameron? You mean the Cameron who met us at the club?"

"Yeah—the redhead. I think that's her name . . ."

"It is—different Cameron, though. 'Club' Cameron is a jet setter—a gig at my father's isn't her style." Maggie glanced at Cummings. *Why would he bring up Cameron,* she wondered. *He only talked to her for a couple of minutes before cutting out.* "Why?"

Cummings finished the last of his coffee, scraping the remnants of his breakfast to the side of his plate. Maggie called him earlier that morning for a quick brunch, and he was more than happy to accept. The conversation with Conrad James didn't go as well as he hoped, placing him in a weak position. He had to come up with something, and it better be quick.

"No reason—I just figured she might be there because she was visiting . . ."

"Nope—I haven't seen her since then. I think she said she was off to Paris in a couple of days."

"That's what she told me . . ."

"She must have made quite an impression on you! Maybe it's the red hair!" She didn't want to grill Cummings, but she had a feeling his interest in Cameron was more than just a passing question.

"I've always been a sucker for redheads!"

"Well, next time she comes to town, I'll make sure you spend more time with her," Maggie teased.

"No need—you're all I need, Baby. You're all I need . . ."

****

"That's it, then? You'll head to Cape Town tomorrow, and I'll wrap up the remaining art theft interviews, and I'll join you—anything else we need to discuss?" Colbie clicked her pen several times, trying to piece together what she needed to accomplish within the following days. Of course, she was used to handling investigations on her own, but she preferred having Ryan there with her. It was always good to have another set of eyes and ears—and, if she were to be completely honest, he was fun to have around.

"Only one I can think of . . ."

"And, that is?"

"Your date tonight with Nigel Blackwell . . ."

Colbie glanced up from her legal yellow pad. "It isn't a date."

"To him it is . . ." Ryan had little doubt about what Nigel

Blackwell was after—he took a liking to Colbie and, as a man who can have any woman he wants, Blackwell was interested.

"All the better—he won't suspect for a second I'm investigating the art thefts. Or, anything else that may crop up . . ."

Ryan closed his laptop, a concerned looked crossing his face. "That's what I'm afraid of . . . anything else that may crop up."

"I'm not sure I know what you mean."

"You mentioned you have a feeling about the art thefts not being the only thing going on here—you think a couple more people are involved. If that's true . . ."

Colbie interrupted. "If that's true, what? I can take care of myself, and I don't need you or anyone else to tell me otherwise!" Colbie felt a flush of anger—'getting her Irish up' Brian called it.

"Hey! Hold on! I didn't mean anything by it—all I meant was if there are two more people involved, we don't have any idea of who they are, what they're up to, and how it changes our investigation. Damn it! I know you can take care of yourself—you don't have to remind me. And, you don't have to chastise me for worrying about you!" Ryan snapped his laptop shut, snatched the rest of his English muffin, and headed for the door.

"Enjoy your evening . . ."

Chapter Eleven

Colbie stood staring at the several choices she had hanging in her hotel closet. Blackwell suggested wearing her finest, but she wasn't exactly sure why. Common sense told her he was going to take her somewhere swanky—but, it could be an intimate bistro, or, for that matter, his place. The truth was she would be more comfortable with Ryan by her side, but he kept his distance since he left earlier that day. *Somewhat in a huff, if you ask me*, she thought as she pulled a perfect little black dress from the hanger. She held it in front of her, liking what she saw in the mirror. *This should do . . .*

****

At five minutes before seven, Colbie turned heads as she walked through the hotel lobby. She checked messages, although she knew she didn't have any—nonetheless, there was a lingering hope there might be something from Ryan. It was unlike him to ignore her, and it wasn't like him to be so sensitive or touchy. *Perhaps something is bothering him*, she thought, heading toward the main entrance while making a mental note to tune in to him when she returned.

As the doorman opened the door for her, a limo rolled up, leaving little doubt it belonged to Nigel Blackwell. It reminded Colbie of him—sleek, and finely crafted. She couldn't dispel the fact Blackwell would turn any woman's head, and she couldn't help feeling a little pleased by his attention to her. *Perhaps Ryan is right—maybe he is interested. But, that's not so bad, is it?*

She waited for the driver to open the passenger door, but, as he did so, Blackwell stepped from the limousine.

"Cameron! You look lovely—perfect for what I have in mind!" Blackwell placed his hand on her back, ushering her toward the limo. "First, a tour of our magnificent city . . ."

"That sounds wonderful! I haven't had much time for pleasure since Regis and I arrived—it's been all work!"

"Well, we'll have to take care of that . . ."

Colbie eased into the limo, waiting for Blackwell to enter from the other side. A quick scan indicated a fully stocked bar with two rocks glasses at the ready—a nice touch, but the cop in her made her wonder if he already knew her favorite drink. As nice as it was to garner Blackwell's attention, the art theft investigation was never far from her mind—Blackwell, as much as anyone else, was a suspect, and she had to keep that thought at the forefront.

Blackwell interrupted her thoughts as he made himself comfortable. "Gimlet?" He reached for a glass, tossing in a few ice cubes.

"Yes, please . . ." She watched as he prepared a Grey Goose gimlet just the way she liked it—a quick squeeze, then a sliver of lime.

"How did you know?"

"Know what?"

Colbie lifted her glass.

"Your preference? It wasn't difficult—I paid attention at Burnett's . . ."

"You paid attention to what I drink? Good heavens! I had no idea my booze preferences are so interesting!" Colbie laughed as Blackwell poured his scotch, neat. *What else does he know about me*, she wondered.

"I'm a firm believer in taking note of everything going on around me—no surprises that way."

"I wish I could be that disciplined—I seldom notice such things!"

Colbie peered out the window, sipping her drink. "It's such a lovely city—it's my first time visiting, and I didn't expect it to be so inviting."

"It is, indeed—I wish it were spring or summer, but there's something vibrant about London, especially after a snowstorm."

As they toured the city, Blackwell adroitly attempted to bring the conversation around to Colbie's work—something she anticipated. But, nothing changed since her evening at Burnett's estate—she needed to steer the conversation in a less troublesome direction. The less Blackwell knew about her trumped up tech company, the better.

"Enough about me—I want to hear more about you! Someone—can't remember who—told me you're in the import-export business . . ."

"I see—I'm flattered you asked about me!" He smiled at Colbie, noticing a slight flush in her cheeks.

"Since Regis and I were newcomers, I asked about everybody . . ."

Blackwell chuckled. "Is that your way of telling me I'm not so special?" His eyes met hers, knowing he was putting her on the spot.

"Perhaps . . ."

Her candor delighted him! Most women who snagged his interest weren't so forthright—unless they came from old money, his bank account was always of particular interest.

He laughed, mixing another drink for both of them. "Well, Cameron, you're right—I am, indeed, in the import-export business . . ."

"Specialty?"

"Nothing in particular—although I handle quite a bit of art for reputable dealers and customers."

"Really? I confess, I don't have much of an eye for art, but I can well imagine your business is exciting . . ."

"It is—but, it has its downside like most businesses."

"Such as?"

"I can think of a few, but Samuel Burnett is a good

example . . ."

"In what way?"

"He's a great client of mine—and, friend—but he's dealing with a situation now that has those in my line of business treading lightly."

"I'm not sure what you mean . . ." *Is he talking about the art thefts?* Colbie wondered.

"I'm not at liberty to discuss it, but suffice it to say I make sure his reputation as an art connoisseur isn't tarnished in any way."

"He's certainly lucky to have you in his corner . . ."

"I wish I could do more, but I'm only in London for a couple of months out of the year—most of the time, I'm in Cape Town."

"I've always wanted to go to South Africa—it sounds fascinating!"

"It is—and, it's home . . ."

"How long will you be in London?"

"I leave in a couple of days . . ."

A pang of disappointment. "Oh . . ."

Nigel Blackwell's eyes met hers. "But, that doesn't mean we can't enjoy ourselves until then!" He offered his glass in a toast, flashing an irresistible smile. "To the next couple of days!"

****

Shortly after midnight, they pulled up to the hotel. Colbie made the excuse she had business meetings the following day, and she needed her beauty sleep. Blackwell helped her from the limo, his hand lingering on hers. "Tomorrow evening?"

"I'd love to, but I'm not sure how my day will play out tomorrow—call me?"

"I understand—I'll call in plenty of time. Promise you'll pick up?"

"Promise—unless I'm in a meeting. In that case, I'll call you back as soon as I can . . ."

"Perfect!" As any British, well-bred gent would do, Blackwell leaned down, kissing her lightly on the cheek. "Cheerio! Until tomorrow . . ." He watched her disappear into the lobby before signaling his driver. *She's different*, he thought. *But, there's something about her that doesn't quite add up . . .*"

****

Brian watched from the coffee shop across the street as the limo pulled up to the hotel, his heart sinking as Blackwell leaned down to kiss Colbie on the cheek—certainly something he didn't expect. If anything, he figured he would see Colbie and Ryan arrive at the hotel together—he didn't expect to see her with some rich guy who looked as if he didn't have to work another day in his life.

From his vantage point, it was easy to keep his eyes on her as she approached the front desk. *Probably checking for messages*, he thought as she thanked the concierge and headed for the lift. He thought it odd Ryan wasn't with her—from what he gathered when they rescued him from his kidnappers, they were inseparable when working on his case. It didn't occur to him she may be interested in someone else. *If that's the case, things just got more complicated*, he thought as he scratched down the license plate number of the limo on a napkin as it pulled away. Maybe he could track down its owner—unless, of course, it belonged to a limo service. If so, he was pretty clear the service wouldn't be willing to divulge who took the midnight joyride.

He sat, thinking and nursing a latte for thirty minutes to make sure Colbie was in for the evening. *It would be unlike her to go out again*, he thought, and he recalled her routine as she got ready for bed—a quick shower, a cup of hot tea, then quiet time as she cued up her intuitive mind. That's always the way it was when she was on the force, and he had no reason to believe it was any different now. Even when success prompted their move to the East Coast, she seldom wavered from her routine. "It gives me peace of mind," she said.

Assured there was nothing more to see, he paid the tab, ready to head for his hotel. As he grabbed his jacket from the back of the chair, he glanced at the hotel across the street just in time to see Ryan greet the doorman. It was three years since he last saw him, and he couldn't help feel a pang of regret at the sight of his old friend. Even so, he couldn't put aside the reason he was there—the mere fact he returned to the hotel after Colbie intimated they weren't spending time together away from the case.

Then, again . . .

****

Colbie tucked her legs under her as she switched on the television. Her evening with Nigel Blackwell played in her mind, and she wasn't quite ready to hit the sack. Until that moment, she had no time to veg in front of the tube, and she welcomed the wee bit of normalcy it provided.

News from across the pond wasn't too different from that in the States. Of course, she couldn't relate to the local stories only because she wasn't familiar with the players, but she paid particular attention to world news—unrest in the Middle East continued to spiral out of control as world leaders attempted to arrive at a workable solution. It dominated the headlines, and it wasn't until the news anchors were ten minutes into their newscast that they reported to their audience there was another found body. According to the report, a string of murders cropped up within the last few months and, at first, it seemed as if the recently-found body was the work of a serial killer. Her ears perked up as the news anchor described the scene. "We have little information, but we can tell you the victim is a young male in his twenties, and he died by an apparent single gunshot. If you have any information, please contact Scotland Yard . . ."

Murder always intrigued her, and she couldn't help thinking about the young man found on the riverbank. *Single gunshot? If so, perhaps a professional hit . . .* even from the limited information provided on the news, it didn't sound

like a crime of passion. Colbie had a feeling it was more—
measured.

As she relaxed, her mind wandered to Ryan. He had
an early flight, but she wasn't sure what time, and what she
heard from him was by a brief note. *Heading out early in the
morning—I'll call when I land. How was your evening?*

At least it was something.

She felt her body merge seamlessly with her intuitive
mind as she focused her energy on her partner. *Is anything
bothering him,* she asked as she centered herself. Instantly, a
face came into view in her mind's eye—except it wasn't Ryan.
It was strange, too—she seldom had visions about people
close to her—they almost always were about situations, or
those she may encounter through work.

Never Brian.

She watched the vision take form and, within moments,
she was in a hospital room teeming with doctors and nurses—
but, from what she could see, the bed was empty. She figured
it had something to do with Brian's suicide attempt, but there
was a feel to the vision she couldn't quite pinpoint.

Something didn't feel right.

                              ****

The following morning, Colbie sat at the small, glass
table in her hotel room sipping coffee, sheets of yellow legal
paper scattered in front of her. Days of the investigation were

slipping by, and the fact was they were no closer to finding anything linking the art thefts. When she compared her current case with those in the past, she and Ryan had far less to show for their efforts. Samuel Burnett's party turned out to be a bust as far as usable information, but she couldn't discount her meeting Nigel Blackwell as one of the highlights. Her evening with him sparked a feeling she hadn't felt for some time and, if she were to be completely honest, she loved every second of it. Life with Brian wasn't exactly loving for the last several years, and it was nice to have someone pay attention to her.

As she suspected, she really didn't have to wear her finest—Blackwell took her to an intimate, upscale restaurant tucked into a quiet corner of the city. Patrons wore everything from finery to blue jeans, and it was clear from the moment they entered, money was the primary concern—not their fashionable or unfashionable manner of dress.

It wasn't hard to figure out Nigel knew he looked his best in black—Colbie suspected, however, he would look great in anything. There was an ease about him she enjoyed, and he didn't press her about business or anything else that might tip her hand. He was content to have her across from him, and he kept conversation to nothing of consequence. And, for the most part, Colbie learned little about him—she went in knowing he was from South Africa, as well as founder of an import-export business. She returned from their evening together knowing little more other than he had a sister, his father died when he was seventeen, and his favorite place to travel was the Far East.

As she dissected the previous evening, Colbie recalled her meditation. She began by asking a question about Ryan, her intuitive visions splintering into so many different directions, she wasn't positive she would remember each symbol as it appeared to her. She remembered seeing Brian and the hospital room and, for several minutes after that, she saw nothing. Then the number 'two' exploded in her mind's eye—the numeral. The word. She envisioned sets of twins, identical in every way. Two elephant tusks. As she watched the symbols, they paired like two elements from the Periodic Table, reminding Colbie of high school chemistry. There were eight 'twos' in all, none standing alone as if two bonded together, forming a circle. In the middle of the circle Colbie saw what she thought was the silhouette of a rhinoceros— she wasn't sure.

By morning, she still wasn't clear on what her vision was telling her, and she accepted the rhinoceros as a symbol of South Africa. But, she was clear there could be two different reasons for the symbol—one, Ryan left that morning for Cape Town, and two, Nigel Blackwell was from South Africa. From her vision, there was no way to tell if the symbol tethered to one or the other and, of course, there was always the possibility her vision didn't involve either of them—but she doubted it.

For the thirty minutes she watched symbols offered by her mind's eye, she couldn't help feeling she wasn't the only one doing the watching. She felt it when Nigel dropped her off the previous evening—so strong, in fact, she scanned the area when she got out of the limo. Nothing caught her eye, although it was late and the only thing open was the coffee shop across the street. A few people entered the hotel ahead of her, but she couldn't put the feeling of being watched out of her mind as she checked in with the concierge. *It was so weird*, she thought, as she scraped a slightly burned section of her English muffin with her knife. *The feeling was so strong . . .*

With only two days left in London, Colbie mapped out her remaining interviews, saving enough free time to see Nigel before leaving. His plans included travel to Bangkok the same day she was leaving for South Africa, and she didn't mind the thought of seeing him one more time. They parted the evening before with the promise to be in touch some time that day, and Colbie found herself looking forward to his call. It would probably be the last time she would see him, so, why not? It weren't as if she were cheating on Brian—he was no longer in the picture, and she was free to see whomever she chose. Ryan, however, was a different story—she couldn't deny the signals, but did that mean she wasn't available to spend time with someone else?

Of course not.

CHAPTER TWELVE

The Detective Chief Inspector stood at the base of the autopsy table trying not to gag—twenty years at the Yard, and he still wasn't used to it.

"So—what do we have?"

"A single bullet to the brain . . ." The coroner pulled back the sheet. "That's it."

"That's it?"

"Well, I know you're thinking this young man is the work of your serial killer—but, I doubt it."

"You doubt it? What the hell are you talking about?"

The coroner pointed to a half-filled black bag. "Check it out—tell me what you think . . ."

Chief Inspector Murray snatched a pair of latex gloves from the wall dispenser, then stretched them onto his mammoth hands, gingerly opening the bag. "Clothes—his?"

"Yes—but take a look at them. Do they look like the clothing peeled off your serial killer vics?"

"Now that you mention it . . ." The inspector poked through the bag containing designer jeans and a leather jacket, the cost of either the inspector could never afford.

"That's not all—take a gander at this . . ." The coroner dangled an I.D. bracelet from his fingers. "Quality stuff . . ."

The Chief Inspector carefully inspected the bracelet, turning it in his fingers. "You're right—this is expensive." He flipped the bracelet to its inside. "Who's Maggie?"

"I don't have any idea—that bracelet is the only thing he had with or on him."

"No license, or I.D.?"

The coroner shook his head. "No, sir—not a damned thing."

CI Murray inspected the bracelet again. *Luv ya big!* He handed it to the coroner. "It's a strange inscription—not the usual sappy stuff from one lover to the other . . . when you're done, we'll send it for prints."

"Agreed. So, to recap—you have an assassinated, well-dressed young man, in his early to mid-twenties, with someone in his life who 'loves him big.' That's it . . ." The coroner placed the bracelet in a plastic bag, sealing it before placing it in a stainless steel wire basket on his desk.

"And, we know the name of the person who wrote the inscription—Maggie."

"That shouldn't be too much of a needle in a haystack now, should it? Good luck, Chief Inspector—you guys have your hands full . . ."

The DCI headed for the precinct, his mind stuffed with information from the coroner. The last thing he needed was a murder investigation of someone who could possibly meet the criteria of the rich and famous. Or, perhaps just rich. Either way, the murder couldn't have come at a worse time—he didn't have the manpower, and it was a sure bet someone would start squawking if he didn't have someone on it—yesterday.

At least he had a name—albeit a common one. Chances of turning up someone named Maggie were slim unless they canvassed every jeweler in London. By its heft, the bracelet wasn't close to a big-box special—substantial and thick, it was obviously crafted by someone who knew what he or she was doing. Mass produced?

No way.

****

"Where should we go?" Nigel placed the palm of his hand at the small of her back, guiding her toward the artists' district only blocks away from her hotel.

"Good heavens! I'm counting on you to show me London! I'm a newbie here—remember?" Colbie laughed as they struck off down the street. Nigel called late morning, and they agreed to spend a quick couple of hours together—then, it was back to work for both of them.

"Ah! I have you completely in my control!"

"Well, I wouldn't go so for as to say that . . ." She grinned, playfully swatting him on the arm. Anyone witnessing their banter would swear they were together for years—Colbie noticed it, too, making her wonder if her relationship with Brian was a complete sham. Her blossoming friendship with Nigel was easy and compatible—but, even though they were in the beginning stages of what could be a good thing, it was prudent for Colbie to maintain her professional decorum.

Within in ten minutes, they crossed the threshold of an intimate, upscale art gallery—so upscale, prices were decided upon during conversation between buyer and seller.

"What do you think of this one?" Nigel asked, guiding her gently toward a stunning painting of an African elephant. Not the traditional pen and ink or charcoal, the canvas in front of them was striking with a palette of reds, purples, and iridescent green.

"This is incredible!" Colbie moved closer, checking the artist information on a plaque next to the large canvas. "It says two young men—twins—painted it together . . ."

"I know—I've been here before, and I actually had the opportunity to meet them—stellar young lads!"

Colbie stood, spellbound by its vibrant colors. "There's something about this . . ."

"Not sure what you mean . . ." Nigel looked at her, eyebrows arched. "Good? Bad?"

"I'm not sure . . ." For the moments she stood in front of the painting, Colbie returned to her visions of the previous evening—the number 'two.' In that vision, she saw identical twins . . . so identical, she couldn't tell them apart. Again, she glanced at the plaque. "You met the artists—the twins—were they fraternal, or identical?"

"Identical—why?"

"Oh, I'm sure it's nothing—maybe I heard of the artists sometime during my travels . . ." '

"The only reason I had the opportunity to meet them is because they're from Cape Town—homeboys, if you will . . ."

Colbie senses were on fire as she stared at the painting, but there was no way she could take a chance of Nigel's becoming suspicious of her intuitive abilities. *If he's as astute as I think, it won't take him long to figure out there's something different about me—if he hasn't already.* She walked a thin line between truth and deception—and, if he were to discover her duplicity, Colbie had a feeling the result wouldn't be pretty.

Again, he guided her toward another piece. "Check these out—same artists, a completely different style—in my line of work, I get to know artists and their works, and I have to admit I was surprised when I discovered they were the same artists as the elephant . . ."

In front of him were two African statues carved from ebony, each identical to the other, the twin identity strong. As they assessed other works in the gallery, most of the pieces had to do with duality, and Colbie understood her vision referred to where she stood at that moment. The only problem was there were options—the actual artists, Nigel, or something else not yet revealed to her. *If it's Nigel,* she thought, *I don't think the vision was complete. Besides, what does he have to do with twins? No—it must be showing me something to do with South Africa . . .*

"Cameron? Hello? Earth to Cameron . . ." Nigel grinned as he waved his hand in front of her face.

She snapped out of her thoughts at the sound of his voice. "What?"

"You looked like you were on another planet!"

"I'm sorry, Nigel—I was just thinking about the kind of talent it takes to create such elegant work . . ."

"I agree . . ."

"Hey! Is it tea time yet? My stomach is telling me it's ready for some good old tea and crumpets . . ."

"Have you ever had tea and crumpets?"

"No—but I'm ready to give them a try!" She laughed, adding a lilt perfect for flirting. The truth was she wanted to get the hell out of there . . . she didn't want Nigel to have too much time to think about the twins and why she was so interested in them.

"Then let's go—I know the perfect place!"

****

It was Colbie's first time in a proper tearoom. Crisp, white table cloths, starched and pristine, were in stark contrast to the rustic wood of the baristas' counter. Loose tea—carefully labeled and stored in glass jars—lined shelves behind the barista, adding to its old-school ambiance. The fragrance of croissants, biscuits, and baked goods wafted to every corner of the establishment, so when Nigel chose a table for two in the back, they didn't miss out on any of the tearoom's charm.

"So, what do you think?" Nigel asked, taking her coat and draping it on the back of his chair. "Is it what you expected?"

"Truthfully? No! I'm such a tourist—when you said 'tearoom,' I pictured something more . . . British!"

"More British?"

"Yes—as lovely as this is, it reminds me of a neighborhood coffee shop I used to spend time in before I moved to the East Coast."

Nigel pulled out her chair, then took his seat, stretching his lanky legs into the aisle. "The East Coast? Where?"

"Virginia . . ." Yes, it was a bald-faced lie, but she couldn't take a chance on Nigel's learning any information other than what she wanted him to know.

"Never been there—although, I get to the States fairly often . . ."

"Really? Do you travel there for work?"

"Once in a while—most of the time, it's purely for fun or special occasions."

"New York City is a blast . . ."

"It is, indeed—I spent my last birthday there."

"What fun! When's your birthday?"

Nigel smiled, a twinkle in his eye. "Well, now, if I tell you that, you'll know how old I am . . ."

"Is that a bad thing? How about if I go first—January. That makes me an Aquarius . . ."

"Into astrology, are you?" Nigel chuckled, delighting in

how different she was than other women in his life.

"Not really—what are you?"

"June—Gemini."

Colbie nearly choked on her croissant. "Gemini?"

"Yes—the Twins . . ."

****

Ryan's plane touched down shortly after six in the evening. Flying really wasn't his thing, and anything longer than a three-hour flight placed it in the 'unbearable' category. Eleven plus hours? That put it in the 'never again unless I have to' category.

He wasn't in the best of moods.

Once on the ground, however, he couldn't help but admire Cape Town's beauty. Touted the oldest settlement in South Africa, it boasts three hundred years of culture—and, the fact there was a national park and game reserves? The brass ring as far as he was concerned—not to mention after the frigid weather in London, he was ready for something warmer. The only drawback was Colbie—he didn't like how they left their last conversation, but there was little he could do. *She's hurting*, he thought as he retrieved his luggage from baggage claim. *She deserves the best—and Nigel Blackwell ain't it!*

The endless flight gave him plenty of time to think about Blackwell, and why he didn't like him. Jealousy? Perhaps. Maybe he was hanging around Colbie too much, but as soon as he saw him at Burnett's gig, his radar pinged. *There's such a thing as too smooth. Too perfect.* When comparing his style to Blackwells', Ryan reluctantly feared he didn't measure up—then again, Colbie never struck him as the type to prefer a fake. And, that was the thing—Blackwell may have been perfect looking, but Ryan felt as if he didn't have a sincere bone in his body. *He's a damned good actor, though . . .*

Ryan considered himself the real deal, and a 'what you see is what you get' kind of guy—but, he couldn't say that about Blackwell. On the surface, he was sleek. Smooth. But he would bet his last dollar Blackwell was nothing more than a snake in the grass.

The buzz of his cell phone interrupted his thoughts as he left the terminal, the name on the caller I.D. a surprise.

"Tammy? Hey—what's up?"

"I'm so sorry to call you, but I haven't been able to get in touch with Colbie all afternoon . . ."

"No problem—what can I do for you?"

"Well, I'm not sure—it's about Brian . . ." Even as she dialed Ryan's number, Tammy second guessed her decision—was she doing the right thing? Still, she figured Colbie would want to know.

"Brian? What about him?"

"He's not at the hospital . . ."

"Discharged?"

Tammy took a deep breath. "Not exactly . . . he walked

out."

"Walked out? How do you know?"

"I called the hospital this morning to check on him because I thought Colbie would want to be kept up on things—you know, just out of courtesy even though they're not a thing anymore."

"And?"

"They didn't tell me much—only that he was no longer there."

"Then how do you know he walked out?"

"I wouldn't have except for the young nurse—at least she sounded young—she slipped, and told me they didn't know where he was . . . I put two and two together."

Ryan fell silent as he considered the possibilities. Did Brian really walk out, or was it simply a case of his striking off on his own to another part of the hospital? Walking out didn't sound like Brian—but, then again, his suicide attempt wasn't the picture of predictability, either.

"So, what do you want me to do?"

"Maybe you'll have more success getting in touch with Colbie—I checked your itinerary, and I know you're in Cape Town, but will you please let her know what I told you?"

"Sure—I'll try to get in touch with her this evening."

"Okay—thanks. I'm sorry, Ryan!"

With that she rang off, leaving Ryan to wonder what the hell was going on. A part of him didn't want to contact Colbie to tell her the news—the last thing she needed was more on her plate. *And,* he thought, *it's not as if she can do anything about it. According to Brian, they're over* . . . Still—it wasn't his decision to make. If Colbie found out later he had information from Tammy—and, she would—he was pretty sure he would be dead meat.

He dialed.

****

"Any luck?"

"Not yet—two men are on the jewelry stores, and Michaels is trying to track down anyone who saw the vic down by the river . . ."

Chief Inspector Murray picked up his subordinate's notes. "I don't have a good feeling about this . . ."

"We've been in this position before, Sir—no reason to think we can't pull this one out of the hat, too."

"I appreciate your confidence, but the truth is this can take months. Years." He stood at his desk, considering his next step. "Any calls? Has anyone reported him missing?"

"No, Sir."

Not good. What started out as a serial killer case quickly turned into something more. His gut told him there was a story behind the young man with the bullet in his brain, and it was his job to figure out the vic's identity—but, with nothing to go on, it was a case that could grow cold within the month.

"When Michaels gets back, tell him I want to see him the second he walks in the door . . ."

"Yes, Sir—I'll send him right in."

****

Colbie was back in her room by late afternoon—in her sweats, she was ready to plan for her interviews the next day. As it turned out, the interview she scheduled for that afternoon had to cancel, pushing her further into an already-cramped following day. After a quick scan of her calendar, it was clear she had her work cut out for her.

First up—Burnett's. Ryan left it to her to wrap up that segment of the investigation, so she was off to the estate first thing in the morning. After all interviews, she and Ryan had little to go on, and she wasn't thrilled about having to report no progress. However, London was only one part of their investigation—she had a feeling Cape Town was going to be more productive.

As she sipped a cup of hot chocolate, her mind wandered to her afternoon with Nigel, and the twin thing. The art gallery was a slap in the face moment, and she had no doubt her vision was providing an answer to their investigation—or, at least part of it. All she had to do was figure out what twins had to do with anything. Intuition pointed her in the direction of Nigel, but, up until then, she had no reason to question his veracity. After spending time with him that afternoon, her concerns faded, and she enjoyed every second they spent together. Besides, she wasn't sure if she'd ever see him again—when they parted that afternoon there were no plans to meet, and Nigel wished her the best in her business ventures with Regis, none the wiser her name wasn't Cameron.

Just the way they planned it.

Twenty minutes into her intense scheduling, her cell buzzed—Ryan. "Hey! How was the flight?"

"Long. Torturous. How about you? How's everything going with the investigation?" Ryan figured it was best to get business out of the way before dumping the news about Brian on her.

"I was just working on my schedule for tomorrow—Clements had to reschedule, so I wound up having extra time today. As far as the investigation, I think we've done all we can do in London—and, I don't mind telling you it really bugs me we're leaving empty-handed."

"I know—I've been thinking the same thing. But, we're going to be in South Africa much longer than London, and my gut says most of the action will be here."

"I agree . . . until today, I felt as if I had nothing. Now . . ."

"What happened today?"

"Blackwell called me, and we spent a couple of hours at a fancy schmancy art gallery and tearoom."

Ryan fell silent at the news she was with Nigel Blackwell.

"Ryan? You there? Can you hear me?"

"Yeah—yeah. I gotcha . . . so what happened to make you think you made some headway?"

"Well, it started last night when I was in my meditation—I

kept seeing the number two. There were two of everything—two elephant tusks. Twins . . ." her voice trailed as she recalled the strength of her vision.

"Twins? What do you think that means?"

"I'm not sure, but when we were at the art gallery, one of the most stunning paintings I've ever seen was painted by twins—twenty somethings. In fact, nearly everything on exhibit was crafted by the twins and—dig this—they're from Cape Town!"

Ryan still wasn't sure he was getting it. "Are you saying you think the twin artists have something to do with it?"

"No. Maybe. I don't know. But, here's the really weird thing—when Nigel and I were shooting the bull at the tearoom, I learned his birthday is in June . . ."

He still didn't get it. "So?"

"June, Ryan. Gemini? The Twins astrological sign?" Colbie waited for her information to sink in.

"Do you think Blackwell is involved?" *If he is,* Ryan thought, *no surprise there . . .*

"I wish I knew—I'll think on it more tonight, and I'll keep you posted . . ."

From the tone of her voice, Ryan could tell she was ready to get off the phone—he couldn't put it off any longer. "Hey—before you go—I had a call from Tammy a little while ago."

"Tammy? Why? What did she want?" Colbie wondered why her assistant didn't call her.

"She tried to get in touch with you, but couldn't get through. Or, you didn't answer . . ." As soon as the words left his mouth, he knew his comment was little more than a mean-spirited dig.

"Oh. Well, what did she want?"

"It seems Brian is on the lam from the hospital . . ."

"What? How do you know?"

It was her question that launched him into a full-blown recap of his conversation with Tammy. By the time he had nothing more to tell, Colbie managed to work herself into a small panic, saying it was her fault.

"It doesn't make any sense! Why would he just walk out?" Such an irresponsible action wasn't the Brian she knew—had he really changed that much without her noticing?

"Who knows . . . but, I told Tammy I would tell you."

"I appreciate it—but, you know what's weird?" She didn't wait for his reply. "When I engaged my mind's eye last night, I tried to tune in on you—except, what I saw wasn't you. It was Brian . . ."

"You tried to tune in on me?"

"Of course, I did—I wanted to get a feel for what you're going to encounter in Cape Town . . ." Her response wasn't what he wanted to hear, but at least she hadn't chalked him up as a done deal.

"Thanks—I guess. You're right—it is weird because I remember your telling me when we were working on Brian's case you rarely see things for people who are close to you . . ."

"True—that's why the image of Brian is sticking with me. Maybe I was picking up on his leaving the hospital . . ."

"Maybe—it's hard to tell. If you don't know what it means, I sure as hell have no idea what it means!"

Colbie laughed. "Point taken—when I figure it out, you'll be the first to know!"

And, that was the good thing about their being friends— moments later they ended their call, satisfied with the timbre of their conversation. No hurt feelings. No unreasonable expectation.

Nothing but friendship.

CHAPTER THIRTEEN

"Sir? Gaines said you want to see me . . ." Inspector Michaels waited by the door for an invitation to enter. He knew better than to simply walk right in—"It's rude," the Deputy Chief Inspector told him the first time he made the mistake. It was also the last time he made such an error.

"Ah! Michaels! Come in—what did you learn? Anything?" Murray prayed his man had something for him.

"Well, Sir, as it turns out—I did."

"Excellent! Sit . . . tell me."

"Luckily, that area by the river was fairly busy—but, no one knew anything until I spotted a young woman sitting by the riverbank."

"And?"

"She said she was at the river the evening before, and she noticed a young man who seemed as if he were waiting for someone."

"Did she say who?"

"No—but she recognized him from the club . . ."

"Club? What club?"

"That's what I asked—she told me there's an upper crust club just outside the city, and she spends a lot of time there. She also said she was surprised to see him by the river . . ."

"Did she notice his meeting with anyone?"

"Negative. But, she does know he belonged to the rich crowd. He hung out with a bunch of what she called 'rich bitches,' and he always had an air of he was better than everyone else."

"It makes me wonder why she was at that club—she doesn't sound like she's one of the rich bitches . . ."

"I wondered the same thing . . ."

"Did you ask her?"

Murray's deputy inspector shifted his weight, looking slightly uncomfortable. "No, Sir . . ."

"Any reason for that?"

"Perhaps not a good one—there was something about her that didn't track, but I can't put my finger on it . . ."

"Meaning?"

"It didn't make sense for her to be down at the river—if she's a patron of that club, the riverside doesn't seem a likely place to be hanging out. It's not the ritziest—it's almost as if she were waiting to talk to the cops. A classy-looking chick like her? No—something isn't right."

Chief Inspector Murray took a couple of moments to digest his deputy's thoughts. "Do you think she saw something?"

"I'm not sure, but instinct tells me she knows more than she's letting on . . ."

"Anything else?"

"Nope—that's it."

The chief inspector sat for a few minutes, thinking about how best to approach the new information. There was no question narrowing the search down to the highfalutin crowd made his job much easier.

"Michaels—start making a list of every rich family in and out of the city. Then, hit the cobblestones—see what you can find out . . ."

"Check—anything in particular?"

"Maggie—you're looking for Maggie . . ."

****

A grey, concrete rain moved in overnight, a considerable disappointment to Colbie as she dressed for her interview. *Two weeks*, she thought. *Two stinkin' weeks, and it's been the worst weather in the last decade . . .* She grabbed her warmest boots from the closet, as well as the navy wool pea coat she picked up for next to nothing at a fire sale stateside. Before she left for London, she questioned if she were packing too much. Right then? Not so much.

She rescheduled her interview with Mr. Clements for eleven o'clock and, after that, she had to hightail it to Burnett's for a quick wrap up, then back to the hotel so she could pack for her flight to Cape Town. The latest possible flight seemed the most prudent so she could grab some sleep before diving into a full day. Ryan said he'd meet her and, if she knew him, their investigation would follow a specific plan—he'd have a schedule in hand that would allow little time for sleep after her feet touched South African soil. At least for the first couple of days . . .

The late flight also allowed an opportunity for her to decompress—in many ways, she couldn't make sense of her time in London, and she could use the flight to think through the time spent with Nigel, her visions, and the disquiet she felt when she considered his involvement. She wasn't prepared to feel disappointment when she entertained the idea of his having anything to do with the art thefts, maybe because she didn't want to believe it. The truth was even though their time together was brief, she was—intrigued. She wanted to learn more about him, and not purely from a professional perspective.

Then, there was Brian. Since Tammy's call to Ryan, it consumed her thoughts. It didn't make sense—if he did walk out of the hospital without being discharged, then why? Why wouldn't he simply check out? *There's something screwy about this whole damned thing,* she thought as she closed her hotel room door. *And, I don't like it . . .*

Not one bit.

****

She looked at the man in her bed, drool dripping from the side of his mouth onto her expensive, Egyptian cotton pillowcase. *It's a good thing you're rich*, she thought as she quietly slipped from under the covers, thinking about the previous evening. He was drunker than she'd ever seen him, and it wasn't a particularly pretty sight. *Disgusting is more like it*, she thought, gently closing the bathroom door.

She stood in front of the mirror, hating the person staring back at her. Three years earlier when she landed in London, her dreams were those of many young women—success in a career and, if it were meant to be, finding a solid guy with whom she could spend the rest of her life. It was a great dream—but, unrealistic. Finding a job was next to impossible, and more than once she lamented the fact she didn't go through the necessary due diligence before making such a drastic move. Months of low paying jobs drained her bank account, and it wasn't until she met Conrad James her life began to change.

They met at a pub—she was serving, he was with a group of crusty older gentlemen obviously from the right side of the tracks. From the beginning, it was clear he liked his women young, and he enjoyed living a young lifestyle—both incongruous since he was at least sixty. She always thought it distasteful when older men hit on women half their age— usually younger. But, circumstances often cause a change of heart and, when he asked her to dinner, she couldn't think of a reason to say no.

That was two and a half years ago.

Although it was her job to listen, his usual drivel was

more like inane babbling. From the minute he walked in the door, he demanded a sidecar cocktail—an indicator he was particularly stressed. She always thought it an odd choice for someone so professorial looking—he seemed more a Guinness kind of guy. *What the hell do I know,* she wondered as she stepped into the shower.

Ten minutes later she stepped out and wrapped a towel around her, steam obscuring the mirror. She liked it that way—nothing to look at, nothing to stare back.

She was halfway through putting on her makeup when she heard him stirring in the adjoining room, ordering breakfast to include toast with orange marmalade—as always. It was the same each week—but, as long as he filled her bank account, he could order as much toast and jam as he wanted—what did she care?

She slipped on a thick, luxurious white terry cloth robe, cinching its thick belt at her waist. Not quite ready to share her time, she sat on the toilet, thinking about what he told her. "It was easy, he said. "Easier than I thought . . ."

"What was easier?"

"Taking matters into my own hands—he was a pilfering little ass . . ." Of course, she had no idea of what he was saying—two sidecars and a brandy later, he was three sheets to the wind.

"Not sure I understand, luv—who?"

He paused, looking at her through heavy eyes. "None of your business . . ."

Minutes later, he was out.

As she replayed their conversation, she knew she did the right thing. She heard about the young man on the riverbank—so, after she was certain James wasn't going anywhere, she tiptoed from the room, and headed for the banks of the Thames. She knew the Yard would be there even though it was in the middle of the night and, at the time, it seemed a good plan—a quick in and out. If she could unobtrusively point the cops in the direction of the club, they would soon find out who was who. And, who did what.

Conrad James was a regular at the club. He enjoyed it's energy, but he wasn't one to participate—always the voyeur. The last time she was there with him only a couple of days earlier, she recalled his having a scalding conversation with a young man who couldn't have been more than twenty-four or five. He had what she thought was a James Dean look to him, only better looking and much better dressed. As she envisioned him while she sat on the toilet, she recalled his expensive leather jacket and designer jeans—pricey on both fronts.

As James and the young man argued, James grabbed the guy's shirt, pinning him to the wall by the restroom, out of sight from prying eyes. Or, so he thought. She positioned herself so she could inconspicuously see them, pretending she was talking to one of the servers.

"Don't screw with me," he warned through clenched teeth, increasing the pressure on the young man's chest with his forearm.

It was a mistake.

The young man's expression turned black as he pushed James into the opposite wall, a stiletto poised at his stomach. "Do that again . . ." he hissed. "See where it gets you . . ." With that, he straightened his jacket, then melded into the crowd.

Before the young man could walk past her, she beat it to their table, hoping she looked none the wiser. James returned and snatched his topcoat, his face crimson with suppressed rage.

She knew better than to ask questions—all she could do was try to make him feel better.

And, she knew just what to do.

As she thought about it, seeing him two evenings in a row was odd—usually, she could count on him for once a week. Although, if she were to be honest with herself, she wouldn't have minded more. At her prices? Twice a week? More money than she needed . . .

She checked the clock on the bathroom counter.

Out of time.

****

"I'm sorry, Samuel—I wish we could have nailed it down before leaving for South Africa." Colbie sat in a stately wingback chair, Samuel Burnett at his desk.

"As am I—but I remain undaunted. It may not be now, but I have no doubt justice will be served."

"I agree—I have a nagging feeling we only discovered a fraction of what's beneath the surface of this case." Colbie took a sip of tea, then set the cup on its saucer. "I leave this evening for South Africa where I'll meet up with Ryan, and we'll proceed much as we did here—dissecting each theft, then interviewing victims."

"Not an easy task . . ."

"True—but a necessary one." She looked directly at him. "Tell me what you know about Nigel Blackwell . . ."

"Nigel? A good chap, really—although I know he has a reputation for being a ladies' man. Why do you ask?"

"No particular reason—I was surprised when he called."

"Ah, yes—I forgot I gave him your number! I hope you don't mind . . ."

"No—as long as it was my investigation phone. He still has no idea I'm not Cameron Carlson . . ."

"Excellent! I guess the question is what do you think of him? It was quite clear he was smitten with you—I could tell that the night of the party."

"Oh, I don't know—I think he was more curious than anything else . . ."

"Curious? About what?"

"Someone new to a crowd of old friends—the fact you never mentioned our names to him prior to that night makes me think he was merely curious about who we are . . ."

"You may be right, but one thing I know about Nigel Blackwell is he knows what he wants, and he goes after it—no matter what, or whom."

"Not surprised—what do you know about his business? Import-export from what I understand . . ."

Burnett took his time, swirling brandy in a warmed snifter, as though thinking about his answer. "Indeed—for many years from what he tells me . . ."

"Does he specialize in anything particular? I confess, I don't know much about the business—how it works, or anything else. All I can do is make an educated guess . . ."

"It's a simple concept, really—import-export businesses match domestic and foreign buyers and sellers of various products and commodities. Overhead is typically low, and they implement lean business models."

"So, what I thought is true—it's a lucrative operation when done right . . ."

"Indeed—sizable profits for minimal investment."

"I can well imagine how successful he is . . ." She paused, thinking about his friend. "But, from what I understand, it can be tricky business—especially legal issues. Has he ever been in trouble with the authorities?"

"Not that I know of, although I seem to remember his telling me about a dust up a few years ago . . ."

"Concerning?"

Samuel Burnett placed his glass on the antique desk. "You can't possibly suspect Nigel Blackwell? I've known him for years, and I can't think of a time I didn't trust him!"

"I'm sure you're right, Samuel—but, in order for us to do our best work for you, I need to consider all possibilities. So far, we don't have much on this end, and the more I know, the easier it will be to bring the case to fruition." *Interesting,* Colbie thought. *Why such a strong reaction?*

"Of course—you're right. It's just that it's an uncomfortable feeling thinking a good friend may turn out to be someone who is alright with betrayal . . . sad, really."

They chatted for another few minutes before Burnett

walked her to the front door. "Let me know if you . . . ah! Maggie! You're just in time to say farewell to Colbie!"

"Thank God, I didn't miss you! It won't be the same—your snooping around!" She laughed, knowing Colbie wouldn't be offended.

She wasn't. "I checked in with security, and thanked him for everything he did to make our job easier. But, I didn't see Nick—will you please tell him it was a pleasure meeting him?"

"I will, but I have no idea when that will be . . ."

"Really? He was around here a lot . . ."

"'Was' is the operative word—I haven't seen or heard from him for several days . . ."

"That's odd—well, I'm sure he'll be in touch soon . . ."

As Maggie walked Colbie to her rental, a black vehicle pulled up, parking behind her.

"Expecting company?"

"No . . ."

"Well, I'll leave you to it—I'll be in touch soon!"

Colbie took her time putting on her gloves, watching the two men approach Maggie. There was one thing she knew . . .

They were cops.

CHAPTER FOURTEEN

B rian continued his surveillance from across the street, sipping a latte as the doorman piled Colbie's luggage in the London taxi. *Why the hell is she leaving so late? She's always in bed by eleven . . .* He grabbed two sugar packets, ripping the tops from both at the same time. *She must be leaving for Cape Town,* he thought as he slowly poured them in his mug, stirring until the sugar dissolved. He watched as she tipped the doorman—then, as if spooked by something, she slowly turned, her focus directly on the coffee shop.

On him.

He knew that look—she said it were as if knowledge passed through her, alerting her to something she shouldn't ignore. "It's different than being in meditation," she once told him. "In some ways, it's much stronger . . ." Either way, it creeped him out. During their last year out west—before his kidnapping—he tried to talk her out of beginning a new career as a profiler. To him, it was all a bunch of crap—a pile of hooey. But, no matter how much he tried to discount it, he had to take her seriously when she located him at the farmhouse in the boonies. She busted the case wide open and, according to her, the only reason she found him was because of her second sight.

He still didn't like it.

Brian grabbed his coat, drained his coffee mug, and strode out the door to a waiting cab.

"Heathrow," he commanded. "Step on it . . ." Obviously, Colbie was heading to Heathrow, so he didn't need to keep right on her tail. The airport was fifteen miles west of central London and, with late night traffic, she could easily make it in twenty to thirty minutes.

On the way, he Googled all flights to South Africa leaving that evening, narrowing Colbie's possible flight to two—one, really, since one of them was slated to take off within the half hour. Checking the departure times, it made sense she was taking British Airways. If he arrived before Colbie, it afforded him extra time to find the best vantage point for surveilling. But, he had to be careful—if he knew her as well as he thought, she would feel his presence if he got too close—the fact she felt him from across the street from the hotel was an indication she's pretty damned good at what she does.

His cab pulled up to the main entrance twenty-five minutes later. Brian tipped the driver, standing back as it pulled away from the curb. There were fewer travelers than he anticipated, making it more difficult to get lost in the crowd as he tailed Colbie to her gate. A quick scan of the area as he walked in the door indicated his concern was valid— the airport wasn't exactly a ghost town, but close enough.

As he checked the ticket counters from a distance, he spied Colbie at British Airways, handing her passport to the agent and, a few minutes later, she was on her way to the gate. If her flight were on time, she had about thirty minutes before boarding. He checked the flight monitor as he edged into his surveillance . . .

He kept well behind her, although there were few places in which he could remain inconspicuous. Unlike some American counterparts, Heathrow was open, sleek, and polished, the floor gleaming twenty-four hours a day. He made it a point to stay away from the middle of corridors, preferring to stick closer to walls. At one point, Colbie turned around again as if trying to figure something out, and Brian knew he tripped her intuitive wire for the second time.

Shit! He ducked behind a man who clearly needed to push away from the table more—Brian walked directly behind him almost completely obscured by the man's width, and he had a perfect view of his mark. He already purchased a ticket, so he followed until she reached her gate and sat down, fishing for her cell which was undoubtedly at the bottom of her purse.

Of course, he didn't have to stay for further surveillance. Where was she going to go? He knew her destination, and there was nothing more he could do until he arrived in Cape Town.

Satisfied he knew where Colbie would be for the next twelve or so hours, he headed for check in—without bags.

****

"Ryan!" Colbie waved as she exited the gate at the main airport. She admitted it was a little weird to be on the same case with Ryan when they worked in different cities. She realized in the last forty-eight hours how much she relied on him, and she looked forward to seeing his smile.

"Welcome to Cape Town!" Ryan grinned as he took her carry-on bag. "I think you're going to like it here—especially after the weather in London!" He paused, looking her up and down. "You don't look any worse for the wear . . ."

"Referring to the flight, I presume . . ."

"No—me. You don't look any worse for the wear being away from me!"

He was baiting her, and she knew it. "It was only two days, Ryan—don't be so sure of yourself . . ." She tried not to smile, but failed miserably. It was probably apparent to anyone in the airport they were good, solid friends glad to be, once again, in each other's company.

As they headed toward baggage claim, he glanced at Colbie. "Tired?" Ryan could tell by looking at her she didn't get enough sleep on the plane.

"Yes, but I know you have a full day planned. Just get me to the hotel so I can shower, and I'll be ready to go . . ."

"Not necessary."

"What do you mean?"

"I scheduled some pleasure time for us—by the time we get to the hotel, you'll have a few hours to grab a nap. Then it's dinner at one of the best restaurants in Cape Town—I made reservations before I left London."

"You have no idea how happy you just made me—my

last day in London got jammed because of rescheduling the Clements interview . . ."

"I figured—tomorrow, we'll take a tour at a game reserve if you're up for it . . . after that, we buckle down."

Colbie stopped, staring at him. "Seriously? A game reserve tour? A mini safari?"

"Yep—I think we deserve a bit of a break, don't you?"

Colbie laughed, throwing her arms around him. "You just made me a happy girl!"

Linking her arm through his, they made their way to baggage claim, then to the rental car. Ryan took the scenic route to their hotel, Colbie marveling at the differences between London and Cape Town—and the States. She wasn't what one might call 'widely traveled,' and her partnership with Ryan promised to open up what were once only dreams. When coupled with the success of her own business, her opportunities were truly limitless.

****

After a quick nap, Colbie lay in the bathtub, bubbles up to her chin, her body relaxing after the long flight. Dinner with Ryan was at seven o'clock, and he wouldn't tell her where they were going. Although, it really didn't make any difference—all she knew about African cooking was the cuisine was often spicy. Ryan did say, however, jeans were entirely appropriate, so all she had to do was throw on a

---

casual top, sandals, and she would be ready to go.

Just when she closed her eyes to fully enjoy the bath, her investigation cell vibrated on the floor beside the tub. *Not now*, she thought. But, as much as she wanted to ignore it, the cop in her said she couldn't.

"Cameron Carlson . . ."

"Colbie? It's Maggie . . ."

"Maggie!" *I just saw her yesterday . . . why on earth is she calling?* Then she listened closely to the young woman's voice—stressed, and higher pitched than usual. "What's wrong? You sound upset . . ."

"I'm a mess!" Maggie's voice caught. "Do you remember when you were leaving yesterday?"

"Of course . . ."

"Those two guys who arrived?"

"Yes—I remember. What about them . . ."

Maggie paused in an effort to compose herself. "They were from Scotland Yard!"

"The Yard? Why? What did they want?" That was enough to pique Colbie's interest, and she shook off the remainder of her relaxation. Her instincts were right about them when they got out of their car—but she didn't think she would be hearing from Maggie. Samuel, yes—Maggie, no.

"Do you remember when you said to tell Nick it was a pleasure to meet him?"

"Yes . . ."

"I said I hadn't seen him for several days—now I know

why . . ."

"Maggie—just tell me. Has something happened to Nick?"

Silence.

"He's dead—shot. They found him by the Thames . . ."

Colbie's mind instantly recalled the London news anchor reporting on a body being found by the river's edge. She also remembered her initial gut feeling about it—a single gunshot, a strong possibility it was a professional hit, and definitely not a murder sparked by misplaced passion.

"What? Are they sure it's Nick?" Colbie thought for a second. "And, what led them to you?"

"They know now it's Nick—they didn't when they showed up yesterday . . ."

"Then how did they track a murder to you?"

"By an I.D. bracelet I gave him last year—I had the jeweler write an inscription with my name . . ."

Colbie was silent, thinking about the enormity of the situation. To narrow it down so fast was unusual, especially when they had next to nothing to go on. At least, that's what she assumed based on the news report—not to mention it happened only a few days prior. The other thing was it wasn't such a long shot that Nick's murder may be connected to the art thefts—at least it wasn't out of the realm of possibility.

"Tell me what you know . . ."

Maggie fell silent on the other end for a few moments before continuing. "God, Colbie—it was awful! Today I had to identify his body!"

For all the confidence and bravado Maggie exhibited for the benefit of her friends, the truth was she sounded like a scared, young girl. Colbie allowed her several minutes to regain her composure before suggesting she start at the beginning.

"Well—I showed them to the sitting room, and asked Cook to bring some tea. Then I asked them what they wanted—it was weird, too. When they got there, they had no idea who I was—it wasn't until they asked my name they knew they were onto something."

"Then what?"

"When I said my name was Maggie, they looked at each other, and then the tall one took an I.D. bracelet from his pocket—he asked if I recognized it."

"Did you?"

"Yes—it was the one I gave to Nick . . ."

As Maggie continued to recount the visit by Scotland Yard, as well as identifying the body, Colbie couldn't help but think something was off. *Either those Yard guys were the luckiest two people on the face of the earth,* she thought, *or, someone pointed them in the right direction.* Her thoughts continued to override Maggie's story—*if that's the case, then who had something to gain by telling the cops whatever it is they knew?*

When Maggie finished, she sounded exhausted. It was a lot to endure, and Colbie appreciated her valiant effort at self-control and composure.

"Where did they leave it? Do they want to see you again?"

"I feel like they understand I told them everything I know, but they'll be back—maybe not right away, but they'll come back sometime . . ."

"I agree—now that they know their victim's identity, they'll focus their attention on who did it." She hesitated, wondering if she should ask the next question—but she knew she had no choice. "Did you call your attorney?"

Maggie squealed, her stress level peaking. "Attorney? Why do I need an attorney? I didn't do anything!"

"I know—but, think about it. You're a smart girl—you know as well as I they're going to start digging, so it doesn't hurt to apprise your attorney of what's going on . . ."

Maggie fell silent as she considered Colbie's suggestion. "You're right—I'll call him first thing in the morning . . ."

"Does your father know?"

"He left this morning for Paris—I left a message for him to call me as soon as he can."

"Good—call me if you need to . . ."

They rang off, Colbie giving Maggie her personal cell number in case she needed to get in touch with her. Maggie promised she would call her attorney in the morning, and Colbie had no reason to suspect she wouldn't keep her word.

She checked the time—six forty-five.

****

Ryan knocked on Colbie's door promptly at seven—reservations were for seven-thirty, so they had plenty of time to walk to the restaurant. When they stopped in front of an American-style diner, Colbie was stunned.

"American?"

Ryan's grin widened as Colbie realized she was about to eat good old American food. "The best burgers in South Africa—or, they're supposed to be. I guess we'll find out, huh?" He opened the door for her, the fragrance of grilled burgers and fries making their mouths water.

"This is perfect!" Colbie beamed. "There's nothing better than a burger and fries!"

"Except having a milkshake with it . . ."

"I'm a chocolate malt girl, "she confessed. "Although I can never drink it all . . ."

They chose the patio—Ryan pulled out her chair, then made himself comfortable. "So—catch me up. What's been going on? Progress?"

"Man—where do I start? And, it's all happened within the last twenty-four or so hours!"

"Then start at the beginning—you already told me about the twin thing—and, Blackwell." He wanted to stay as far away from him as he could—Colbie was in a good mood, and it was best to keep it that way. The last thing they needed was tension between them.

"Right—well, there are two—no, three—things we need to pay attention to . . ." Colbie paused to take a sip of water. "The first has to do with the murder of Nick Cummings . . ."

"What? Nick Cummings was murdered? When?"

"According to Maggie, a couple of days ago . . ."

From there, Colbie spent the next few hours bringing Ryan up to speed about London's Cummings investigation, how she had a strange feeling someone was watching her before she boarded her flight for Cape Town, as well as her idea that Cummings may be the first possible link to their art theft investigation.

"The way I see it," she continued, "For Scotland Yard to wind up on Maggie's doorstep only a couple of days after the murder . . ."

"I know where you're going with this—that barely gives them time to review any information they obtained from the launch of the investigation."

Both paused as the server freshened coffees, placing the tab on their table.

"Exactly—nobody can be that lucky. My theory? Someone knows something, and he or she put the Yard onto it . . ."

"Agreed—the question is who . . ."

They spent the waning sunset hours discussing Colbie's latest information, finally heading for their hotel as the sun faded. A quick check with the concierge, and they were in the lift to the seventh floor.

Colbie stood in front of her room door, facing her friend. "What do you think is going on with Brian?"

Ryan thought for a few moments. "I don't know—but I don't think we know enough about who he is at this point in his life to anticipate or discount anything . . ."

Colbie looked him in the eye. "You may not believe this,

but I really think he's following me . . ."

He cocked a brow. "Really? Just because you got a feeling someone was watching you in London?" It seemed far-fetched—if Brian cut her loose, why would he follow her? It didn't make sense to him, and he didn't hesitate to tell Colbie so.

"Maybe you're right," she agreed. "But when I felt that—feeling—it was one of familiarity."

They stood outside her door, each not wanting to say goodnight. Colbie enjoyed how he made her feel, but she also recognized how different he was from Nigel Blackwell. Ryan was safe. Secure. Solid. Blackwell was just the opposite—exciting. Intriguing. Magnetic. The differences between them couldn't be more obvious.

Or, confusing.

CHAPTER FIFTEEN

By eight o'clock the following morning, Colbie and Ryan stood in front of a private tour guide employed at the black rhino reserve—somehow, Ryan managed to make arrangements for a personal tour rather than go with a group of people they didn't know. A few minutes later, they were on their way to an experience neither would forget—to witness any wild animal in the wild is an incredible experience, but when Colbie spied a black rhino, it took her breath away.

She turned to their guide, unable to contain her enthusiasm. "He's magnificent!"

The guide grinned, hands on hips as the three of them stood in the morning light. "He is, indeed—theirs is a terrible plight . . ."

"I'm not sure I understand . . ."

"Poaching—their horns bring a tidy sum."

Colbie was horrified. "I know there's a problem with poaching elephant tusks, but I had no idea black rhinos are facing the same thing!"

"Oh, yes—in the early seventies, there were somewhere around sixty-five thousand." He paused, watching Colbie's expression turn from curious to disgusted. "Today? A mere forty-eight hundred remain . . ."

Colbie focused on the enormous beast in front of their safari Jeep. "That makes me sick . . ."

The guide nodded. "You'd think their extinction would be due to habitat loss—but, it's not."

"Poaching?" Colbie asked.

"Yes—overexploitation."

"So, what's so great about rhino horn? Is it ivory?"

"No—it has nothing to do with ivory . . ."

"Then, what?" Colbie covered her eyes as she looked into the morning sun, observing the large, male rhino in front of them.

"Medicinal purposes."

Colbie and Ryan glanced at each other, each thinking the same thing. Colbie's vision. Medicine droppers.

Their guide continued. "It has been that way since the fifth century—in Southeast Asia, they used it as a antidote for certain poisons, but they used it for thousands of years without impacting the populations . . ."

"When did poaching become a problem?"

"The rhino maintained until the seventies—but, the

reason for their demise is different than you may think . . ."

"And, that is?" Colbie and Ryan asked in unison.

"Oil."

"I'm afraid I don't understand," Colbie admitted. "What does oil have to do with it?"

The guide focused on his clients. "Young Arab men covet rhino horn for dagger handles, as well as symbols of wealth and status in their countries. As you can imagine, few of them could afford something so prized . . ."

"That's when the poaching really got going?"

"Oh, yes—chasing rhinos became quite the black-market business."

"Where does the oil come in? Those countries are usually swimming in it," Ryan commented.

"True—but, at that time, there was a massive oil shortage, and prices for black rhino horn escalated. 'Black gold' they called it . . ." He paused as the magnificent animal moved from view. "The result? A seven-year increase in per capita income in Yemen that made rhino horn daggers within reach of nearly everyone."

"Holy crap," Ryan muttered. "What about today? What are the conservation efforts?"

"How much is a rhino horn worth? Colbie interrupted. "It must be pretty damned expensive!"

"The black market was—and, is—alive and well. Twenty-five to fifty thousand in 1990 . . ."

Colbie and Ryan stared at the guide, dumbfounded.

"The good news," he continued, "is due to conservation efforts including monitoring and protection, numbers nearly doubled from the twenty-five hundred in 1990 . . ."

"That's good . . ." Colbie commented. "Is Asia still a big market for poachers?"

"Indeed . . ."

"Where?" Colbie had a sinking feeling she already knew.

"Thailand, mostly . . . "

She shot a look at Ryan, raising her eyebrows. Since the beginning of their investigation, Colbie had visions of Thailand—then, she had no idea why. At that moment, clarity washed over her.

Another piece to the puzzle.

****

Inspector Michaels knocked on his boss's door loudly enough for the entire floor to hear. No one minded, however, for everyone knew DCI Murray had a tendency to bury his head in every case he investigated, and he was seldom aware of anything or anyone.

Michaels rapped again. "Sir?"

The deputy chief inspector looked up. "Michaels—I hope you have something worth hearing . . ."

"I think you're going to like this, Sir . . ."

Murray studied his colleague for a moment deciding if he really wanted to be interrupted. The serial killer investigation was nearing a breakthrough, and he wasn't sure if he wanted to take the time.

He watched as Michaels took a seat in front of his desk. "Well?"

The inspector leaned forward, handing a manila folder to his boss. "We found Maggie."

"You're kidding!" He hesitated a moment to consider the ramifications. "Who is she?"

"Maggie Burnett—daughter of Samuel Burnett . . ."

"I know that name—big into art. He has quite the reputation for being a connoisseur . . ." Murray flipped through the file—not much to it yet, but he had the feeling there soon would be. "So—fill me in . . ."

Michaels spent the next half an hour relating the details of his visit to the Burnett estate, including seeing someone leave just as they got there. He could have kicked himself for not asking Maggie Burnett who she was—but, in the long run, he figured it probably didn't matter.

"Do you think Maggie had anything to do with it?" the deputy chief inspector asked.

"Not really—but, the fact she was close enough to Cummings to give him an I.D. bracelet warrants a closer look, don't you think?"

Murray turned his chair so he had a good view of the window. He stared through it, unaware of the pigeon perching on the sill, his thoughts racing as he compared the similarities between the serial killer victims and Nick Cummings. "I don't think they're related," he commented as he returned his focus to the inspector. "The coroner was right . . ."

"I agree—but there's something that bugs me about Cummings. I think that young woman I met at the riverbank knows a whole lot more than she's letting on. I thought so before, but now I'm sure of it . . ."

"You're sure?"

"I am, Sir—I think we need to pursue finding her in order to find out who murdered Nick Cummings—I think she's our link . . ."

Deputy Chief Inspector Murray leaned back in his chair, his gaze fixed on the young inspector sitting across from him—sending Michaels out on such an important case may prove to be a little much for his level of experience. On the other hand, maybe he would have a new perspective—a chance he needed to take.

"Run with it," he ordered. "And, keep me posted . . ."

****

Colbie and Ryan headed back to their hotel by late afternoon, both thinking about their day at the game reserve.

"Think about it . . ." Ryan suggested. "When we start peeling back the layers, I'm beginning to think Nick Cummings is the missing puzzle piece to really get our investigation going . . ."

"Maybe—but, why? What did he have to do with anything? Just because he's from South Africa . . ."

"Cape Town in particular," Ryan interrupted.

"Okay—just because he was from Cape Town isn't enough to go on . . . and, we have to remember we met him in the context of the Burnett art. Plus, there isn't any evidence to suggest he has—had—a hand in it."

"You're right, of course, but I have a feeling he's linked to the art thefts—and, I have a feeling there's something else going on here—in South Africa. Cape Town, specifically . . ."

Colbie thought for a second about Ryan's suspicions. "Like what, though? We haven't heard of anything going on here, and we're here to investigate the art thefts—that said, I think we need to concentrate on what we have in front of us."

"Right, again—I'm still going to keep my eyes open, however. And, I know damned well you will, too . . ."

"Let's just say if anything piques my interest, I'll let you know—in the meantime, let's go over our plan for tomorrow. Who's first on our list?"

Ryan flipped through the pages of his binder. "Conrad James . . ."

"What do we know about him?"

"Nothing, really, other than he's another victim of art theft . . ."

"That's it?"

Ryan continued flipping through his binder, stopping suddenly as he reached the end of his notes. "And—he has a home in London and Cape Town . . ."

They looked at each other, both realizing the significance.

"You think?" Ryan asked.

"I don't think—I know . . ."

****

Kristi took extra care to please the man in her bed. He was, after all, her only source of income—well, perhaps not the only source, but he certainly was the main source. If she had any intention of keeping up her lifestyle—at least for a little while—she needed to keep him close to the vest.

"Hey, Baby . . ." As she left the bathroom, the man sitting on the side the bed looked completely unfamiliar. Yes, his features were the same, but his classy British style changed to one of a haunted man. He looked as if he'd been on a three-day bender—one he didn't weather particularly well.

He grunted, grabbing a half-smoked cigarette from the ashtray next to the bed, lighting it with the butt of another. *Weird*, she thought. *He never smoked cigarettes before—always a pipe . . .*

She sat beside him. "How about if I order from room service?" She rubbed his back gently with the palm of her hand.

"Not today—I have to go . . ."

"Go? Where? We hardly had any time together!"

He looked at her, his eyes cold and empty. "None of your business . . ." He took one, long drag before crushing the butt to smithereens in the ashtray. "Where are my pants?"

Even though she had only a couple of years' experience in her—field—she knew better than to provoke him with provocative questions. "Okay—I understand. When will you be back," she asked as she fetched his slacks from the seat of an easy chair.

"I'm not certain—maybe never."

Her worst fear smashed into her gut like a cannonball. "Never? What about me?"

"What about you?"

She hesitated, knowing her next question was out of line. "Are you going to see me again?"

He snatched the pants from her, making a feeble attempt to put them on, one leg at a time. "Don't worry—I'll send an allowance. You'll be pleased to know I'm quite good at keeping people on my payroll . . ."

Kristi's back stiffened as she understood the full force of his words—she was nothing but a piece of property to him.

****

Inspector Michaels stopped in front of the club, its heavy steel doors exactly like every other building on the block. If he didn't know better, it wouldn't occur to him there was a club of any sort there—let alone a club for only the rich and, possibly, famous. In the late afternoon, there was little going on—in fact, the street was bare except for a food supply truck parked in the alley. But, he figured it not unusual—the club wouldn't get going for another several hours, and there was no better time to get a feel for the place without interruption.

He walked a few blocks in all directions, surprised at the swanky high rises only blocks over from his target—the area tested the boundaries of his usual turf, and the truth was he wasn't familiar with the district, at all. That, however, couldn't come into play—it was his job to get familiar with it as of yesterday. DCI Murray stuck his neck out allowing him the opportunity to show what he could do, and he wasn't about to screw it up.

In the investigation biz, there's a fine line between tipping one's hand, and getting what's needed. If Michaels decided to puff his chest a little and approach the owner or manager of the club, it could shut his investigation down in a heartbeat. No—the more prudent approach, he decided, was to hang back, and visit the club when it was in full swing. Without doubt, there would be a bouncer checking identifications or personal invites, and Michaels knew getting in wouldn't be a problem once he discreetly flashed his credentials. It was a good bet he would have only minutes inside the club before upper management would know of his presence—and, it was within those minutes he would glean the most information. He wanted time to observe without the obvious stigma of being a cop—only then could he see things as they truly were.

He checked his watch—if he planned to return at midnight, he had a few hours to catch some shuteye, and grab a bite to eat. As he climbed into his car, he couldn't help but wonder what the girl at the riverbank had to do with everything—yet, he knew she did. She certainly seemed to know quite a bit about the club, although she didn't admit she spent time there. Was she a regular? Did she ever go to the club by herself? Did she work there? Michaels instinctively knew his answers were directly tied to her—the only problem was he had no idea who she was, and it would be another needle in the haystack gig if he weren't careful. Hell, he didn't even have a picture—all he had to go on was his memory.

And, his ability to draw.

CHAPTER SIXTEEN

66 You look like hell . . ." Nigel Blackwell watched his friend make himself comfortable in a chair across from him, the ironwood desk an impressive expanse between the two men.

"Thanks, mate—nice to see you, too . . ." Conrad James pulled his pipe from his pocket, placing it on the desk as he fished for his pouch of tobacco. His wife considered it a filthy habit, and he was relegated to smoking outside or in pubs. That day, however, he had the pleasure of partaking in the office of his good friend.

Blackwell sat back in his chair, studying the man sitting across from him. There was a day, he supposed, James was a sturdy, confident sort—he knew he was because that's how he portrayed himself since the day they met. But, clearly, something changed—as James lit a match, Nigel noticed a tremor in his hands not previously apparent. Had it always been there? He wondered. Then, doubted. *I would have noticed it*, he thought as he watched his friend search for a comfortable position in his chair.

"So, what brings you here? You're usually not one to call on the spur of the moment . . ."

"Who said it's the spur of the moment? I figure we didn't have time to catch up at Burnett's shindig, so now is as good of a time as any . . ."

"You're right. What do you have to report? Are we ready for delivery to Thailand?"

"Indeed, we are—two weeks. Three, at the most."

"What's the hold up?" Blackwell rolled his chair closer to the desk, a move that could be interpreted as intimidating.

"Cummings—I haven't been able to reach him . . ." James fidgeted with his pipe, refusing to look Blackwell in the eye.

"When's the last time you saw him—or, talked to him?"

"About a week ago . . ."

Nigel took a moment to consider his friend's story. It didn't make much sense because he knew Conrad James to be relentless when it came to keeping the underlings on a tight leash. Cummings had the personality of an incorrigible brat, and it was no secret James hated his guts. "That long? It's rather unlike you, isn't it?"

James held Blackwell's gaze, refusing to succumb to surreptitious grilling. But, just as he was about to explain his side of things, they were rudely interrupted by the constant, annoying ring of Nigel's phone. "I like the old-fashioned ringtone," he said more than once. "Besides, it's tough to ignore . . ."

Nigel excused himself, taking the call as he walked from his office. "Yes, yes—how can I help you?"

Before Nigel returned, Conrad James had a little under ten minutes to figure out how best to orchestrate the shipment to Thailand without the help of Nick Cummings. There wasn't any reason he couldn't make things happen on his own—after all, he hadn't tipped his hand thus far, and there was no reason to think he couldn't handle it. *As long as Blackwell doesn't find out,* he thought, *I have it made . . .*

Just as James was ready to swing into a full-fledged plan in his brain, Nigel returned, a grim look tightening his jaw. Without word, he again sat opposite his good friend.

"Please accept my apology—I don't like to interrupt time with colleagues unless I have to . . ."

"I understand—now, where were we? Oh, yes— Cummings." James paused for dramatic effect. "The way I see it, we don't need that miserable little shit . . . if he had any brains, he'd answer my calls and messages." As James prepared to walk Nigel through a possible plan for Thailand, he noticed the look on his friend's face didn't change. "Nigel—you okay?"

Blackwell drew a long breath. "It seems we have a problem . . ."

"Problem? What kind of problem?"

A pause. "It appears Nick Cummings won't be joining us for the delivery . . ."

Conrad James froze in his chair. *How the hell does he know,* he wondered. *Who the hell was on the phone?* He figured the best approach was to play stupid. "Where the hell is he? I'll kill him . . ."

"It seems someone already has . . ." Nigel didn't break character. If he were to get to the bottom of Nick's murder, it was critical he remained in control at all times.

At that moment, Conrad James had to pull on every bit of acting experience he had. He lit his pipe, and sat back in his chair as casually as possible. "Any idea of who did it? Or, how?"

Nigel eyed James, assessing the man's level of stress. "Murder, you think?"

James considered his question. A trap? Perhaps. "Well, from what I know of Nick Cummings, it's hard to believe it would be anything else . . ."

"You're probably right . . ." Blackwell sat, fingers tented as if he were contemplating mysteries of the universe.

"How did you find out?"

"You mean who was on the phone?" Nigel saw no reason for anything but candor.

James nodded, taking another puff from his pipe. "Based on our conversation, I can only assume you didn't have that information before I arrived . . ."

Nigel sat in silence for a few moments, thinking about the voice on the other end of the line. "I don't know who it was—all I know is it was a woman . . ."

That, James thought, *is a problem.* He considered the ramifications, and no matter how he cut it, someone outside of their circle had Nigel Blackwell's phone number. And, he couldn't think of one woman who would call Blackwell on his business cell. In itself, that raised serious questions— how did she get the number? And, for what purpose?

One thing was clear—it was time for Conrad James to get the hell out of there. He looked at his watch, feigning surprise at the time. "I'm sorry, Nigel—I have a previous appointment, and I must be on my way . . ." He rose, placing his empty pipe in his pocket. "Let me know what you find out, right?" With that, he strode out the door none the wiser he was already on Nigel Blackwell's radar.

Nope—he didn't catch on to that, at all.

****

The line outside the door of the club wrapped around the building, Michaels estimating at least one hundred or more partygoers. It inched slowly toward the massive door, everyone fully aware they could be turned away at the whim of the bouncer. Usually, there was a guest list he consulted each time a hopeful reached him and, when Michaels cut in line showing his credentials, the bouncer wasn't any too happy. He compared the investigator to his picture, making sure he was who he said he was—the owners of the club made it a point to instruct all bouncers, managers, and bartenders to make nice with the cops if and when they showed up for any reason. The last thing they needed was the cops snooping around, and the sooner they could get rid of them, the better. The bouncer unhitched the theatre rope, allowing Michaels entrance into the club as those he cut off in line voiced their lack of appreciation.

"Thank you," Michaels commented as he approached the door. "I promise to not cramp anyone's style . . ." The bouncer nodded, resuming his duties as the inspector disappeared into the bowels of the club.

As with most hot spots, the dance floor was in the middle, the D.J.'s booth to its right. Tables and chairs were elevated like theatre seating, allowing all patrons to have an unobstructed view of the grinding moves, all of which Michaels thought were disgusting.

He pegged the median age from twenty-five to thirty-five or forty, although the forty set seemed a bit old for the atmosphere. Servers snaked through the dancers, trays loaded with beers and cocktails—and, from the look of it, they probably made damned good money.

Scanning patrons at the bar, Michaels noted there was something different about them—even though they were young, they clearly had enough bucks for an evening at one of the swankiest clubs in town. Girls didn't look like sluts, and the twenty-something men were well-groomed—both were fashionable, their finery on parade.

Michaels took a spot at the bar, and ordered a pint. Sipping a brew offered ample opportunity to watch comings and goings, as well as the actions of those who seemed to be right at home. He devised a plan should he see the girl from the riverbank, but he had the gut feeling if he approached her she may book—that was the last thing he needed. She was his only link to discovering why Nick Cummings was slapped on a slab in the morgue and, if he scared her away, it could be the last opportunity to learn what she knew.

As luck would have it, an hour and a half later—just as he was ready to wind it up—Inspector Michaels hit pay dirt. She walked through the front door and onto the dance floor, servers greeting her by name. "Hey, Kristi," some called to her as she wound her way to the bar through the dancers. *Interesting*, he thought. *She doesn't look anything like she did when I met her at the riverbank . . .* Instantly, he knew the person she presented to him that night was a farce. The young woman he watched flirting with young and older men was in her element—she knew that club inside out, and there was no mistaking her comfort with it.

She gracefully eased onto a barstool next to him, eying him up and down. "Hello—I haven't seen you here before . . ."

"That's because it's my first time . . ."

"Ooh—I like first timers . . ." Her voice dripped with innuendo. "What brings you here?"

As he hatched a reasonable story, Michaels made a mental note of everything about her—jet black hair styled in a sleek, swing cut brushing the lower part of her jaw. Stick-straight bangs cut across her forehead, lightly touching her eyebrows, perfectly framing her small face. Her smile revealed a slight gap between her front teeth, making her appear genuine and instantly likable. She was tall and thin—what some might call 'willowy,' and Michaels instantly recognized her level of sophistication and elegance.

"Haven't I met you before," she asked. "You look so familiar . . ."

"No—don't think so. I'm in London on a business trip—another first time . . ." Michaels figured if he flirted with her, he may have time to get a handle on her game. And that's exactly what it was—a game. He knew as soon as she sat down, she had the information he needed—the trick was how to broach the subject with her.

"Do you come here often?" *Oh, Jeez*, he thought. *The worst of all pickup lines . . .*

Kristi smiled, finding his blush endearing. But before she could comment, a server slid between them, turning her back to Inspector Michaels. "Hey, girl! It's been a while—where's Conrad?"

Michaels noticed Kristi shifting in her seat as if she didn't want to have that particular conversation. "He's out of town—business," she snapped, letting the young woman know the topic was out of bounds. Moments later, the server was on to someone else, hoping to score a few more tips in the process.

"I'm sorry—where were we?" She turned to Michaels, a sweet smile on her face. She hoped he hadn't heard—what happens in her life was nobody's business, and she didn't want some scrawny businessman to be an exception.

But, it was too late. "I couldn't help but overhear," Michaels admitted. "It sounds as if there's someone else in the picture . . ." He distinctly heard the name 'Conrad,' but he hoped if he played stupid, he could gain information without her knowing he was scrutinizing everything coming out of her mouth.

"Oh, she doesn't know what she's talking about—Conrad and I broke up several weeks ago . . ." She smiled her most seductive smile. "So—I don't have anyone . . ."

Michaels always thought it best to let an investigation take it's course without having to force it—he believed it was the best way to gain accurate information.

"Drink?" he asked.

"Of course! A sidecar, please . . ."

He thought her drink an interesting choice—not the usual, and not often the preference of poison for someone so young. Michaels remembered his grandfather ordering a sidecar when they went to restaurants when he was a boy and, since then, it never entered his mind.

He smiled at the beautiful girl sitting beside him. "I haven't heard of that drink for years!"

"I never heard of it until a couple of years ago," she commented as the bartender placed a cocktail napkin in front of her. "If it weren't for Conrad, I never would have tried it . . ."

****

Colbie and Ryan mapped out their plan for the next morning, and it was shortly before they called it an evening she brought up what neither wanted to discuss. "Do you think Blackwell is involved in any way," she asked, clicking her mechanical pencil to extract more lead.

"I'm not sure—what do you think?"

Colbie paused for a minute before continuing. "I'm with you—I don't really know, but I think he's worth checking out."

Ryan was stunned at her suggestion. He knew without question Blackwell piqued her interest, so it must be with some trepidation she suggested such a thing. "In what way? Should we run a full-blown investigative report on him? You might not like what you find out . . ."

"I know—that's the point. But I can't shake the feeling he's involved somehow."

"Any ideas? What would he have to gain?"

"Who knows? But I do know one thing—I want to take a spin past his business—you know, just to see what's what. The closer I get, the more I'm going to pick up on whether he has anything to do with this whole thing . . ."

"Do you know the name of it?"

"No—but it can't be that hard to figure out. How many import-export businesses are there in Cape Town?"

"I have no idea, but I'm sure as hell going to find out," Ryan promised as he made his way to her hotel room door.

"I'll Google his name," Colbie offered, "and it shouldn't be too difficult to find out the name and address of his business . . ." She thought for a moment before continuing. "I really should have done that before . . ."

Ryan thought he detected a sadness on her face as she realized the man who swept her off her feet may have a nefarious bent to his nature. It didn't make him feel good— he hated seeing life take another swipe at her. But, he also thought it was his job to protect her—with Brian out of the picture, who else was going to do it?

No one.

****

"All in all, it was successful . . ." Michaels flipped his small, spiral notepad open with a snap. "I know she's involved as least as far as we're concerned—but, I don't think she's a participant in the murder."

DCI Murray raised his eyebrows. "You're sure?"

"One hundred percent . . . she was definitely trying to conceal her true identity when I met her by the riverbank."

"Meaning . . ."

"Just this—the girl I met looked as if she were at home there—nothing like the girl I met at the club."

"Name?"

"Kristi—that's all I know. I would have been pushing my luck if I asked for her last name . . ." Inspector Michaels was quiet for moment as he recalled Kristi's sitting beside him.

"Working girl?" DCI Murray suspected that was the case, but it was never a good idea to assume in his line of work.

"Now, that's the interesting thing—I usually have pretty good sixth sense about that. And, although I suspect she's a high class call girl, there's a part of me that says it's not the truth . . ."

Murray considered his inspector's intuition. Although he didn't have a great deal of experience, he exhibited good sense and instinct, so there was no reason to discount his initial observations and impressions.

"What does she look like—and, what did she look like when you approached you at the riverbank?"

Michaels smiled. "Got any copy paper?"

"Copy paper? Why in the hell do you need copy paper?"

The inspector laughed. "I'll show you—just grab me a couple of pieces of paper from your printer . . ."

DCI Murray swiveled his chair and grabbed several sheets of paper, sliding them across the desk. "Okay—printer paper. Now what?"

"Give me a few minutes . . ." Inspector Michaels plucked

the only pencil from a cup on Murray's desk filled with pens. Ten minutes later, he held up two, very different portraits of the same young woman. "Meet Kristi . . ."

DCI Murray took a long look at the drawings which were professional quality—in his opinion, Michaels could make one hell of a living being a police sketch artist. "Nice that you decided to show me this side of you," he said smiling. "And, you're right—they look completely different."

Inspector Michaels grinned, pleased he had something to offer the department that may set him apart from his aspiring colleagues. "At the club, she was a real looker—at the riverbank? Not so much . . ." His boss agreed. "But, tracking her down wasn't the best part—one of the servers asked her about someone named 'Conrad,' and, Kristi didn't like it. She turned her attention to me as fast as she could while she sent the waitress packing . . ."

"Any idea of who Conrad is?"

"No—but I don't think that will be too difficult to find out—one more trip to the club tonight, and I should have all the info we need to move the investigation . . ."

DCI Murray grabbed a folder on his desk. "Keep me in the loop . . ." That could only mean one thing to Michaels.

Dismissed.

Chapter Seventeen

Brian waited down the street from Colbie's hotel, afraid he was being too obvious. At that time of the morning, nothing was open except a few small cafés, so he sipped a cup of Kenyan coffee and picked at scrambled eggs with fresh mushrooms. Since his arrival nearly two days before, he had little luck catching Colbie by herself—she was always with Ryan, and tangling with him didn't seem like a good idea.

The plan was to talk to her as soon as possible, but the more he thought about it, the more he considered it prudent to hang back. He wasn't sure how she would react, and the last thing he wanted to do was alienate her. His tactics to get her back were questionable—he knew that—but with her planning to be out of the States for so long, time away from each other didn't bode well for rekindling their relationship.

After an hour of nursing breakfast, his patience paid off. Colbie and Ryan exited the hotel, Colbie checking a map while Ryan handed his parking chit to the valet. As he did in London, Brian had a cab at his disposal and, by the time their rental car pulled up, he was in the back seat, ready to shadow them as they quickly headed for the outer edges of Cape Town.

Fifteen minutes later, the target vehicle slowed significantly. "Drop back," he ordered his driver. He couldn't take any chances on her seeing him—or, worse, noticing they were being tailed.

****

"This is it—Gemini Imports. Let's go a couple of blocks then turn around—we can check it out from there . . ." There was no way Colbie wanted Nigel Blackwell to see her and, even though he said he was headed to Thailand when they were last together, she didn't put it past him to do exactly the opposite. Being away from Blackwell's influence had considerable effect on her—there was something about him that was mesmerizing, but, knowing she would probably never see him again, she gained clarity about him, as well as his business. She had no doubt—Blackwell was involved.

Big time.

Ryan eased into a parking space a block from Gemini Imports and, as she and Ryan watched the storefront of his business, Colbie realized the full significance of her vision weeks earlier—the number two surfaced in several ways, one of which was 'twins.' When she learned Nigel's birthday was in June, she attributed her vision to just that—his birthday. She never dreamed it was the name of his business! She smiled, comforted by the thought her intuitive senses once again led her in the right direction.

Ryan interrupted her thoughts. "Check it out—someone is leaving Blackwell's . . ."

Colbie peered through her surveillance binos, focusing on the figure walking toward them. "Holy crap! That looks like the guy we saw at Samuel Burnett's, but we didn't talk to him. She handed the binos to Ryan. "What do you think?"

Ryan adjusted the binos to fit his eyes. "You're right—the British professor-looking guy. James—I think his last name is James!" Ryan thought for a moment. "Conrad—Conrad James." He continued to track him for a few seconds before realizing James was headed right for them.

He grabbed Colbie. "Kiss me!"

"What?"

"He's coming right toward us—kiss me!"

Colbie didn't hesitate—she and Ryan locked lips, staying glued together until James was well past them. She pulled away, lingering slightly, scanning the area behind the car.

Gone.

They sat for a moment, each replaying what just happened. Ryan spoke first. "Sorry—it was the only thing I could think of . . ."

"I get it—I wonder why he was at Blackwell's? And, perhaps more important, does he have a legit reason to visit when Blackwell is supposed to be out of town?"

Ryan nodded. "That's the sixty-four thousand dollar

question, isn't it?" Ryan glanced at Colbie. "Do you . . ."

"Wait! Get a load of that . . ." She pointed to Gemini Imports. "What a stinkin' liar . . ."

Ryan and Colbie watched as Nigel Blackwell paused to lock the front door, then climb into a black, new-model Porsche.

"Thailand, my ass . . ." Colbie muttered.

"Maybe he had to change his plans . . ."

Colbie stared at her partner. "Why are you defending him? He lied to me, and you know damned well he did!"

He recognized the disappointment on her face—he saw it many times while they investigated Brian's kidnapping, and again when Brian called to tell her it was over. Ryan wondered if it were more guilt than disappointment—when Brian dumped her, she questioned her ability to make the right decision when it came to men. She confided in Ryan and, as he looked at her, he knew how much a slap in the face Blackwell's duplicity was—*for that, he'll pay*, he thought.

"I'm not defending him—I'm just not jumping to conclusions. Maybe he had to cancel his trip for legit reasons—you don't have any proof he lied to you . . ."

Colbie looked at him, knowing he was right—it was easier thinking he did her wrong. It was a reason for anger, as well as a reason to slip her true feelings to the back of a drawer, forever out of sight.

"I know," she admitted. "You're right . . ."

"So, let's operate on the assumption he canceled his trip—what we need to look at is why. Why did he return to Cape Town when he said he was heading for Thailand?"

Colbie buried her head in the map, and Ryan leaned over her shoulder as Blackwell sped by. Ryan glanced in his side mirror, watching the Porsche make a right turn onto the main highway.

"Shall we?" Ryan asked as he flipped a u-ey.

****

Several cars behind Blackwell, Ryan and Colbie recognized the scenery after they turned onto the main highway heading north—the previous day, Ryan took the same road to the game reserve.

"You don't think he's headed there, do you?" Colbie asked as she kept track of Blackwell's Porsche several cars ahead.

"We'll soon find out . . ."

Twenty minutes later, Blackwell confirmed their suspicions. He pulled into the game reserve, parking in one of the best spots where guests check in for luxury accommodations. *Either he's a big deal here,* Colbie considered, *or, he's incredibly arrogant and parks wherever he damned well pleases.*

Due to lack of traffic in and out of the reserve, Colbie and Ryan decided to hang back at the entrance until Blackwell disappeared into the building. They couldn't risk his seeing them, and they had two choices—hang around until he came out, or head back to the hotel to revamp their game plan.

The latter won.

****

Nigel Blackwell relaxed in his favorite leather chair swirling brandy in a vintage crystal snifter, his thoughts toggling from Cameron Carlson to his current dilemma— Conrad James. In all the years he knew him, he could count on one hand the number of times James dropped in to see him at Gemini Imports—and, each time he did, it was because he needed something. But, that day was different. There was a nervousness about James he hadn't noticed before— an insincerity—and it confused him. No matter how much James attempted to look casual and relaxed, it didn't work and, after he returned from the phone call, James couldn't wait to beat feet. *No,* he thought, *there's something afoot, and it's time I find out what it is . . .*

First, however, he needed to make a call.

Drink refreshed, he dialed, his party picking up on the third ring. "Andrew! So glad I caught you! It's Nigel . . ."

"Nigel? You son of gun—I was just talking about you the other day!"

"I wanted to get in touch when I was in London recently, but you know how it is—next time, right?"

Andrew Michaels laughed. "Yeah, right—nothing's

changed since university. But, not to worry—I have my hands full with an investigation . . . "

Nigel Blackwell hesitated. "That's what I want to talk to you about . . ."

"What? You know I can't divulge information of a case—but to satisfy my own curiosity, what is it you want to know?"

"Off the record?"

"Yep—on my mother's grave . . . "

Blackwell gave his glass another swirl. "Well . . . I left London a couple of days ago, but I recently heard of a murder case involving a young man." Nigel paused, weighing his words. "Do you know anything about it?"

"Like I said, I can't divulge that information—why do you want to know?" Michaels knew his old friend for many years, and he knew he wouldn't ask a question just for the hell of it. If Nigel Blackwell wanted to know something, he had a damned good reason for asking.

Nigel again hesitated, thinking about how far he wanted to take the conversation—there was something to be said for not opening up a can of worms. "Between you and me, off the record, I got a phone call today from a young woman— British accent—advising me a young man I know met with a foul end . . ."

Michaels swallowed hard. "The young man's name?"

"Cummings. Nick Cummings."

Michaels' silence was all Blackwell needed to know—there was no question he knew something about the case, if not working on it directly. Knowing that, he had to tread lightly. "If you're working this case, Andrew—and I suspect you are—I'm thinking we can help each other . . ."

"How? What do you have in mind?" He could always consider Blackwell a protected source . . .

"What can you tell me about the girl who called me? I'm certain you know who she is . . ."

Michaels hesitated, thinking about the possible ramifications. On one hand, he couldn't divulge investigation particulars—on the other, he could have Nigel Blackwell in his hip pocket, funneling information to him whenever he needed it. It was truly the lesser of two evils. "One thing—why do you think she called you?"

"Good question—I'm not sure, but it was under the auspices of letting me know about Nick Cummings's death—but there was an ulterior motive, I'm certain . . ."

"Why would she want you to know? And, how did she get ahold of your number? If I recall, you don't give it out to just anyone . . ."

"You recall correctly . . ."

Michaels thought for a moment before continuing. "All I know is her name is Kristi . . ."

"Last name?"

"No idea—but I intend to find out."

Nigel had to think twice about his next question, finally convincing himself he had to ask. "Andrew? Ever heard of a woman named Cameron Carlson?"

"Cameron Carlson? No, I don't think so—why?"

Exactly what Nigel wanted to hear.

****

Colbie and Ryan picked at their appetizers, both thinking about what transpired earlier that morning.

"When we saw James coming out of Blackwell's business," Colbie commented, "it didn't occur to me he was first on our list for interviews . . ." Colbie doodled on her cocktail napkin as she thought through seeing James at Gemini Imports, as well as coming to grips with the fact Nigel Blackwell lied to her purposefully. Or, not. Maybe it was something as simple as a change in plans, but she didn't think so. "So, let's recap what we know . . ."

"Roger that—I think we should start with your visions over the past few weeks to see how accurate they are—and, if I know you, they're pretty accurate . . . "

"Thanks—but, no matter how much I convince myself otherwise, there's always the possibility of my being one hundred percent wrong."

"Maybe—but, if you think about it, how many times have your visions turned out to be crap?" Ryan held Colbie's gaze, daring her to come up with an example.

"Well . . ."

"That's right—pretty much never . . ."

Colbie thought back to her first visions when she accepted the assignment with Ryan. "Okay—I agree. Let's go over them—the first time I meditated, I saw waving grasses—which, as I think about it, represents South Africa. I think it was nothing more than confirming location."

Ryan scratched notes into his notebook. "I remember that—okay, that's one. What else?"

"I remember seeing a broken, white gate hanging off it's hinges and, at the time, I didn't have a clue as to what it meant . . ."

"Now?"

"I think it represents my breaking off from Brian—a white gate brings feeling of comfort and home, and I think the vision was telling me to prepare for the worst—my relationship with Brian was on the skids."

"Makes sense to me—that's two . . ."

Colbie searched her memory banks for each vision, but they weren't clear—not surprising when they occurred days or weeks earlier. "I'm not sure when I saw this one, but I know it was a while ago—probably when we first began the investigation . . ."

"What's that?"

"I saw bamboo huts—you know—the kind with thatched roofs. Or, something like them. And, in that same vision, I remember seeing medicine vials . . . dark, dropper-type small bottles." Colbie paused as she tried to dig deeper.

Ryan stopped writing, thinking about the game reserve. "What do you think they mean?"

"I didn't know it at the time, but I think it has to do with the rhino poaching here—didn't the guide at the game reserve tell us the primary recipient of bootleg rhino horn is Thailand?"

Ryan threw his pen on the table with a whistle, and leaned back in his seat. "You're right—and, if that's the case,

Nigel Blackwell could be in it up to his neck . . ."

"Agreed, but why do you think so?"

"Because he has the perfect front—an import-export business . . ."

Colbie thought about Ryan's observation, certain they were on the right track. "The problem is how do we prove it?"

Unfortunately, there were no simple answers, and it wasn't until after dinner they agreed on a new plan.

"You're one hundred percent on board with this?" Ryan asked. "It's dangerous, and you know it—so don't pull the 'I used to be a cop' crap on me. Cop, or not—you need to have your head straight before going in—if you have any feelings at all for Nigel Blackwell, now is the time to address them."

Colbie looked at her friend with a steeliness in her eyes he hadn't seen before. "Oh, I'm over him, alright—he played me for a fool . . ."

Ryan chose not to comment. He knew she would beat herself up for a while as she processed her attraction to Nigel Blackwell, and there was nothing he could do to help her. "Alright then—we're agreed. You'll resurrect a relationship with Blackwell . . ."

"Yes—I don't see any other way . . ."

"Then I'll take the interview tomorrow with Conrad James about his being a victim of an art theft here, and you'll swing by Gemini Imports . . . right?"

"Check. But, if you find out something, be sure to text me immediately—I don't want to be in the dark about anything." Colbie thought about everything she needed to accomplish within the next hours. "Now, get out of here! I won't get anything done if you don't—I need to get some sleep!" Colbie laughed as she shooed Ryan out the door.

The truth was she needed time to herself to prepare.

CHAPTER EIGHTEEN

The following day dawned hotter than usual for the time of year. Compared to London, Colbie would take Cape Town any day just based on the weather. *On the other hand*, she thought as she leaned over the bathroom counter to put on mascara, *London does have its charm . . .*

She stepped back, taking a long look. *Not bad . . .* the thing she appreciated most was a casual look accentuated her porcelain skin and auburn hair. A sundress and sandals were perfect for a meeting with Nigel—although he didn't know about it yet. From what she gleaned from their surveillance the previous day, he was in the office during the morning, so a drop-in visit about ten-thirty seemed right. With luck, he would invite her for a quick lunch, offering her the opportunity for innocent flirting. Except it wouldn't be so innocent—since the last time she saw Ryan, all she could think about was how Nigel lied. *And, no matter what Ryan thinks,* she thought, *I'm sure Nigel's smooth for a reason— there's a 'sleight of hand' quality about him . . .*

By ten o'clock she was ready to go, and Colbie slipped on a white cotton shrug and grabbed her purse, heading out the door. Ryan left earlier in order to make his nine-thirty with Conrad James, agreeing to meet up with Colbie no later than midafternoon. They spent time on the phone that morning reviewing their dossiers on James—his background was impressive. But, until the previous day, neither Colbie nor Ryan considered James a real player in their investigation— an admitted mistake, especially since both of them knew better than to discount anyone or anything until the evidence corroborated the decision.

At Burnett's party, they didn't have an opportunity to chat with him and, once Nigel Blackwell caught Colbie's attention, James slipped through the cracks. The important thing, however, was they were currently on track with Nigel Blackwell and Conrad James in the crosshairs. *Then,* she thought as she climbed into her rental, *there's Nick Cummings—how does he fit into all of this? And, who decided to do him in?*

As she headed for the city's perimeter, she considered contacting Scotland Yard to see if she could learn more— perhaps, if they put their heads together, they could solve the art thefts and a murder in one sweep. *Wouldn't that be nice,* she teased herself as she pulled into a parking space in front of Gemini Imports.

She sat for a moment, centering herself before entering the lion's den. Colbie no longer felt anything for Nigel Blackwell except contempt, although she was certain he would try his best to recapture what they had in London. She wasn't going to lie—it would be difficult to see him again. But, she had to remember the investigation wasn't about her—it was about art thefts, and she had to find out how Blackwell was involved. If it turned out he had a hand in the rhino poaching? Well, all the better . . .

****

Ryan couldn't remember a time since his foray into private investigation when he was so ill-prepared going into an interview. There was no question Conrad James wasn't on their radar when he should have been, and Ryan felt as if he didn't have enough information going in despite his researching well into the night. As he walked up the brick walkway to James's home, he made a mental note—*investigate everything!*

The doorbell sounded exactly as Ryan expected from a classic British-looking chap—nothing cheap or tinny, only the deep rich sound of low-toned, church-like chimes. He waited for several minutes before a pleasant, plump woman pulled open the heavy door with some difficulty—she couldn't have been more than five feet or five one. *Almost the same height as Colbie,* he thought as she ushered him into a formal sitting room.

"Please—have a seat," she invited. "I'll let Conrad know you're here . . ."

"Thank you . . ." Ryan instantly knew the woman was James's wife—a quick glance at her left hand, and the style of her clothes tipped him off, as well as her calling her husband by his first name. Clearly, she was an added piece to the puzzle—what stories did she have to tell? He scratched down a reminder to return to their home when Conrad wasn't there—if he could have a private conversation with her, he might get info about the inner workings of their relationship. *And, why the hell didn't I know he was married,* he chastised himself.

A few minutes later, Conrad James entered, extending his hand to Ryan, then stopping short. "Haven't I met you before?" He held onto Ryan's hand as if it would help him remember.

"I don't believe so—it's my first trip to Cape Town . . ." Ryan suspected James might remember him from Burnett's party even though they didn't have the opportunity to chat.

"London? Did I meet you there?" James wasn't going to let it go.

"Nope—never been there. But, my mom once told me when I was about ten I looked like every kid on the block—maybe she was right!"

James relaxed his grip, accepting his mistake. "Perhaps she was," he said with a smile. "Please—have a seat. I'm not sure what I can tell you because I was out of the country at the time of the theft . . ."

Ryan nodded. "I know—but it seems rather irresponsible of me not to talk to you while I'm here . . ." he explained as he took out his small notepad and pen from his jacket pocket. "So, I'm thinking the best place to start is at the beginning—where were you when the theft occurred?"

"London." James wasn't comfortable talking to anyone about the theft, let alone a private investigator. He regarded them as slimeballs, scurrying around in the dead of night, exploring dark corners of people's lives. He told Burnett he didn't want to report the theft—but Samuel wouldn't listen and, for some inexplicable reason, Burnett added James's name to the list of victims, anyway. That was what they were to discuss the evening of Burnett's party, but it turned out there was no time nor opportunity.

"Was anyone home here when the theft occurred?" Ryan

decided to ignore James's monosyllabic response—he'd press him later.

"Just my wife—Corrine."

"Is your wife available to talk with me today?"

"I doubt it . . ."

As Ryan jotted down sparse notes, he implemented a technique Colbie taught him three years ago. "Let yourself go," she said. "Don't just listen to or think about a vic or perp," she said. "Feel what they have to say . . ."

To him, Conrad James seemed a guarded, careful man, measured in everything he did. Ryan had the feeling he couldn't trust him as far as he could throw him, and there was a distance about him that made the room feel thick. Uncomfortable. Plus, he had a difficult time looking Ryan in the eye—he glanced to the floor often as if the young man sitting across from him could see into his soul.

Then, there was the way James dressed—when Ryan saw him prior to that day, he wore a tweed sport coat made of fine wool, and that day was no different. Definitely an odd choice considering the winter temps in Cape Town—*although*, he conceded, *the house does feel a bit cool . . .*

Still, it seemed out of place.

From James's clipped answers, Ryan had the sinking feeling he wasn't going to get anywhere, and he questioned how far he should go with his interrogation. There was a lot to be said for coming back to talk to Corrine when Conrad wasn't home, and he revamped his attack within minutes of taking a seat in James's sitting room. But, James couldn't know that—so, he spent the next thirty minutes listening to nondescript answers that wouldn't help him, although he did get to see where the stolen painting hung in his library.

Ryan stood, again extending his hand. "Thank you very much, Mr. James—I think I have everything I need. But, on the off chance I need to get in touch with you, will you be here, or in London?" It was a risky move, one Ryan hoped wasn't too transparent.

"Neither—I leave tomorrow for Switzerland . . ." With that, Conrad James stood. "And, as I'm sure you understand, I have many things to do before I leave . . ." Just then, Corrine entered the room as if one cue. "Corrine—will you please show our guest out?"

His wife obliged, Ryan thanked James for his time and, as he walked to his car, he noticed James's wife wasn't in so much of a hurry to get rid of him. He fully expected to say goodbye at the door, but, instead, she escorted him all the way to the driver's side door. "Mr. Fitzpatrick?" she inquired, her voice purposefully at a whisper.

Ryan turned, looking her in the eye. In that moment, he knew he and Colbie were on the right track—fear in Corrine's eyes belied a happy marriage, and he knew all he had to do was acknowledge it. "What is it, Mrs. James?"

She looked at him, tears in her eyes. "Are you here because of what happened in London?"

Ryan's first response was to hold the diminutive woman in his arms, letting her cry her heart out. But, he couldn't— for all he knew, her husband was peering at them from the house.

"Perhaps . . ." He watched her carefully, trying to read the source of her pain—did she know something she wasn't supposed to know?

"She called here . . ."

"Who? Who called here?"

Corrine James could barely keep her pain inside. "That girl . . ."

"What did she want?" Ryan thought it best not to ask who she was talking about—he was sure she would drop a name if given the chance.

"He didn't know I was listening—I picked up the extension, and I heard her say she knows what he did . . ."

Ryan tried not to show his surprise. "What did he do? Do you know?"

Corrine shook her head. "No—but I'm scared."

Now was the time. "Do you know the girl's name, Mrs. James?" He softened his voice as a cue he knew her heart was breaking.

"Kristi—her name is Kristi Parker . . ."

****

Colbie poked her head around the corner to Nigel Blackwell's office. "Knock, knock . . ."

He looked up, stunned. "Cameron! Good heavens—what are you doing here?"

"Surprised?" Colbie smiled, as she took off her sunglasses.

"More than surprised—I thought you were off to Paris. Did I misunderstand?"

"And, I thought you were off to Thailand," Colbie countered.

"Touché!" It took a moment or two for Blackwell to regain his composure. He crossed to her, planting a kiss on her cheek. "Please, sit—tell me what you've been up to for the last few days . . ."

"Well, after our trip to the art gallery, I received notice my appointment in Paris had to cancel—since Regis was already booked on a flight to Cape Town, I decided to ride shotgun . . ."

"Regis has business in Cape Town? Lucky man . . ." Blackwell eyed Colbie, uncertain if her story were kosher. "Who is he seeing here?" He knew everyone in town and, if Colbie rattled off a name he knew, he could easily check the veracity of her statement.

"Oh, good heavens, Nigel—I have enough to worry about with my own clients! Regis and I have an understanding— one that makes our business work, I think—he does his thing, I do mine. It was really quite unusual we were together in London—in fact, I'm only going to be here for a couple of weeks, and then I return to the States.

"Is he staying here?"

"No—both of us are leaving at the same time. Or, close to it—I head back home, and Regis heads back to London . . ."

Blackwell relaxed a bit, especially as he looked at the lovely sight sitting across from him. "Well, then—I guess I'll have to show you the best Cape Town has to offer!"

"Honestly, I wasn't sure if I should stop by—I know it's a

drag to have someone drop in when they're least expected."

"Don't be silly—I'm glad you're here . . ." Nigel checked his watch. "How about an early lunch, and we can catch up—even though it's only been a couple of days . . . "

"Perfect!"

"Just let me tell my guys in the back I'm going out . . ."

"This is my first time—seeing an import business, I mean . . . do you mind if I tag along?"

Blackwell paused before answering. "Of course—come with me!" He was pissed at putting himself in that position—he held a steadfast rule that no one was allowed in the warehouse portion of Gemini Imports and, until then, it was a rule unbroken.

"Excellent!" Colbie hooked her arm with his. "That's one thing I love about you, Nigel—you show me a side of life I don't know . . ."

A look of pleasure flitted across his face before he opened the door to the warehouse. "After you . . ."

****

Before Colbie met with Blackwell that morning, she and Ryan decided it would be a quick get together. Both had a feeling Nigel Blackwell liked to call the shots, so if Colbie wrapped up the afternoon lunch before he was ready—well, it could serve as a point of intrigue.

Their plan went off without a hitch—Nigel took Colbie to a little known authentic restaurant in Cape Town, and they took their time eating, chatting, and laughing. She was sure if she hadn't pulled the 'I have to go' move, Blackwell would have been content to stay on the patio, sipping drinks for the entire afternoon. As it was, Colbie agreed to meet him for dinner the following evening, but she was the one to request the restaurant. "How about the game reserve?" she suggested. "It's so beautiful there . . ."

Her request didn't surprise Blackwell in the least—the reserve was one of the widely touted tourist attractions around Cape Town, and it was always first on many lists. He agreed, offering to pick her up at five—plenty of time to enjoy a glass of wine and spectacular sunset before dinner.

She kicked off her sandals, poured a glass of wine, and waited for Ryan on the small patio adjoining her room, thinking about what they had in front of them. She wasn't comfortable being alone with Nigel—why, she wasn't quite sure, but it was an uncertainty that surfaced after she learned his true colors. He never did offer an explanation as to why he didn't travel to Thailand, although she told him why she didn't fly to Paris. A purposeful move? She thought so . . . he was curiously quiet during lunch, and she had a distinct feeling he was holding her at arm's length—all while being charming. Or, so he thought . . .

Colbie closed her eyes, hoping to gain clarity about Blackwell, but it would have to wait. She heard Ryan's key card flip the lock as he entered, arms filled with take out containers.

"Hey, you!" she called. "Out here . . ."

Ryan plopped the takeout on the patio table, then pulled up a chair beside her.

"Vino?" Colbie asked, scrutinizing the bottle. "2010 . . ."

"God, yes—what a day!"

"You're telling me—you go first . . ." she suggested, handing him his glass.

"Ah—but you've had more time to relax. How about if you go first while I decompress?" He lifted his glass in a toast.

Colbie shielded her eyes from the afternoon sun, noticing the twinkle in Ryan's eye. "Decompress, huh? That bad?"

"Nice try—you go first . . ."

Colbie grinned as she answered his toast. "Well—it's safe to say Nigel wasn't expecting me to show up!"

"I bet! What did he say?"

"Nothing—although I did manage to get in a 'gotcha' when he tried to call me out for not flying to Paris . . ."

"In what way?"

"I called him out on not flying to Thailand . . ." Colbie paused, smiling at her memory of Nigel's face—just like a little boy getting caught in a lie.

"Nice! So, what was the highlight of the day? Did you come up with anything we can use?"

"There wasn't a highlight, really—as you know, I had to mind my Ps and Qs. It worked because he asked me to dinner for tomorrow evening . . ."

Ryan was quiet for a moment. "Are you okay with that? I'm not sure how I can have your back if something goes south . . ."

"I know—I thought of that."

"Where's he taking you?"

"You'll like this," Colbie said as she took a last sip of wine. "I asked if he would take me to . . . wait for it . . . the game reserve!"

Ryan took a long look at his partner. "Nicely done—I'm assuming you want to see how they treat him there . . ."

"Precisely—at the least, he'll be a VIP . . . we have to remember Nick Cummings worked at the game reserve, and I'm certain there's a connection between Cummings and Blackwell."

Ryan adjusted his chair so he wasn't looking into the sun. "Speaking of Nick Cummings . . ."

"What about him?"

"I had a brief chat with Conrad James's wife—and, unless he were peeking out the window, he doesn't know anything about it."

"Does she know something about the art theft?" Colbie reached for one of the to-go containers. "Napkin?"

"Of course I need a napkin—you've seen how I always manage to dribble something down the front of my shirt!" He laughed as he recalled the time Colbie teased him because he wore more spaghetti sauce than he ate.

"True—don't remind me," she kidded, handing him two napkins to be on the safe side. "So—don't keep me in suspense . . . what did she say?"

Ryan paused—not for effect, but to make sure he recalled everything Corrine James told him. Then, he told Colbie everything—from Conrad James's showing him the spot where the painting used to hang to Corrine's saying a woman called the house telling him she knows what he did.

"Holy crap!" Colbie stared at Ryan. "You know what this means, don't you? We might have a connection to Nick Cummings's murder!"

"I know—that's what I thought. I'm thinking you need to get in touch with Scotland Yard . . ."

"Me? Why, me? You're the one who had the conversation!"

"Yes, but you're the ex-cop . . ." He winked at Colbie. "Gotcha!"

CHAPTER NINETEEN

A fellow officer behind him, Inspector Michaels drew his weapon as he allowed the manager of the building to unlock the door, ordering him not to enter the flat. Michaels' training as an Authorized Firearm Officer permitted carrying a weapon at all times, and it provided more than a small comfort when entering unknown situations.

Getting to the point where he stood before Nick Cummings's door was no small task—after considerable effort, he finally learned the address—it turned out when they fished his partly exposed body out of the river, the only thing on him was his clothes. No wallet. No phone. No nothin'. With little to go on, his only hope was to return to Maggie Burnett—with what he knew so far about the case, she was the only one who knew Cummings well and, undoubtedly, she would have been to his place before.

He was right.

Heading back to Burnett's also provided the opportunity to ask who was leaving as he arrived the first time they were there to inquire about the bracelet. His question put Maggie in an awkward spot—she didn't want to blow Colbie's cover, but, considering the circumstances, she couldn't lie. "Colbie Colleen . . ." she said, telling herself she should call her the second they left.

You'll just have to wait, Colbie Colleen, Michaels thought as he stood back, pushing the door open with his left hand, surveying the tiny room in front of him. Canvases—at least ten—stood in various stages of completion, the artwork of an incredibly talented individual. A small, twin bed piled with dirty clothes was jammed against the far wall, a tiny refrigerator next to it—a two-burner hotplate laden with burned-on grease was pushed to the back edge of a dilapidated card table.

Whatever Inspector Michaels expected to see, the scene before him wasn't it.

****

"Murray . . ." The inspector crooked the phone under his chin, putting his biscuit down as he reached for his coffee.

"DCI Murray, my name is Colbie Colleen . . ." Colbie paused, listening carefully to the inspector's response.

"What can I do for you, Ms. Colleen?"

"Well—I'm not sure, but I think this is a case of what we can do for each other . . ."

Thirty minutes later, Colbie wrapped it up. Murray understood the particulars of her art theft investigation, as well as Ryan's and her suspicions that Nigel Blackwell, Conrad James, and Nick Cummings were involved in illegal poaching, art theft, and black market sales.

"Do you have photographs of the stolen art?" Murray asked.

"Of course—as well as detailed, professional descriptions of each piece. I'll fax them to you as soon as we hang up—or, do you prefer email?"

"Either is fine—I'll be on the lookout for it. Is there anything else?"

"Just one more thing—when my partner interviewed Conrad James earlier today, James's wife wanted to have a private conversation . . ."

The hair on Murray's forearms stood at attention—something that always happened when he was about to crack a case. "Private? In what way?"

"I'm thinking this may be of particular interest to you—she told Ryan she picked up an extension phone when her husband took a call from a woman—a woman with a young voice . . ."

"And?"

"She heard the woman tell James she knew exactly what he did . . ."

"What did he do?"

Colbie sighed, thinking for a minute. "That's just it—
we don't know if she's referring to his involvement in the
art thefts, poaching, or both. Maybe it's about something
completely different . . ."

"I don't suppose you have a name . . ."

Colbie smiled because she knew she was about to make
his day. "As a matter of fact, I do . . ." She paused for a moment,
giving him enough time to grab a pen.

"Kristi Parker . . ."

****

Neither Colbie nor Ryan slept well that night. Colbie's
dreams were wracked with discontent, and Ryan was just
plumb worried about her being alone with Nigel Blackwell.
Of course, he planned to remain out of sight as they dined,
but, not knowing the layout of the restaurant, going incognito
would prove a challenge.

Both had their marching orders for the day—Colbie
needed to check in with Maggie to surreptitiously pick her
brain about Nick Cummings, and Ryan was to conduct two
theft interviews, promising to check in every three or four
hours.

As sure as Colbie was a redhead, she knew Cummings
was the hinge linking the art thefts and the rhino poaching.
The fact he worked at the game reserve made him even more
interesting, and she intended to work meeting Nick at the

club in London into dinner conversation. The evening, she surmised, would be tricky—*Nigel is an intuitive man*, she thought as she brushed her hair, *and he'll pick up on any insincerity.*

****

The fax machine spit out ten pages, each one a different photo and description of the missing art pieces. One, in particular, caught Murray's eye—a water color, it was an impressionistic street scene dating back to the late 1800s. Another was an oil painting of a young woman standing at a dilapidated farmhouse gate, her dress a vibrant orange. It stood in such stark contrast to the desolation of the artist's work, Murray couldn't help but admire it.

Twenty minutes later, he memorized the salient points of each missing painting, reminding himself to show them to Michaels just in case . . . just in case what, he wasn't sure. However, he learned early in his career discounting anything only proved a fool's folly.

He sat back, thinking about his conversation with Colbie—she was gracious enough to provide him with her website which included a complete bio, as well as the services her firm provided. Having a stellar rep as a behavioral profiler didn't hurt, either—something he should have known just by speaking with her. Her voice was pleasantly measured, making sure she got her point across and, the one time she laughed, he found it more of a chuckle. He suspected she was damned good at her job, and he welcomed the opportunity to work with her.

"Sir?" Michaels waited. "Sir?" A knock.

"What? Oh, yes—Michaels. Come in—have a seat . . ."

Michaels settled into the only chair in front of DCI Murray's desk. "You were lost in thought . . ."

"Actually, I was just thinking you might be able to use these . . ." Murray stuck the fax pages in a folder, sliding it across the desk.

"Use them for what?" Michaels flipped through the pages, his face blanching as he came to the photo of the girl in the tangerine dress. "Where did you get this?"

"Colbie Colleen—she's a behavioral profiler working an art theft case in London and Cape Town . . ."

Colbie Colleen? Michaels immediately recalled his conversation with Maggie Burnett. "I've heard that name before—Burnett's daughter mentioned it. Colbie Colleen was the person leaving Burnett's estate just as I arrived . . ."

"Makes sense—she told me she and her partner were investigating an art theft at Burnett's."

Michaels studied each photo, then looked at his boss. "You're never gonna believe this . . ."

"Try me . . ." Murray sat back, taking a sip of cold coffee.

"I've seen these paintings before . . ." He flipped through the fax pages for a third time, making certain he wasn't making a mistake.

"Where?"

"Cummings's' flat . . ."

Murray stared at Michaels for a moment, weighing the enormity of what he just heard. "You mean you found the stolen paintings at Nick Cummings's flat?"

"Not quite—I saw partial canvases in various stages of completion." He pulled the photo of the girl at the farmhouse gate from the folder. "This one is nearly done . . ."

The two men sat in silence, each considering what was at stake. First, there was a real possibility a high-caliber art scam was in full swing—why would there be duplicate paintings of those stolen from reputable art collectors?

Murray chewed on that one, finally turning to Michaels. "You realize what this means—I'll swear on my mother's grave at some time in the near future, miraculously the paintings will be located and returned to their owners. Or, would have been had Mr. Cummings not met with an unfortunate, early demise."

Michaels picked up the thread of Murray's thought. "Only those paintings wouldn't be the originals, would they?"

"Bingo . . ."

Michaels glanced up from the photos of the paintings. "Now what?"

Murray swiveled, and gazed out the window. "Now, Inspector Michaels, we find out who stands on the tip of the pyramid . . ."

"I sealed the flat, Sir, and I'll have forensics on it, first thing . . ." Michaels rose, and headed for the door.

"Michaels?"

"Sir . . ."

"You might want to start with Kristi Parker . . ."

Michaels turned to Murray with an obvious look of surprise. "Parker? Kristi Parker?" He paused to let Murray's bombshell sink in. "How do you know that?"

"Colbie Colleen . . ."

****

Ryan stood in front of Conrad James's home, hesitating slightly before opening the wrought-iron gate. If he were to take James at his word, he should be winging his way to Switzerland. With his luck, however, it was a good idea to always have a Plan B—so, if Corrine weren't by herself, he needed to have a reason for being there. Revisiting the library sounded like a good one—the scene of the crime. Ryan smiled as he thought of his backup plan—it was cheesy, and sounded like a crappy line from a Grade B movie. Still, it would work.

The previous day, it took Corrine just about as long to answer the door. As she invited Ryan into the sitting room, he guessed her age to be in her early '70s, age rearing its ugly head. She didn't seem the athletic type, and there was something about her that seemed—defeated. Drained. Diminished.

She motioned for Ryan to sit. "I knew you would come by today," she confessed as she poured two cups of tea.

"Really? Why did you think that?"

She held his gaze. "Because I can tell you're a bright young man—and, I'm guessing you figured out there's something going on with Conrad." As he listened, he watched her morph from a woman who looked like a whipped puppy to someone steeled by anger.

Ryan was motionless. Her demeanor wasn't exactly the same as the prior day—there was a coldness to her he didn't previously detect. "Well . . . yes. I'm hoping you can provide information I desperately need . . ."

Corrine James chuckled. "Desperately? I suppose that's rather dramatic, but I know what you mean . . ." She paused. "Biscuit?"

He accepted her offer, placing it on the teacup's saucer. "So—I'll be blunt. What happened in London?"

"I don't know exactly—but, I'm convinced Conrad is running from something. And, that call from Miss Parker certainly confirms my suspicion . . ."

"Why do you think he's running?"

"Because since he returned from London, he's virtually locked himself away in the library. He won't take calls, and, frankly, I'm surprised he agreed to speak with you—he was none too pleased about your being here, either."

"So . . . that's what you're basing your suspicions on—a call from Kristi Parker, and ignoring you?"

Corrine leveled her gaze on Ryan. "That—and the blood I found on his pants . . ."

Ryan nearly spit his tea across the room. "Blood? When?"

"On the pair of pants he had on when he walked in the door from London. They were small stains, mind you, but there was no mistaking it."

"But, why would he wear blood-stained pants on an airplane? Doesn't it make sense he would have changed clothes?"

"Oh, I don't think he was thinking too much about making sense—it was disgustingly obvious he had been on a bender, and he looked as if he hadn't slept a wink." She hesitated for a moment before continuing. "And, his shirt smelled like perfume—not the cheap kind. There was a sophistication to the scent, although I don't know what it is." She paused again. "Not that I care . . ."

Ryan sat back in his chair. He didn't believe for a second she didn't care—his gut told him her emotions were in ribbons. "Pardon me for being blunt—but do I understand you correctly? You believe your husband is having an affair with Kristi Parker?"

"Oh, good heavens, no! I wouldn't call it an affair—my guess is she's on his payroll. Conrad pays for everything he gets . . ." Corrine changed positions, as if trying to get comfortable. "Besides—it takes the heat off me."

More bravado, Ryan thought as he studied her. "Have you heard of Nick Cummings?" he asked.

"Nick Cummings? Of course—I always classified him as a wannabe. Sadly, he will never achieve a higher station in life . . ."

As Ryan listened, he couldn't help but wonder if Corrine James were simply parroting what she heard her husband say a million times—Nick Cummings was a miserable little sot who would never amount to anything.

"Let me ask you this—do you know Nick Cummings is dead?" Ryan watched her reaction closely—she didn't know.

"I do now . . ."

"Again, pardon me for being blunt—but I see no reason to tap dance around what both of us are thinking. Do you believe your husband is capable of murder?"

Corrine James straightened her dress, folding her hands in her lap. "Oh, yes, Mr. Fitzpatrick—it wouldn't surprise me in the least . . ."

****

Colbie was running a bit late, so answering a ringing cell wasn't on her list of things to do as she tried to get ready. One shoe on, the other in her left hand, she limped to the coffee table, and snatched her phone.

"Colbie Colleen . . ." There were few people who had her personal number, so it had to be someone worth speaking to.

"Ms. Colleen? DCI Murray speaking . . ."

"Chief Inspector! I didn't expect a call from you . . . has something happened?"

A hesitation on the other end. "Not so much happened as what we uncovered."

Colbie sat on the couch, shoe still in hand. "Uncovered?"

"Indeed—I figured it would be a good idea to bring Inspector Michaels up to speed on the Nick Cummings case—you know, the Kristi Parker connection."

"Did you?"

"Yes—and when he reviewed the photographs you sent of the paintings, he said he'd seen them before . . ."

"Seen them before? Where?"

"That's what I asked—he said he saw partially completed canvases of the missing art pieces in Nick Cummings's flat."

Colbie couldn't believe what she was hearing! "What?" Her brain sped through possible scenarios, and it didn't take long to figure out there was only one that made sense. "An art forgery scam?" she asked, still incredulous by what Murray told her.

"That's my take on it—and, Ms. Colleen, since we now seem to be joined at the hip regarding our individual investigations, I think it might be a good idea if we keep in touch—regularly."

"I agree, Chief Inspector. I certainly agree . . ."

****

Ryan walked in the door ten minutes after Colbie hung up from her call with the Chief Inspector. "Hey!" he called as he kicked off his shoes. "You about ready?"

Colbie exited the bathroom looking like she stepped from the pages of a high classed fashion magazine. "I'm ready—and you're not going to believe what I have to tell you!"

"Likewise—you want to go first?"

"I went first last time—your turn!" Her eyes twinkled as she tilted her head slightly to put on an earring.

Ryan grabbed a beer from the mini fridge, filling her in for the next fifteen minutes. Then, it was her turn. By the time they were ready for Colbie's dinner with Nigel Blackwell, their investigation shifted considerably.

"Now," Colbie said as she closed her hotel room door, "I need to steer the conversation in a totally different direction at dinner tonight . . ."

Ryan stopped.

"What?"

"Just be careful . . ."

Colbie noted his concern. "I will—I promise. I always am . . ."

CHAPTER TWENTY

The restaurant was much smaller than Colbie anticipated—and, while luxurious, there was still an indescribable feeling of being in the middle of a powerful, raw nature.

Nigel picked her up shortly after six so they would have an opportunity to watch the sun set. "There's nothing like it," he said, guiding her to a lovely table on the patio. "Of course, you have your tourist attractions in the States, but there is nothing quite like seeing a black rhino in safe environs . . ."

Colbie allowed him to scoot her chair forward so she was comfortable at the table and, as soon as they were seated, a server appeared with a bottle of wine and two glasses. Nigel checked the year—apparently a good one—nodding to the server to continue the pour. Colbie noticed he delighted in being a connoisseur—perhaps self-educated—and he took his time reveling in the fragrance of the local sparkling wine.

"I love a fabulous bouquet, " he commented, as he held

his glass up in a toast. "To you, Cameron—the loveliest woman in Cape Town!"

Colbie answered his toast silently, taking her time easing into conversation, and blushing appropriately at his compliment. Nigel was clearly pleased he could have such an effect on her.

"It's so relaxing," Colbie commented. "Everything seems to move at a slower pace—much slower than the States . . ."

"Indeed . . ." Nigel studied his dinner partner, aware she was slightly uncomfortable. The time he spent with her in Cape Town wasn't as easy as their time together in London and, sitting across from her, he picked up on something he didn't quite understand. It bugged him, too—he prided himself on being able to tune in on anyone if given half a chance. But—with Cameron—he felt as if he were being held at bay.

As the sun rested on the horizon, anyone bypassing Nigel's and Colbie's table would see an easy-going couple, enjoying each other's company. And, if Colbie had to be one hundred percent honest, she was enjoying herself. If nothing else, Nigel was a charmer in addition to being a fine piece of eye candy.

"Nigel—will you please excuse me?" She looked at him apologetically. "Too much tea . . ."

"Of course," he graciously agreed, rising.

Colbie flashed him a stunning smile, scanning the restaurant for the restrooms. "I'll ask the hostess," she said as she left the table. "I'll be back in a few—pour me another, please?"

She headed for the hostess stand, then disappeared around the corner near the entrance of the restaurant.

"How's it going?" Ryan stepped from the shadows just as she was about to enter the ladies room.

"Ryan!" She paused a moment to catch her breath. "You scared the crap out of me!"

"I know—I couldn't resist . . ."

She should have been annoyed, but she appreciated his take on trying to lighten up the situation. Both knew their investigation recently catapulted to a dangerous level, and neither trusted Nigel Blackwell as far as they could throw him. They suspected he was the brains of the forgery scam as well as rhino poaching for rewards obtained from a lucrative black market, but the reality was they had no proof. No evidence. All they had to go on were partially completed paintings, and the murder of Nick Cummings—bupkis as far as Blackwell was concerned.

"Where are you hanging out?" Colbie whispered, glancing over his shoulder to see if anyone were coming.

"Outside for the most part—I'm making like I'm a tourist, and I have a pretty good view of your table."

"Cool—now get out of here . . ."

Minutes later she was back at her table. As soon as she sat down she sensed something was different. "Hey— is something wrong?" she asked. Colbie thought she saw a fleeting look of irritation.

"Wrong? Of course not—I just received a message from a colleague and, I'm afraid, I must respond. Do you mind?" Nigel got up, cell in hand. Clearly, his was a rhetorical question—he was halfway to the lobby of the restaurant before Colbie had time to pick up her wine glass.

****

Inspector Michaels stood at the door, hesitating before knocking. There was a good chance the conversation he was about to have would be difficult and, as with most investigative interviews, there were only two ways it could go. *Although,* he thought, *if she decides to tell the truth, she can be done with this. At least, for now . . .*

He quickly reviewed his notes, jammed the tiny notepad in his jacket pocket, and rapped four times in quick succession. Moments later, he felt an eyeball peeking at him through the peephole, making his skin crawl slightly.

The door opened. Slowly. Not all the way.

Kristi Parker stood before him, her face revealing someone used it for a punching bag.

Michaels held up his identification.

"I knew you were a cop . . ."

"How?" He didn't move toward her.

"Seriously?" She looked him up and down. "Take a good look in the mirror . . ." Kristi turned, revealing bruises on her throat and back. "Come on in . . ."

She showed him to the elegantly decorated living room, gesturing for him to take a seat.

"Pardon me for not looking my best . . ." She touched her cheek gingerly.

Michaels sat in a plush leather chair as he handed her his card. "You know I have to ask—what the hell happened?"

Kristi attempted a smile. "Well—let's just say it was an unsatisfied customer . . ."

He took a long minute to look at her. "I understand. Well—let's get down to business, shall we? Are you sure you're up to it?"

Kristi nodded. "I knew you would be here eventually—I just didn't know it would be so soon . . ."

"Thanks to you," the inspector acknowledged. "Without your information that evening on the riverbank, I wouldn't be here . . ."

"So—what do you want to know?" She sat back on the couch, the down pillows cradling her small, bruised frame.

"Everything . . ."

There was no hesitation. After the previous evening, she had no desire to ever see Conrad James again and, as far as she was concerned, he could rot in hell. And, if she helped him get there? Well—that was just fine with her.

Nearly two hours later, Kristi got up and grabbed a Ziplock bag filled with ice from the freezer. "The only thing that doesn't leak," she advised, pressing the bag to the base of her jaw as she returned to the couch. "So—there you have it. That's everything I know . . ."

Michaels wasn't sure his brain could process everything he just learned. "Let me be absolutely certain I understand— you believe Conrad James murdered Nick Cummings. Correct?"

"Yes. I'm certain of it."

"Why? Did James tell you?"

"He didn't—but he often spoke of Cummings as if he

were nothing more than a low-grade irritant. Except, for some reason, he couldn't quite shake him off . . ."

"What do you mean?"

Kristi switched the icepack to the other side. "I mean, he hated Cummings with a passion, and I heard Conrad threaten him on the phone more than once."

"But, why? Why was James threatening him?"

"Because Nick Cummings knew a hell of a lot more than he was supposed to . . ."

"About what?"

"I think it had to do with Cape Town. He told me one time—in a drunken stupor, or course—that some guy needed to be taken down a peg, and he was just the one to do it."

"Do you know who that guy was?"

"I'm not sure—but it seemed from the conversations Conrad felt this guy had the thumb on him, and Conrad was getting tired of it." Kristi paused. "Conrad also said there was no way in hell he was getting paid enough for having to deal with Cummings . . ."

"Paid enough? Is Conrad on this guy's payroll?"

"Probably—he certainly isn't hurting for money, that's for sure!"

Michaels scribbled a few more notes, his pad nearly filled. He paused, looking squarely at the young woman on the couch. "And," the inspector continued, "I may be going out on a limb here, but James is the one who decided to use you as his boxing partner?"

Kristi hesitated. "Yes . . ."

"Let me guess . . . he found out you called Corrine."

"That, and just to serve an overall threat . . ."

"Keep your mouth shut, or else?"

"That was pretty much it . . ." Kristi placed the plastic bag on the coffee table. "And, now, Inspector, I'm afraid I need to rest . . ."

Inspector Michaels stood, offering his hand with respect. "I understand—please call me if you remember anything else." He hesitated. "Do you want to file a report against James?"

"No—I don't think that would be wise . . ."

****

Nigel Blackwell gripped his cell, knuckles whitening. "You told me we were good to go within two to three weeks— now you're telling me something else?" He felt his mouth turn to cotton as he waited for a response. "Well?"

"I told you Cummings was going to be a problem . . ."

"What the hell does he have to do with it? He doesn't have anything to do with Thailand . . . is there something I don't know?"

"There are cops swarming all over his flat, and I'm praying to God our names aren't written on anything—

shopping receipt. Napkin. Anything!" Conrad James hoped his answer served as an undetected diversion.

Nigel paused, considering the response. "Don't screw with me, Conrad—set up delivery for two weeks." He waited. "Do it—now!"

****

As Colbie waited for Nigel to return, she slipped on her wrap, aware Ryan was watching every move. She scanned the area beyond the patio, scoping out every shadow—an unfamiliar feeling coursing through her. Without warning, her prior vision of the lion racing toward her leapt to life, and it were as if she were reliving those moments of her meditation.

It was then she knew.

The symbol in her vision boiled down to two things—she would either be devoured by a lion, or she was being stalked. The first possibility she doubted—chances of her being anywhere close to where a lion could do her in was next to impossible. Stalked? Possibly. By whom was the question. Nigel? No—of that she was certain. Conrad James? Highly doubtful, and the only other player was Nick Cummings. She supposed anything could be possible as she waited for Nigel, but none of it made sense. Realizing that, she returned to the first possibility—no way. *What am I missing*, she wondered. *There has to be something else . . .*

Moments before Nigel rejoined her, Colbie thoughts turned to Brian. *How he would have loved looking over the game reserve as the sun dips in the sky!* A part of her missed him, and she couldn't help but grieve for a relationship lost.

"Please accept my apology—business. I'm sure you can relate . . ." Nigel's face was taut, his eyes cold. "I'm sorry to interrupt—you looked as if you were miles away . . ."

"Oh, good heavens—it's not a problem! It was lovely watching the last of the sunset . . . wine? I'll pour . . ." While Nigel was gone, she surreptitiously dumped her wine over the rail of the deck—she couldn't take a chance of losing her faculties, but Nigel was another story. A little wine—a little food. Who knows what he might say in the presence of a woman whom he barely knew?

"Problems at work?" she asked as she filled his glass.

"Not really—well—a few. Delivery issues."

"I know the feeling—a couple of months ago we ran into delivery difficulties, as well. It damned near took me three days to get it sorted out . . ." Colbie offered her most sympathetic smile.

Nigel softened, his anger subsiding as Colbie feigned understanding.

"You said yesterday you had a delivery to Thailand happening in a couple of weeks—is that the one?" She sat back in her chair. "Do you mind if I order a coffee? And, I wouldn't mind something chocolate for dessert . . . feel like sharing? One sinful chocolate torte with two forks?"

"Sounds perfect!" Nigel signaled a waiter.

An hour later, they pulled through the main gate of the reserve, heading for Cape Town. As Nigel drove, both were mired in their own thoughts—his probably about the delivery debacle, hers about the transformation she noticed in her dinner companion that night. She was certain she hadn't raised his suspicion and, for all he knew, she was Cameron Carlson, successful business woman.

Pulling up in front of the hotel, Colbie waited for Nigel to open her door, her legs the purposeful focal point of her exit. She glanced at him as he took her hand, noting his look of appreciation.

"Nigel," she said, "I don't know how to thank you for such a lovely evening . . ." She kissed him lightly on the cheek. "Until next time . . ."

He watched her disappear into the lobby, heading straight to the concierge's desk. Then, she turned, gazing past him—it was the same feeling she had in London.

Someone had her on their radar . . .

****

Ryan pushed his plate to the middle of the coffee table, settling back on the couch with a full cup. "He may be charming, but, I gotta tell ya—he gives me the creeps. I had a good, unobstructed view of your table, and when he came back . . ." Ryan paused for a moment. "Where the hell did he go, anyway?"

"He had a phone call—it was weird, too. He must have been gone about ten minutes . . . "

"Or, longer . . ."

"You're probably right—but, no matter how long it was,

when he returned to our table, everything felt different." Colbie poured the little remaining tea, curling her legs underneath her in the chair big enough for two. "I don't know—he was a different man. A Gemini quality, don't you think?"

"You don't really believe in that crap, do you?"

"Whether I believe in it is of no consequence—all I need to know is what changed. Who was he talking to on the phone? He said it was about a delivery problem, and the only person I can think of is James . . ."

"Maybe. We did see him leaving Gemini Imports— maybe there was more to his visit than two friends catching up . . ."

Colbie nodded. "Let me ask you something—when you went to James's house, what did it look like?"

Ryan's forehead creased as he tried to recall the details of Conrad's home. "It was pretty big—kind of ostentatious. Then again, you have to consider my point of reference—I live in an apartment the size of this room. Anything will seem big to me . . ." He looked at his partner. "Why? What does his home have to do with anything?"

Colbie thought for a few seconds before answering. "Probably nothing—but did it fit for an older, professorial type? Remember—his dossier said he's retired . . ."

Ryan was quiet as he considered James's lifestyle evidenced by the interior of his home. "Now that you mention it—it was pretty fancy on the inside. I'm guessing it costs a bundle for upkeep . . ."

"So," Colbie suggested, "the question becomes how does he maintain that lifestyle on a retired professor's income?"

Ryan glanced at his partner. "Damned good question—does he simply live above his means, or does he have another source of income?"

"Precisely my thought . . ." Colbie rested her head on the back of the chair, staring at the ceiling, thinking about the possibilities. "Precisely my thought . . ."

Ryan reached for the coffee pot. "You're empty—switch to coffee?"

"Sure . . ." She waited as he refilled her cup, handing her the cream. She smiled. *He always remembers the little things,* she thought as she took a sip.

CHAPTER TWENTY-ONE

Nigel Blackwell walked in the door, throwing his keys into an artisan-made bowl on a table in the foyer. A man on a mission, he headed straight for the bar in his library, mixed himself a drink, then pulled his cell phone from his pants pocket.

Moments later, the call connected. "Get your ass over here . . ." He tapped the screen, and stood in front of the French doors leading to the garden, drink in hand, thinking about his evening. It bothered him he couldn't put his finger on what was bugging him—*maybe it's about the delivery*, he thought, promptly discarding the idea. As he gazed into the dark, he remembered his father saying, "Trust your gut, my boy—it's the only thing that will get you through . . ." his voice ringing true in Nigel's memory. *And*, Nigel thought, *there's something about you, Cameron Carlson, that doesn't quite ring true . . .*

Within thirty minutes his man arrived. "I got here as

fast as I could . . ."

Blackwell didn't turn around. "I appreciate it—I'm a firm believer every man must have his own life. Tonight, however, you belong to me . . ."

"So—what's going on?"

"I need you to investigate someone, and I need results on my desk by noon tomorrow."

His investigator plucked his notepad from his pocket. "Name?"

"Cameron Carlson . . . she's staying at the Bel."

"What does she look like?"

"Small—red hair. Gorgeous . . . I'll send a picture by the usual method." Nigel referred to his undisclosed cell number—one that couldn't be traced.

"What else can you tell me?"

"Not much—I met her at Samuel Burnett's not too long ago. She was there with a guy she said is her stateside business partner . . ." Nigel paused, as if trying to access something stubborn in his memory. "Regis . . ." Another pause. "Pat . . . Patrick!"

"Cameron Carlson and Regis Patrick—check." His man stood, waiting.

"You're not still here, are you?" Nigel asked, still staring out the French doors.

Nothing but footsteps.

****

The following morning and with little to go on, Nigel's investigator instantly knew surveillance was in order and, being intimately familiar with the hotel, he knew the only way to really get anything on Cameron Carlson was to take advantage of his network. By the time he got back to his place, he had only enough time to grab a few tools of the trade—fingerprint powder, and tape. He also checked his phone to make certain it was in perfect working order, as well as his tablet as a backup. The one thing he didn't want to do was face Nigel Blackwell, telling him his phone died, so he stuffed the car charger in his pocket, just in case. *Always good to be prepared*, he thought as he closed his office door. *And, anything can happen . . .*

His contact at the Bel was usually on the morning shift, and he couldn't see any reason for things to be different—and, letting him know the particulars was first on his list of things to do. Considering the twenty minutes it would take to get to the hotel, he had to plan for the possibility the target would be in and out of the restaurant before he got there. Granted, it wasn't a huge possibility considering she was out late with his boss the night before, but he would be a fool if he didn't have plan.

He dialed. His contact didn't go on shift until seven, and there was a good chance he would have an opportunity to talk before clocking in.

"It's me," he said when his party picked up on the second ring. "Listen up . . ."

****

Colbie was up early. She and Ryan agreed to meet at the hotel restaurant for a quick bite to eat, then head out to the game reserve to see what they could dig up on Nigel Blackwell. The trajectory of their investigation changed when they found out about Nick Cummings's secret life as an art forger, but Colbie and Ryan instinctively knew Cummings wasn't bright enough to carry out such an operation on his own. There had to be someone else—someone with brains.

And, money.

The only one who filled that bill was Nigel Blackwell. From everything they could figure out about Conrad James, he leaned toward being weak rather than strong. If given a chance, he could probably be bought, too—so their standing reasoning and focus was on the smooth South African. They were sure Blackwell embedded Nick Cummings at the game reserve to be his eyes and ears, but, as with everything else about their investigation, again there was no proof.

Colbie wanted to stay on the down low for their trip to the reserve, so she slapped on a bit of mascara and some lip gloss, scrunching her hair so it looked half-way decent—jeans, a light sweater, and hiking boots were perfect to look like a typical tourist. With just her cross-body bag and light jacket, she quietly closed her room door, making her way down to breakfast.

She thought about calling Ryan for a friendly wakeup call, but decided he was a big boy and he didn't need a reminder they were going to meet for breakfast. Besides, there was no reason they should always be seen together—no one in Cape

Town knew of their investigation, and it would be easy for a casual onlooker to think she and Ryan were a couple. *Not that it would be that bad*, she thought as the hostess showed her to a booth in the nearly empty dining room.

Within a few minutes, a friendly server appeared, asking if she'd like something to drink.

"Coffee, please . . ." After her late night with Nigel, she needed a little pick-me-up. " . . . with cream. I'm waiting for someone, so it may be a few minutes . . ."

Before he left, the waiter rattled off the breakfast special, telling her he would be right back with the caffeine. While she waited, Colbie flipped through the menu, but she couldn't keep her mind on anything. Ever since she returned from her evening with Nigel, she had a feeling of being violated—not in the usual sense, of course—but she felt as if she were being probed in some way. *Good heavens—before I know it, I'm going to believe in alien grays abducting me for experimental purposes!* She chuckled at the thought of a space ship beaming her up.

"Hey!" Ryan grinned as he pulled up a chair, placing his backpack on the seat next to him.

"Hey, yourself—a backpack, eh?" She eyed him with a budding grin. "You look like you're going on an archaeological dig . . ."

"C'mon—that's a low blow! I took a long time picking this out—I think I look pretty good . . ." He winked at her, grabbed a menu and, from nowhere, their server appeared. He and Colbie ordered Eggs Benedict, Virgin Mary's, and coffee, hoping the meal would carry them until at least midafternoon.

"And," Ryan advised, "I have a few snacks from my hotel

room if we get hungry—they're in my pack."

"Do any involve chocolate?"

"Of course . . ."

"Good—I'm not sure if we're going on a wild goose chase by scoping out the reserve," Colbie commented, "but, it certainly can't do any harm . . ."

"Did you give any thought to how Mr. South Africa is involved in this whole thing?"

Colbie sipped her coffee. "Are you kidding? I couldn't think of anything else!"

"Me, too—I know in my gut he's masterminding the art forgery scam as well as the rhino poaching. And, I don't have any doubt he's dangerous should someone cross him . . ." He paused, looking seriously at her. "You know, don't you, if he breaks our cover, we're in for a world of shit . . ."

"I thought of that, and I think it's a good idea if we aren't too far from each other whenever possible. However, I suspect I need to meet with him by myself again to figure him out . . ."

Ryan glanced at her from over the rim of his cup. "You're kidding . . ."

"No—I need to somehow get him to accept me as non-threatening. Right now, I have a feeling he's beginning to get suspicious . . ."

"Oh, swell—that's what I needed to hear. Why do you think that?"

Colbie paused, thinking about the feeling of her being watched—the only problem was she didn't know if someone were really watching, or if her feelings were stemming from intuition. "I noticed it when we were in London, too, and it happened when I spent time with Nigel—kind of creepy . . ."

"Well, let's narrow it down—who would actually be watching you? No one other than Tammy and Brian know you're here—and, I'm pretty sure it's not either one of them."

"You're right. So, if it's someone—such as Nigel—then we have a huge problem. That goes for Conrad James, too . . ."

"Speaking of Conrad James, it might be a good idea if we surveil him—I think he's the one who is going to lead us directly to Nigel . . ."

Colbie finished the last of her breakfast, placing her knife and fork diagonally on the plate. "Agreed—is he back in town?"

"I'm not sure, but it won't be hard to find out—I'll put it on my list for tomorrow . . ."

"Good." She grabbed her fanny pack, and slid from the booth. "This one's on you," she teased as she booked it out the front door.

Ryan laughed and paid the bill, leaving a hefty tip for the server before he headed for the car. Their waiter watched as they pulled out of the parking lot, then inconspicuously slipped Colbie's coffee cup under his shirt.

Fifteen minutes later, he was with Nigel's top man.

****

The investigator locked his car door, setting up a makeshift table on his lap with a magazine. With gloved hands, he gently placed the cup on it, and began twirling the soft brush dipped in fingerprint powder yielding pay dirt after a few moments—a clear print appeared on the body of the cup. Next, he carefully applied clear tape to lift the print, then positioned the tape just right on the screen of his phone.

One click, and it was done.

As an ex-cop, he knew he would have everything he needed within a matter of minutes.

He was right.

But, the person's bio wasn't what he expected.

Bingo, he thought, as he realized the seriousness of Nigel's situation. *Bloody, freakin' bingo . . .*

****

Conrad James stood in front of the mirror in his Cape Town master bedroom, staring at his reflection. There was no doubt about it—the way he saw it, he had three options, all of which weren't the best. Option number one—getting the hell of there, and heading to a country without extradition treaties. Option number two—admit to everything, and spend the rest of his life in jail. Option number three—do himself in.

As he considered how his life would probably proceed, he regretted only one thing—leaving Corrine. No matter what he chose, she would be left to pick up the pieces, dealing with snide looks, gossip, and exclusion. *It's not fair to her,* he thought as he sucked in his gut. *How will she get along?* But, no matter how guilty he felt, her feelings really didn't amount to dirt—he couldn't help it, and she would be his only true casualty.

Being a rather cowardly man, sticking the barrel of a .40 cal in his mouth and pulling the trigger didn't sound like a great idea. Nor did popping a few pills. So, in his mind, the third option wouldn't work, and he trashed it based on lack of guts. Cowardice again came into play as he considered his second option—used to the open spaces of South Africa, could he endure the rigors of prison life?

Doubtful.

That left a clear choice—option number one was the way to go. When and where wasn't an issue—there were plenty of countries in South America that wouldn't extradite, and the weather was warm. The only thorn in his side was Kristi Parker—if she chose to flap her jaws, the law could be on his doorstep at any time. *She probably will,* he figured, and *it will be sooner than later.* He never did trust her, and the possibility of cops showing up posed a problem—he would have to leave as if nothing unusual were going on. He'd walk away from his home—his wife—for the last time, only to vanish completely.

And, so it must be, he thought as he reached for a clean undershirt.

****

"We have to move—now. If we don't, our opportunity is lost . . ."

"Agreed, Sir. If he took the time and made the effort to return to England to beat the crap out of Kristi Parker, that tells me he's not confident she won't rat him out." Michaels sat in his usual chair, thinking about Conrad James. "And, I don't trust him not to run . . ."

"Exactly my thought—take a few men with you to check out his London residence. If you turn up nothing, then we'll head to Cape Town. In the meantime, I'll get in touch with Colbie Colleen to let her know we may soon be in her current neck of the woods . . ."

Michaels stood, hesitating before leaving. "And, Kristi Parker? What about her?"

DCI Murray looked at his colleague. "Kristi who?"

****

He arrived at Blackwell's just before noon, as expected. For previous assignments, he rarely stuck around to witness his boss's reaction to whatever information he gave him. That time, however, he wasn't in a hurry to head back to his office. The folder contained info Blackwell didn't want to see, and it would certainly be enough to anger him in a way that wouldn't yield a pleasant result for whomever was on the receiving end of his upcoming tirade.

He sat in his car, waiting.

****

Nigel Blackwell rested his fingertips on the manila folder in front of him. *It's worth it*, he thought, *to pay for the best. No sense in fooling around* . . . The folder was thicker than he thought it would be—not a good sign. That meant there was much more information than just a business report on a woman from America. *Okay, Cameron Carlson—who the hell are you?*

He opened the folder.

On top was a picture of Cameron Carlson—or, as the caption indicated, Colbie Colleen. Blackwell wasn't sure what he expected, but Cameron's name being an alias didn't enter his mind. He stared at her picture, his blood pressure spiking as he realized he was being cast as a pawn in a very dangerous game. *It should be the other way around,* he thought, as he read her bio. *Behavioral profiler? Ex-cop?* His man prepared an extensive report—surprising, really, since he had such little time.

Nigel flipped through the pages, then settled in to read every word—within the hour, he knew Colbie Colleen's career inside out. Where she worked. Brian's kidnapping. Her successful career as a profiler. He knew of her stellar decade as a cop, as well as where she lived—all due to a bit of extra effort from his investigator. No—by the time he closed the folder, he knew everything concerning the woman he considered a candidate for being more than an just an ornament on his arm.

And, he didn't like any of it.

He sat, thinking. Of course, there was no way he could

let the situation stand—the question was what was he going to do about it? With Cummings dead, he certainly couldn't call on him to take care of business. *He wasn't good for much, but he would have been perfect for this,* he thought. Conrad James didn't seem the best choice either—*if he can screw up a delivery, I doubt seriously he'll be able to handle something of this caliber. No—I better handle this myself if I want it done right . . .*

His plan began to germinate as he considered which was most important—Colbie Colleen or Conrad James. Without question, she posed the most danger to him and, when he thought about it, her behavior at dinner made perfect sense. He felt she put up her guard, but he didn't know the reason—but, after reading her dossier, it gelled. Unfortunately, as often happens with arrogance, he didn't fully accept she may prove to be his Achilles heel. The fact she was a woman decreased the threat somewhat, but he still considered it a worthy idea to get rid of her altogether.

Even though Blackwell's gut reaction was to set his plan into action immediately, such a thing would have been foolhardy as well as risky. Colbie mentioned during dinner she was most likely going to remain in South Africa for at least another two weeks, so her timetable provided the opportunity for a well-thought out plan. He had the salient points in place, but, in order to carry it out, he needed to lay the groundwork. In some ways, it was easier because he wasn't going to rely on anyone to help him—however, it would be nice if someone had his back. Again, he considered Conrad James—unfortunately, he, too, was a risk to his operation.

Just not as much as Colbie Colleen.

By the end of the day, Nigel Blackwell pulled the trigger on his plan.

Call number one.

He tapped in Conrad James's number on speed dial. "Conrad! Nigel here . . ."

James wasn't too happy to hear from him. "Nigel—what can I do for you?"

Nigel swallowed, hating the words about to come out of his mouth. "I believe I owe you an apology—I was too worked up about the delivery, and I know there are bound to be delays. For the most part, we run our operation on time."

"I appreciate that . . ." Conrad James immediately knew something was up, instantly wondering if Blackwell figured out why the delivery was delayed. It wasn't because his man couldn't get the product—the truth was James had a private buyer for the rhino horn at a considerably higher price and, by delaying the delivery, it gave him time to procure more product from his private vendor. A second poaching expedition was in place, and his man assured him he could have it within the month. All James had to do was buy a little time, and he'd be seventy-five grand richer—considerably more than the going rate. At first he thought it odd someone would pay the inflated price—but, in reality, it wasn't any of his business. He could care less about what happened after the money greased his palms.

"I'm thinking of traveling to London this week—how about if we get together this evening to iron out the delivery. I'll leave it in your hands . . . "

"This evening? Not sure that's possible, Nigel—I promised to take my wife to dinner . . ."

"Well, you can't squirrel that now, can you?" Blackwell chuckled. "How about if you pop by after dinner—probably best for me, now that I think about it. I need to get a few things together before my trip . . ."

James hesitated. Meeting Blackwell was the last thing he wanted to do, but he didn't see any way out of it. "How about nine or so—I expect both of us will be ready to get home by then . . ."

"Excellent! Give Corrine my best . . ."

Nigel disconnected the call, thinking about the next several hours.

So much to do.

****

The raid on Conrad James's London house yielded nothing, and within hours DCI Murray and Inspector Michaels were winging their way to Cape Town. Murray contacted the appropriate agencies apprising them of the situation—which he summed up in two words.

Murder one.

The flight was long and, once on the ground, they headed straight for the Metropolitan Police Department Headquarters. Even though they anticipated a fairly straightforward apprehension, the possibly of a screw up still existed, and they needed to be certain the paperwork was in order. At least South Africa and the UK had extradition treaties, so there shouldn't be any hiccups if everything went according to plan. After that? Surveillance, and working in tandem with Metro police. They wanted to execute the warrant within twenty-four hours—that's if Conrad James were in Cape Town. If not, it was back to the drawing board.

"What about his wife, Sir?" Michaels triple checked his notes, not wanting anything to be left to chance.

"What about her?"

"We don't really know much about her—do you think she has any idea we're on James's tail?"

Murry thought for a second before answering. "I'm not sure about that—but, if she doesn't, she's fooling herself. She knows damned well—according to Colbie—her husband was up to no good when he was supposed to be in Switzerland."

Colbie? Michaels glanced at his boss—it surely didn't take him long to be on a first-name basis. "Plus, she noticed the blood on his pants when he returned to Cape Town—however, I question the admissability of her claim."

"I do, as well. We don't know for sure if those spots were, indeed, blood—and, I have a feeling the pants are long gone."

"Agreed. That doesn't leave us with much, other than the phone call from Kristi . . ."

Kristi? That didn't take long, Murray thought as he eyed his colleague. "The good thing about apprehending guys like James? Their arrogance is what takes them down . . ."

"I think you're right about that—Kristi told me James is insufferably arrogant, and he can't see beyond himself . . ."

"What I find interesting is the relationship between your Kristi Parker and James—from what you said, I got the distinct impression she thought James would be around for a long time—in fact, she was counting on it."

"That was my take on it, too," Michaels agreed.

Both men sat in silence for a few minutes, thinking about Conrad James and how they were going to take him down. Each had the feeling they were only scratching the surface of something, only they didn't have a handle on it.

"Are we meeting up with Colbie and her partner?" Michaels asked.

"Not sure—I tried getting in touch, but she didn't pick up. That was last night, however . . . but, I know they're working on the art theft case on their end, so I think it's a good idea . . ."

"I agree—how about I leave checking in with her to you?"

Michaels' superior shot him glance. "I will . . . and, check your notes—what did Colbie say about the guy who runs the import-export business? She thinks he's involved somehow, but, the last time I spoke with her, she was still in the process of figuring it out . . ."

The young inspector leafed through the pages in his folder. "Blackwell. Nigel Blackwell . . ."

"Ah, yes—I've heard of him. See what you can find out— let's lend a hand while we're here, if possible. We may not have time, however . . ."

"Roger . . ."

Chapter Twenty-two

"Don't forget—our reservation is at seven . . ." Conrad looked at his wife, then continued stuffing suitcases with more than enough clothes.

"I know, Dear—I made them," Corrine teased.

"Indeed, you did—I should have known you wouldn't forget . . . but, always good to check, don't you think?" Conrad winked at his wife, and continued packing.

"Where are you going this time?" Corrine asked, noting he wasn't packing the usual.

James wasn't planning on her being around when he filled a couple of luggage pieces with clothing he didn't normally include. "Australia . . . I have a new client who, unfortunately, is unable to fly and he insists I go to him . . ."

Corrine studied her husband. A line of bullshit? Most likely. Did it matter?

Not much.

****

Call number two.

"Cameron! I'm glad you picked up—I'll be traveling at the end of the week, and I'm hoping we can get together one more time before I go . . ."

Colbie glanced at Ryan.

"Nigel—how delightful to hear from you!" She paused, motioning to Ryan to hand her a piece of paper and pen. "How long are you going to be gone?"

"That's the thing—I'll most likely get back after you return to the States . . ."

"Well, then, dinner sounds great—when and where?"

"How about my place? You've never been here before, and I think you'll quite like it . . ."

"Your place?" She shot a look at Ryan who was emphatically shaking his head no. "Perfect—you'll send a car, or pick me up yourself?" Colbie wanted to know what to look for because she had every intention of Ryan's tailing their vehicle.

"I'll send a driver—since this will be our last evening together, I want to make sure everything is perfect. I'll wait for you here . . ."

A couple of minutes later, Nigel rang off. There was a twinge of sadness as he thought about how the ex-cop duped him into thinking she was the CEO of a tech company stateside. *That was your first mistake*, he thought.

The second is thinking you could get away with it . . .

****

Colbie stared at Ryan. "I wasn't expecting that—and, I don't have a good feeling about it . . ."

"Neither do I—but, I also have a feeling we're not going to get the information we need if you don't go . . ." He looked at Colbie knowing damned well there was no way he could talk her out of it.

"Well, it's not the best situation, that's for sure . . . but, we'll see . . ." They stood looking at each other for a moment, each aware of the danger.

"Here's my question—and, please answer honestly . . ."

From his tone, Colbie knew he was concerned. "What?"

"Do you think Blackwell is capable of . . ." He didn't want to voice what he knew to be true—Nigel Blackwell didn't care about anyone other than himself, and he wouldn't hesitate to dispose of anyone who got in his way.

"Harming me?" Colbie glanced at her friend, somewhat surprised he asked the question. "I know he is . . ."

****

Conrad James pulled up to Blackwell's estate shortly after nine, cutting the headlights as he drove up the long drive—after two hours with Corrine, he needed a little time before dealing with Nigel. Although Blackwell sounded sincere when he called, James knew him well enough to know his friend and colleague was a chameleon, changing his persona whenever it suited him. In James's mind, Nigel wasn't a man to be trusted.

Ten minutes later, he knocked.

Blackwell opened the door, greeting him as if it were a month of Sunday's since he'd seen his good friend. "Conrad! Please come in . . ." He stepped to the side of the massive door, allowing room for his guest to enter.

"Thank you, Nigel—don't mind if I do!"

Blackwell closed the door, carefully latching it. "Can't be too trusting these days," he said as he headed for the library. "Drink?"

"The usual . . ."

"You're the only man I know who drinks a sidecar—you know, don't you, I learned how to mix it because of you . . ."

"Well, my friend, you learned a valuable skill!"

Drinks in hand, both men settled into chairs, their conversation inane and inconsequential. Nigel purposefully chose two classic wing backs so they could sit side by side, separated only by a small table. Sitting across from James at his desk didn't seem quite right—too much of a judging atmosphere, and that was the last thing he wanted. Besides, the seating arrangement was more conducive for small talk.

"How is Corrine," Nigel asked. "It's been quite a while since I've seen her . . ."

"She's fine—busy, as usual . . ."

"I imagine she has a lot to keep her busy when you're traveling . . ."

"Indeed . . ."

Both took a sip of their drinks, knowing the main conversation was yet to come.

"So," Nigel began, "bring me up to speed on the delivery—when is the date?"

James tried not to fidget. "Three weeks—it's the best I can do . . ."

Nigel took a second before answering. "Three weeks, eh?" He swished his drink, then leveled a long look at the man seated beside him. "Well—I'm afraid that's bullshit, Conrad—and both of us know it."

At that second, Conrad James's world crashed. "Bullshit? I'm not sure I know what you're talking about, Nigel—I tried for an earlier date, but it simply could not happen . . ."

"Unfortunately, I beg to differ—you see, Conrad, I placed a couple of calls . . ." Nigel met Conrad's eyes. "And, what I learned was interesting . . ."

Conrad tried not to shrivel under Nigel's stare. "What was that?"

"Oh—I think you know. But, just to clarify, it appears you've been running a little scam on your own." He paused for effect. "You can imagine my disappointment . . ."

Conrad swallowed. "I can . . ."

"Explain?" Nigel interrupted. "No need, Conrad—no need, at all . . ." He paused again, looking at his friend. "Unfortunately, I'm afraid this means I must sever our relationship—business and personal."

Conrad took the last sip of his drink, unaware of the irony. "I'm sorry you feel that way—we've been friends for a long time . . ."

"Indeed—only I now question the depth of that friendship. Apparently, you had no compunction about horning in on my business—pardon the pun." Nigel quelled a slight smile. He watched James turn his glass in his hands as if he were trying to figure out what to do next. To Blackwell, he looked like a pathetic, sniveling man destined to follow in the footsteps of their compatriot, Nick Cummings.

The sad thing was James didn't realize it.

"How about one more for the road," Nigel suggested, reaching for Conrad's glass. "Then we can discuss how to deal with your current problem . . ."

James nodded. As Nigel mixed his drink, he scanned the room looking for the best exit should a quick escape be necessary. Then, he remembered Nigel's carefully locking the front door—chances of any window or door remaining unlocked were next to nil.

Before he fully comprehended his situation, Conrad James accepted the drink, wondering how the hell he was going to get out of there.

"Perhaps," Nigel interrupted his guest's thoughts, "perhaps we can rectify the consequences of your poor judgment, Conrad—if, of course, that's what you choose to do."

"What do you have in mind? What are my options?"

"Options—now that's an interesting word, isn't it? Clearly, you gave me no options when you decided to fleece me—my business. I'm sure you understand it's going to be difficult for me to forgive—or, forget."

James remained silent, nearly downing his drink.

Nigel paused as he watched his friend. "But," he continued, "I'm not above trying—what I need to know is how you are going to repay me." He took a sip, stealing a side glance at the man sitting beside him. The tremor he noticed when James dropped in at Gemini Imports was becoming increasingly pronounced—and, it was just the beginning.

Conrad James clutched his throat, desperately trying to breathe. "You—son of a bitch!" he screamed as his eyes rolled back in his head. Just then his body seized, and he dropped to the floor, arms and legs convulsing uncontrollably.

Nigel calmly watched as Conrad James attempted to gulp his last breath, foam streaming from the side of his mouth. "Conrad—you stupid man. You should have known better . . ." He reached under the table beside his chair, and pushed a small buzzer. Moments later, two men appeared, both the size of an eighteen wheeler. "You know what to do," he ordered as he finished his drink.

Unfortunately, that was your only option, my friend . . .

****

DCI Murray and Inspector Michaels waited, knocking three times before Corrine James answered.

"Mrs. James?"

"That's right—what can I do for you?" She didn't recognize either men, although she thought the Metro Police officer looked familiar. The Brits appreciated the back up, especially since they weren't sure what they had in front of them.

"Is your husband home, Mrs. James?" DCI Murray flashed his identification.

"No—may I give him a message?" Her demeanor changed as she scrutinized the men.

"Do you know where he is?"

"He's on a flight to Australia . . ." She wasn't going to provide any information—if they wanted to know something, they were going to have to fish for it. But, she was adamant about one thing—she wasn't going to lie.

"Australia?" Murray and Michaels glanced at each other. *What the hell is he doing there*, the Chief Inspector wondered. "When did he leave?"

"Last evening."

It was clear to both men selling out her husband wasn't in the cards.

"Where in Australia?"

Corrine James steeled herself, standing her ground.

"I'm afraid I don't know what this is about, gentlemen. And, until I do, I'm afraid I'm going to ask you to leave . . ."

DCI Murry turned to the Metro Police officer. "The warrant, please . . ." The officer complied, handing the search warrant to the British Chief Inspector.

"I'm afraid that's not going to happen, Mrs. James . . ."

****

Colbie and Ryan decided to spend the afternoon crafting several plans just in case one—or, all—went south. An hour before the limo was to arrive, Colbie showered and dressed while Ryan fine tuned how the evening would shake out. She decided it was a good idea to wear flats instead of heels just in case she had to get the hell out of there—that, and because Nigel was a man of considerable means, it would have been disrespectful to wear something allowing her to make use of her police training—flats were the best she could do.

"You look nice," Ryan commented as she performed a half-hearted twirl in front of him.

"Do these shoes look dopey with this?"

Ryan checked her out, up and down. "Not really . . ." He instantly knew why she made the choice. "I gotta tell you— I'm not sure about this whole thing . . ."

"I know—I feel as if I'm walking into the lion's den . . ." She plopped into the chair beside him. "But, I really don't see any other way—and, I know I can take care of myself."

"Still—I'm going to be right behind you . . ."

"That's if—and I emphasize 'if'—you can get close to

the house. If not, I'll be on my own." Hers wasn't a pleasant thought—she had no means of protecting herself if something went wrong. *If this were happening in the States*, she thought, *at least I could go in with a weapon* . . .

Ryan checked his watch. "It's time . . ." He helped her up, then drew her close. "Colbie . . ."

Her hands lingered in his. "Not now, Ryan . . ."

"I just want to . . ."

Just then Colbie's hotel room phone rang—she answered and, after a quick thank you, she turned to her good friend.

"The limo is here . . ."

Neither spoke as they headed for the main lobby, each going over their plan one last time.

"I'm going to be right behind you . . ." Ryan said, kissing her lightly on the cheek. "There's nothing to worry about . . ."

"Right—nothing to worry about . . ." They exchanged a long look before the doorman opened the door, and she turned to look at Ryan one last time before disappearing into the limo.

As soon as it started to pull away, Ryan hopped on his rental scooter which he strategically positioned, ready to go. He kept several cars behind the limo until they reached the perimeter of the city—after that, he kept as far behind as he could, still keeping Colbie in sight.

Twenty minutes later, the limo pulled into a long, estate, circular drive tastefully decorated with just the right amount of flowers. The sun had yet to set, and there was still enough light to pay attention to her surroundings, so Colbie assessed all access points as the limo rolled to a stop, making a mental note of entrances and exits.

Nigel greeted her before she got to the front door. "Cameron—you look magnificent!"

Colbie offered her best fake grin. "Thank you, Nigel— but, I'm afraid my choice of footwear doesn't show off of my ensemble—I have a blister, and these were the best I could do!"

"Well, it's a good thing you don't have to do any running this evening—I'll make sure you're comfortable and pain free . . ." He held the door open for her. "Please, come in . . ." he invited, gently latching the door once she was inside.

She noticed.

Colbie crossed the threshold into one of the most magnificent homes she'd ever seen—white carrara marble tile stretched from the entryway into various rooms, each decorated impeccably with what Colbie assessed to be millions of dollars' worth of original art.

"This is breathtaking!" she exclaimed as Nigel showed her to the garden.

"Thank you—it's taken me years to get it exactly the way I want it . . ."

"You have exquisite taste . . ."

"Again, I appreciate the compliment—I think I inherited my love for art from my dad . . ."

"Was he in the import-export business, as well?"

"No—no, he was an artist. He never could pull away from his creativity long enough to carve a place in the business world—besides, he really didn't have the heart for it, so I guess it was for the best . . ."

They stepped down into the garden, Colbie crossing to a handwoven rattan chair with a subtle limp. *No harm in keeping up the story,* she thought as she settled in.

"I could get used to this," she said as Nigel headed for the bar set up in the southwest corner of the patio.

"Well—maybe we can make that a reality," he replied with an engaging smile. "Would you like that?"

She blushed at the intimation. "Perhaps it's a bit premature for that—but, it's certainly worth thinking about," she commented, accepting a drink.

"You're right—but, you can't blame a chap for trying, can you . . ." Nigel took a seat next to Colbie, much like he did with Conrad James.

Then a strange thing happened. As Colbie feigned relaxation in Nigel's garden, her intuitive mind leapt to the forefront, consuming her with the feeling of someone watching her—the same feeling she had in London. It was so strong, it made her shift in her chair as if doing so would make it go away. *Not now!* she thought, glancing at Nigel hoping he didn't notice.

But—he did.

"Is there something wrong?"

"Good heavens, no! How could anything be wrong? Look where I am—such a gorgeous setting!"

Nigel smiled. "Good . . ." He paused, looking at the stunning woman sitting beside him. "So, Colbie—where do we go from here?"

Colbie's heart dropped.

"I imagine you're rather shocked—my knowing your

real name . . ."

Colbie stiffened, preparing her body for battle. "A bit—yes."

"And, that's not all—I know everything about you. Your career as a police officer. The kidnapping of your lover. Your move to the East Coast . . ."

"Your thoroughness is impressive—but, I can't help but wonder why you went to so much trouble . . ."

"Why? Surely, Cam—Colbie—I could ask the same question of you . . ."

As she was about to answer, the vision of weeks previous flashed—the lion stalking her. Its attack. *What the hell?* Colbie felt the warning streak through her, stronger than the first time, and she flinched as the lion leapt directly at her.

Keeping her composure was a struggle. "It's really quite simple, Nigel—I'm on a case, and I couldn't risk anyone learning my true identity. You know as well as I, when someone knows too much about you . . ." Colbie hesitated. "Well, it can hamper things, if you know what I mean . . ."

Nigel held her gaze, trying to deftly determine if she were telling the truth. "Perhaps—but something tells me your subterfuge is much deeper than a simple masquerade."

"I'm not sure I understand—what does my investigation have anything to do with you?" Although it went against everything she believed in, Colbie figured playing stupid just might work.

Nigel hesitated. *What if she's telling the truth?* If she is and he spouts off, he'll certainly be placing himself in a precarious position.

"Nothing, of course—I'm sure you can understand my surprise when I learned you aren't who I thought you were. It's a bit of an understatement, I imagine, to say it's disconcerting . . ." At that moment, there was a lot to be said for backing off to let things play out.

As Nigel spoke, Colbie quickly decided she must meet Nigel on his own ground—if he perceived her as weak, the chances of her getting out of there unscathed tanked.

"Trust me, Nigel—this has nothing to do with you . . ."

"I want to believe you . . . Colbie. And, please forgive me if I stumble over your name—I'm certain I'll get used to it."

Colbie sipped her drink, trying to maintain a semblance of control. She found the man beside her nothing less than repugnant, and she couldn't wait until she and Ryan busted their investigation wide open. However, given the new wrench of Nigel's discovering her true identity, she may have to speed things up.

She thought of Ryan, her intuition in full gear telling her she was in danger, although she wasn't sure how it was meant to play out. The lion receded to the depths of her intuitive mind, leaving her to figure out if it represented Nigel, or something else. If it represented Nigel, she was in a load of trouble for she realized Ryan may not be able to help. Of course, she noticed when Nigel latched the front entrance door, and she put her money on every window and door being latched, as well.

Nigel wasn't ready to let it go. "Perhaps it will help if you tell me about your investigation—then, I will decide if it involves me . . ."

Perspiration beaded on the back of her neck. "I believe doing so will breach the contract with my client—I'm sure you understand."

He remained silent for a moment. "I want to believe you—however, I'm afraid I can't unless you decide to trust me with confidential information. So, Colbie, the decision is yours . . ."

That was about as much of a trap that Colbie could imagine. If she confided to Nigel about the art theft investigation, Conrad James would undoubtedly come into the conversation—something she couldn't allow, unless necessary.

"Well, Nigel, I'm equally disappointed—so, it seems we're at a stalemate. I will not compromise my investigation because of your unfounded suspicions . . ." She squared her eyes directly on him, refusing to back down or give in to his intimidation tactics. If he needed information from her or had the predisposed idea to take her out of the picture, it was going to be his decision.

He momentarily backed off, thinking about her statement. She was a feisty one, and he liked that—however feisty didn't mean trustworthy. He wanted to believe her, but, in his gut, he knew she was attempting to turn the tables by making him feel guilty for what he knew to be true—he was at the pinnacle of her investigation.

And that simply would not do.

"It seems we're at an impasse," she continued, reaching into her clutch for a cigarette. She took her time taking it from its gold case, flicking the lighter three times before the flame steadied. As she inhaled, she tried not to cough—the truth was she never smoked a day in her life, but she and Ryan agreed the flame of the lighter would be easy to see— provided she were outside. Inside? He would have no idea if she were in trouble.

"I didn't know you smoked," Nigel commented, his tone slightly accusing.

"Not all the time . . ." Colbie held the cigarette between her fingers as if it were a natural thing to do.

It worked perfectly. Stashed at the side of the estate, Ryan remained concealed by flowering bushes as well as a few small trees. Twilight was fading and, as he saw the lighter flicker three times, he stealthily moved closer, keeping an eye on Colbie at all times.

From Colbie's perspective, there was little she could do to improve her situation, so it came down to blathering small talk, or learning as much as she could from her now adversary.

"Tell me about Conrad James," she suggested, carefully observing his reaction.

"Conrad James?" He eyed Colbie. "What does he have to do with anything?"

She didn't bite. "You tell me . . ."

Nigel Blackwell paused, considering why she wanted to know. "Conrad and I have been friends for years . . ." He didn't like the direction of the conversation—what did she know about James, and how did he factor into her investigation? "In fact, we met through Samuel Burnett . . ."

"So I understand . . ."

He glanced at her as she finished her drink. "Not to change the subject, but it's getting chilly—shall we go inside?" He preferred having his guest in a more private environment for such a conversation.

Colbie put down her drink, dabbing her lips with a

cocktail napkin. There was nothing she could do—if she declined, doing so would appear odd for the temp was beginning to dip, and she may further aggravate Blackwell's suspicions if she didn't agree to his suggestion. The problem was she didn't like being out of Ryan's line of sight—but, what she needed most at that time was to determine whether Nigel Blackwell knew anything about Conrad James's art scam.

"Yes, let's . . ."

Nigel picked up her clutch bag from the small side table, handing it to her as he placed his hand at the small of her back. *Checking for a weapon*, she wondered.

Or, a wire?

CHAPTER TWENTY-THREE

The sweep of Conrad and Corrine James's home yielded little. Nothing, really—and, no matter how many times her husband wronged her, Corrine stood by her man. Naturally, she had no idea where the pants with the alleged blood stains were, telling the inspectors Conrad probably packed them for his trip. When asked if those particular pants took a side trip to the dry cleaners, she pleaded a faulty memory. But, that wasn't truly a lie—she had no idea what happened to the pants, although she suspected Conrad disposed of them in an appropriate manner.

She dutifully showed the blank space on the library wall where the stolen piece of artwork once hung, and she answered their questions with respect. But, in the end, the inspectors and one Metro Police officer left with nothing to show for their efforts.

Perhaps you should stay in Australia, my dear, Corrine suggested silently to her husband.

Yet, as much as she didn't want to admit it, there was one, small thing bothering her—as she walked them to the door, Inspector Murray turned, locking his eyes with hers. "Mrs. James—perhaps you should think a bit more about your husband's whereabouts. I suspect both of us may be surprised . . ."

She returned the gaze. "I doubt it, Chief Inspector. Nothing my husband does surprises me . . ."

****

Nigel escorted Colbie through the garden doors into his private library, its walls home to four stunning art pieces, all oil on canvas. His taste was striking, and the obvious contrast between the art on the wall and various pieces throughout the room should have felt discordant, yet, somehow, they functioned in harmony.

"You really do have exquisite taste, Nigel . . ." Colbie stood in front of a painting reminding her of the girl in the orange dress standing by the farmhouse gate. It wasn't the same, of course, but the feeling was there. "Who's the artist?"

Nigel rattled off a name she didn't know, his pride obvious as he explained the artist, his works, and untimely demise in the early 1900s. "It was a shame, really—there's only one other painting of his I know of that achieved the same critical acclaim . . ."

Colbie studied the canvas. "I saw a photo recently of a

painting that reminds me of this—it was rather foreboding except for a young girl in an orange-colored dress . . ."

Nigel looked at her, startled. "The Girl in Tangerine? Where did you see that?" Before Colbie could answer, he realized the enormity of her investigation. *Art theft! It has to be!*

In the same moment, Colbie realized Nigel had nothing to do with the art thefts. As strange as it was, he knew nothing of Conrad James's second career—or, first career, for all she knew. Since he managed to elude authorities, he remained something of an enigma. But, what she did know was Nigel wasn't involved, and a small sense of relief pricked at her as if to warn her of things to come.

She turned to Nigel. "How well do you know James? I mean, really know him?"

He determined from her tone there was something she needed to know. "As I said, we were friends for a very long time . . ." He was certain Colbie had no idea of his last encounter with James in that very room. "Both of us love art and, it was through that love we met via Samuel Burnett."

Colbie paused, considering what Nigel told her. "What about Nick Cummings? What do you know of him?" It was clear Cummings was involved in the forgery scam as a master artist, but did Cummings have anything to do with Blackwell? She wasn't sure—but, with the one common factor of both being from Cape Town, it was all she had to go on. Did Nick have anything to do with the rhino poaching scam? Maybe. But, in order to know for certain, she had to hear it from Nigel himself.

And, for that, she wasn't going to hold her breath.

"Nick Cummings? No—I don't believe so. Why? Who is

he?"

Colbie noticed Nigel stiffen at Cummings's name, recovering a brief moment later. "Before we get into that, Nigel, I want to know something—and, I don't mean to insult you . . ."

Nigel frowned at her comment. "And, what is that?"

"How do you know these paintings are the real deal? Again, I mean no offense—clearly, I don't know dirt about art, so, for me, the question is sincere."

They stood in front of a painting strategically lit above the built-in bar. "Tell me what you know, Colbie . . ."

With that, Colbie sat in the wing-backed chair previously occupied by Conrad James, fishing in her clutch for a pen and paper. "Do you mind if I take notes?" And, there it was—the question of trust. She may have surprised Nigel by posing as a successful business woman from the States, but his answer to her question would determine whether she should worry about getting out of there, or try to signal Ryan.

He held her gaze for a moment before answering. "Not at all . . ."

For the next hour, Colbie laid out her case against Conrad James, as well as the murder of Nick Cummings. She left nothing out except for the possible connection between Blackwell, Cummings, and rhino horn poaching. *There's no sense in combining the two cases—at least, not right now,* she thought as she retrieved her pen that fell from her lap onto the hand-knotted rug.

"You see, Nigel—I'm not the Delilah you think I am—all I'm trying to do is solve an art theft case . . ."

Nigel took a sip of his drink. "So, let me see if I have this right—you were contacted by Samuel Burnett, art theft victim . . ."

Colbie nodded.

"And," he continued, "it turns out the paintings reported stolen were actually going to be replaced—sometime down the road—with forgeries. Forgeries painted by Nick Cummings—right?"

Another nod. "Precisely—I believe Conrad James hired Nick Cummings to paint the forgeries, and he—Conrad—would save the day by 'finding' the stolen art. Only they wouldn't be the original paintings—only forged pieces."

Nigel shook his head. "Undoubtedly for a huge reward—and, I assume Conrad was in charge of the thefts in the first place?"

"That's why I asked you if you knew your painting are originals—did you ever happen to report a theft?"

Nigel's face set. "Indeed—last year . . . "

"One of the paintings in this room?"

Nigel nodded. "Conrad James was the one who recovered it for me . . ."

Colbie watched anger seethe as Blackwell realized the painting hanging above the bar may not be the original.

When was the last time you saw James?" she asked.

Nigel glanced at her. There was no way she could know of his last—conversation—with James, so playing it safe seemed the best bet. "He stopped in at Gemini Imports a day or so ago . . ." Nigel poured himself another drink as he replayed his conversations with James at Gemini and in his home—*more corrupt than I thought*, he recalled as he visualized the man writhing on the rug, spittle oozing from his mouth. But, having the wool pulled over his eyes wasn't what bothered him most—no matter how he cut it, Conrad James got the best of him.

The mere thought of James outsmarting him was more than he could bear and, as he thought about him—and Colbie—well, it was then a new plan materialized.

"I don't know about you, but I'm getting a bit tired—you gave me much to think about, the first of which is having my painting verified as authentic. So, how about if we have one more for the road, and I'll take you back to your hotel . . ." It wasn't a question—rather an indication of how the rest of the evening was going to go.

"That's fine—and, for what it's worth—I'm sorry. I hope you understand why I had to keep my identity from you . . ."

Nigel reached for Colbie's empty glass, replacing it with a clean one as he mixed their drinks. "I'm a businessman, Colbie—sometimes it's prudent to keep things close to one's vest . . ." He handed her the glass, his fingertips lightly brushing hers. *We could have been good together,* he thought as he watched her take a sip. *You're exactly what I needed . . .*

They spent the next ten minutes in casual conversation, Nigel keeping a close eye on his guest. He noticed her eyelids flutter as her face lit up with recognition.

"You son of a bitch!" she cried, as she realized the blooming effects of a powerful sedative.

Just what Conrad said, he thought as the glass slipped from her hands, its contents spilling onto the rug. "Come, come, Colbie—surely you didn't think you were going to walk out of here?" He laughed, delighted he played his role so well.

He made it a point to give his men the evening off,

knowing he wanted to take care of things himself. *My plan is flawless*, he thought as he hoisted Colbie's ragdoll body against his, carrying her much as he would a mate who had too much to drink. She struggled slightly, only to meet with a firm hand and stern voice. The floor scuffed the tips of her shoes as he lugged her across the room to the door leading to the garage, her body completely limp. Yet, she was aware—whatever drug he gave her, it allowed no muscle memory, but her mind was alert, conscious of everything. Silently, she cried out to Ryan with the unreasonable hope he would catch her plea as Nigel stuffed her in the trunk, zip tying her hands behind her.

****

He dropped to a prone position as a black sedan emerged from the garage. From his vantage point, it seemed as if there were only the driver, but light was fading—he couldn't be sure. As the vehicle approached, Ryan felt the hair on his arms rise and, instinctively, he knew Colbie was in trouble. As it passed, he could have sworn he heard her voice, and there was no doubt—the driver was Nigel Blackwell, and Colbie was no where to be seen.

Once the vehicle rounded the bend to the main gate, he pulled his scooter from nearby bushes, and slipped on a helmet—more for cloaking his identity than anything else—making certain he kept a good distance behind as he tailed the sedan. Within a few minutes, he knew the vehicle's destination.

The reserve.

****

A quarter of an hour later, he pulled up to the gate, but not through it. Instead of heading toward the main buildings, he turned onto a dirt road leading far into the reserve, away from prying eyes. He veered from the road minutes later, toward the reserve's darkest recesses—where life was natural, and without apology. As he cut the engine, Nigel sat for a moment considering the eventual fate of Colbie Colleen. *If only you would have been truthful with me,* he mentally chastised her, *we could have made it work.* It was a long time since he met someone with her spunk—her enjoyment of life—and it saddened him she had to wind up like the others.

As he opened the car door, the scent of the African veldt was strong and powerful, yet comforting. The reserve was a place of his youth—where his father took him when he needed to commune with nature to inspire his art. Nigel knew the dangers, yet he never ceased to feel the thrill when spying a pride of lions in the distance, or the single silhouette of the black rhino at sunset.

He got out, and opened the trunk. Colbie lay in a fetal position, her body flaccid. Her eyelids flickered and she tried to speak, but there were no words. *This will be easy,* he thought as he lifted her from the vehicle, again balancing her body against his.

Colbie's senses were on full alert as he dragged her

through high, swaying grass, eventually laying her down with no consideration of her comfort. As much as he hated to admit it, he enjoyed the fact she comprehended everything happening to her. *Certainly,* he thought, *she realizes the extent of her peril.* If he didn't know better, he'd think she were sleeping like a baby—except for the zip ties, of course.

"I'm sorry, my darling, but you see how it is, don't you?" He grinned, not waiting for a response. "It's quite a troubling position you're in and, unfortunately, I don't see any way out for you . . ."

No response.

He kicked her leg with the tip of his shoe—nothing.

"Right, then—I so hope your end is swift . . ." Nigel blew her a kiss before heading back to his car, almost tripping over something in his path. He picked it up, looked at it for a moment, then threw it on the ground—nothing but a large shred of tweed.

****

Ryan drew to a stop where the road forked by the game reserve. *It doesn't make sense for Blackwell to go where there may be people,* he thought as he decided which road to take. He inspected the road to the left—in filtered moonlight he noticed fresh tire tracks of a street car, not those typically used by the reserve and, in the distance, dust kicked up from an approaching vehicle.

He quickly laid the scooter on its side in tall grass, then, barely breathing, took his position behind a large, low scrub. As it approached, he recognized it as the sedan Blackwell drove—again, no sign of Colbie.

The car sped past, its driver unaware of anything but himself. As soon as it turned onto the main road, Ryan righted the scooter and hopped on, following the fresh tracks of Blackwell's car. Minutes later, he entered what could be termed the dark side of the moon—death lingered in the air, the spirit of the wild unsettling.

He followed the tracks to their end. As he turned the key to cut the engine, the back of his neck tingled, and he was aware of something—or, someone—watching him. He scanned the area in all directions, shuddering as he got out and stood silently, listening to the night. To his right, a barely discernible trail of trampled grass—*what the hell?* It was then he realized the nature of Blackwell's sick plan.

Colbie was bait.

****

She lay in the grass, unable to move, her thoughts racing. As she saw it, her only hope was Ryan, but the chance of his being unaware of Blackwell's car leaving the estate were, unfortunately, high. She counted from the time the vehicle left the garage to what she could only relatively gauge as fifteen or twenty seconds before it turned onto the main road. So, if Brian weren't in sight of the garage, he may have missed Nigel's exit altogether.

Her body refusing to move, she considered the truth of her situation, and had to believe she was living the last hours of her life. Without question, her end would be gruesome and, thinking about Nigel Blackwell, she had no doubt she wasn't his first victim. Then, suddenly, her intuitive mind erupted with visions of the past—her childhood. Meeting Brian. His kidnapping. *So,* she thought, *this is what they mean by my life flashing before my eyes* . . . Tears spilled as she realized she would leave many things unresolved—her greatest regret being Brian. In those moments before her life was to end, she recalled what it felt like when they got together, talked about marriage, and planned their future. Tears stung her eyes as she realized she wouldn't have the opportunity to say she was sorry—or, show him how much she cared.

It was somewhere between thinking of her mother and Brian she felt the ground around her move—the slightest vibration. At least she thought she felt something, but, in her state of mind, accuracy wasn't a given. She lay as still as possible, listening. There it was! Again! Her senses straining, Colbie tried to hone in on the barely discernible crunch on dried grass . . .

Slung low to the ground, the female lion approached, her body tensing as she stalked her prey. Another mature female in the pride did the same, the scent of distress beckoning them to their target. If theirs a normal kill, two lions would lead the prey into the waiting, hungry jaws of the pride, killing it by latching onto its neck. Many times, however, they simply attacked their prey's spinal cord, rendering it useless. Both were successful tactics, and hunting techniques were often implemented in tandem to ensure a clean, efficient kill.

The lion crept closer, its shoulder muscles quivering slightly as it maintained position. Suddenly, she lunged forward, her timing perfect as her body arched upward, eyes locking with Colbie's!

God, help me! God, help me! Colbie screamed silently as she lay defenseless, moments away from the lion's sharp incisors sinking into her flesh. She envisioned Brian, saying a quick goodbye.

Then—a loud, echoing crack!

The lioness crumpled on top of her, heartbeat slowly fading, its lifeless head lolling beside Colbie's,

Then, another! *Holy shit! Somebody's shooting! Help me!* She tried to scream, but her voice was nothing more than a pathetic squeak.

Then—silence.

Colbie struggled to move her legs, but the lion's three hundred and fifty pounds of dying weight rendered her efforts unsuccessful.

"Colbie! Thank God! She's here!"

The voice sounded familiar.

"Colbie! Colbie!" Blurred hands struggled to drag the lion from her, one voice barking orders. "Hurry! I think she's alive! Hurry, damn it! Hurry!"

Colbie felt the weight of the lion subside as she flexed her legs, again struggling to move.

"She's alive! She's alive!" The voice sounded familiar— Ryan?

"Get your knife—slice through the ties!"

The cool blade of a pocket knife brushed her hands as two, gentle hands slit the hard plastic. "Colbie . . . can you hear me?"

She nodded.

"Thank, God!"

It was then she recognized the voice with the gentle hands . . .

Brian!

Colbie tried to focus on two men standing side by side— she instantly recognized Ryan, but she couldn't believe who stood beside him. "Brian . . ."

"I'm here, Baby. I'm here . . ."

CHAPTER TWENTY-FOUR

Colbie opened her eyes. "Hey . . ." She tried to focus on the figure sitting beside her, stroking her hand, the touch reassuring.

"Hey, yourself . . ." Brian tenderly held her left hand, careful not to jostle the IV. "You know you scared the crap out of me . . ."

She struggled to focus a jumble of thoughts, her memory blurred. Tears slipped down her cheeks as she recalled what she thought were the last moments of her life. Nigel. The lion. Gunshots.

"I don't understand . . ."

"I know—the doctors say you'll eventually regain full recall, but, for now, it's probably better you take it easy . . ."

She shook her head. "That's not what I mean . . ." Colbie searched the room, barely moving her head. "Where's Ryan? Is he okay?" She felt uncomfortable alarm as she thought of her friend.

"He's fine—right now, he's at Metro Police HQ, From what I gather, they're figuring out the best plan to nail Nigel Blackwell . . ."

"What? You're telling me he's not in custody?" Colbie's anger erupted. "That bastard left me to die! Why the hell didn't they haul him in?"

A nurse rushed in, throwing a scathing look at Brian as she realized the spike in Colbie's vitals. "Are you upsetting her?"

"Not guilty! I promise!" He chuckled, as he swept a stray hair from Colbie's forehead. "I think she can do that all by herself . . ."

Colbie grinned and, in that moment, he knew she would be alright. "Tell me . . ."

Brian hesitated. "Tell you what happened?"

Colbie nodded. "I want to hear everything . . ."

****

By the time the sun set, Colbie knew the whole story—Brian's walking out of the hospital so he could find her to make amends, his arriving in London and Cape Town, and tailing Ryan as he followed Nigel Blackwell to the reserve.

"So—it was you! I can't tell you how many times I felt as if someone were watching me . . ."

"I thought about that, but I had to risk it—unfortunately, I could never get you alone so we could talk . . ."

Colbie searched his face. "That's what I mean when I said I didn't understand—did you . . ." She could barely choke out the words. "Did you try to commit suicide because of me?"

Brian squeezed her hand, and hung his head. "I don't know what I was thinking—maybe my failed attempt was what I needed to wake me up . . ." There was no mistaking his shame as he looked up. "Colbie?"

Her auburn hair lay in strands on the pillow—asleep, her head tilted toward him, a small smile on her lips. *We have all the time in the world*, he thought as he sat back, not letting go of her hand.

All the time in the world . . .

****

DCI Murray, Inspector Michaels, and Ryan sat at a small conference table, each flipping through his respective files.

"Okay—let's get to it," Murray began. "We can't risk misinformation leading to a botched arrest—therefore, Inspector Michaels and I need to know everything . . ." DCI Murray sat back and looked at Ryan, clicking the end of his pen on the table. It was an annoying habit, and it drove Michaels nuts—but, he figured it was a small price to pay for having the privilege to work with such an accomplished investigator.

Ryan took a swig of water, collecting his thoughts before launching into the details of their investigation. "You have to admit," he commented, "Conrad James had a pretty good racket going, and he was damned good at it . . ."

"Agreed. But what happened to make James want to get rid of Nick Cummings? That's the one thing that doesn't make any sense . . ."

"It didn't make much sense to us, either—but, after Colbie was safe in the hospital, I placed a call to Maggie Burnett . . ." Ryan paused, mentally rewinding his conversation with her.

"And?"

"I asked her to tell me everything she knew about Nick Cummings . . ."

"We tried that, too," Inspector Michaels interrupted, "and we didn't get to first base—she was convincing, and I thought she was telling the truth . . ."

Ryan nodded. "I'm not surprised—but, you have to remember Colbie and I had a different relationship with Burnett and his daughter. In many ways, as soon as we arrived in London, we were in Burnett's inner circle—he was missing a multi-million dollar painting, and he wanted it back." Ryan glanced at DCI Murray. "No matter the cost—and, Maggie was in on our ruse."

Murry held Ryan's gaze for a moment, thinking about Nick Cummings. "So—what did she have to say?"

"You know, of course," Ryan continued, "Colbie had the

opportunity to meet Cummings at one of those high brow clubs outside the city—she posed as a friend of Maggie's, and Cummings was really the first person she talked to . . ."

"Where were you?"

"I ordered a drink, and hung out by the lounge near the restrooms—a perfect view of Maggie and her gaggle of friends."

"Including Cummings . . ."

Ryan nodded. "Including Cummings."

"How long did Colbie talk to him? Did he strike up the conversation, or did she?"

Ryan ran his fingers through his hair. "She did, I think." He looked at the Chief Inspector. "Why?"

"It just helps me to get a handle on the type of person Cummings was—that's all."

"Colbie said Cummings had a distinct South African accent, and that raised her antenna since she was scheduled to join me in Cape Town within a few weeks."

DCI Murray clicked his pen. "Okay—but that still doesn't tell me what I need to know. What did Maggie Burnett tell you about Nick Cummings? Does she have any idea why anyone—James—would want to kill him?"

Ryan leveled his eyes on the British Chief Inspector. "I'm getting to that—after Colbie left the club and met me at a coffee house around the corner, Colbie mentioned she had the distinct feeling Maggie was more attached to Nick Cummings than he was to her. At the club, Cummings up and left with barely saying goodbye to Maggie and—according to Colbie—Maggie was hurt, although she tried not to show it."

"Do you think she was in love with him?" Michaels asked. "If that's the case, chances are good Maggie Burnett knows a whole lot more than she let on when we questioned her . . ."

"Unfortunately, Inspector, I suspect that's the case . . ." He paused, ticking off the bullet points in his brain about what he needed to cover with DCI Murray and Inspector Michaels. "When I spoke to Maggie late last evening—as I said, after Colbie was settled in the hospital—I asked her why Nick Cummings was murdered. She didn't answer at first, but I explained it was in her best interest to come clean."

"Did she?"

"Yep—and, she admitted to having feelings for him beyond that of being just friends."

"That's it?"

Ryan took another drink of water, draining the water bottle. "She also said Cummings changed over the last couple of months . . ."

"Changed how?" Finally—something the Deputy Chief Inspector could chew on.

"According to her, he used to be a gentle, fun guy—but, as of a few months ago, he seemed edgy and he was always looking over his shoulder . . ."

DCI Murray flipped through his notes, thinking about what Ryan just told him. "Did she say why? What changed him?"

"I asked her, but she didn't know—but, she did say she thought it had to do with Conrad James. In a way, Cummings's knowing James seemed natural because James was a friend of her father's—Cummings was always around the estate. It made sense their paths would cross . . ."

"Did she have any idea Cummings was an artist?"

Ryan smiled slightly, recalling his conversation. "That's the thing, Chief Inspector—she didn't have any bloody idea!"

"But, she knew where he lived—are you telling me she was never inside his apartment?"

"That's exactly what I'm telling you . . ."

The three of them sat at the table thinking about how that could be.

"So, where does James come in?"

"Apparently, about a week before Cummings was found on the riverbank, Nick was agitated and he couldn't stop yammering about 'the guy in the damned tweed jacket.' Of course, Maggie knew instantly he was talking about James— it was all the bogus professor ever wore." Ryan shifted in his chair. "He also mentioned to Maggie that 'if he had half a chance, he was going back to Cape Town—such confessions, of course, uttered after several pints."

"Did she say why?" Inspector Michaels asked the question as he scribbled on his tiny notepad.

Ryan waited to make certain his revelation had maximum impact. "She said Cummings had a better gig with an import dealer in South Africa . . ."

Both British inspectors stopped writing, looking expectantly at Ryan.

Michaels already knew the answer to his question, but he figured he should ask anyway. "Blackwell?"

Ryan took the opportunity to let the question sink in, more for effect than anything else.

"Yep—none other . . ."

CHAPTER TWENTY-FIVE

" So—where are we?" Colbie carefully propped her legs up on the coffee table in her hotel room, Brian seated beside her. After three days in the hospital, she was ready to get back to work, and she couldn't wait to hear about the investigation progress. A meeting with DCI Murray and Inspector Michaels was scheduled for the following day, and she needed to know everything Ryan knew.

"Are you sure you're up for this?" Ryan glanced at her. "Shouldn't you be taking it easy?"

"Oh for God's sake, Ryan! I'm perfectly capable of understanding everything you have to say . . ."

"I see her hospital stay didn't slow her down much," Ryan teased, focusing on Brian with a slight grin.

"I tried—but you know her as well as I do. She's not going to rest until Nigel Blackwell is stuffed and cuffed . . ."

"As much as I hate to bring up what happened," Ryan

commented, "I need to know exactly what went on while you were inside Blackwell's home . . ."

Colbie clutched a mug of coffee, thinking about where to begin. "Well . . . you know we were at a table in his garden until the air took a chill . . ."

Ryan nodded.

"As the sun set, Nigel escorted me inside, and I actually had the feeling everything would be okay. In fact, I'm embarrassed to admit I had no idea he was planning on doing away with me—an 'in the library with the candlestick' sort of thing." Colbie smiled as she recalled her favorite game as a child, having no idea *Clue* would lead her to a career she dearly loved.

"What did you talk about?"

"Art, mostly—but, I recall there was a defining moment when I realized he had nothing to do with the murder of Nick Cummings. He said he didn't know him, but that was a pile of crap, I'm pretty sure—still, I have no doubt he didn't know anything about the forgery scam."

"Did he say anything about Conrad James?" Ryan glanced at Brian as Colbie's expression changed.

"Oh, he admitted they were friends, and had been since the time Samuel Burnett introduced them years ago—and, I'm certain he figured out we're here on an art theft case. That's why I didn't feel as if I were in danger . . ." Colbie paused for a sip. "It was when I asked him if he ever filed an art theft report with the cops that everything changed—that's when I told him about James's art scam and forgeries, as well as James's most likely spearheading the entire art theft ring . . ."

"What was his reaction?"

Colbie squirmed at the memory. "Not good—and it got worse when he realized Conrad James played him for a fool. I watched his face darken when he recognized James scammed his sorry ass . . ."

Ryan thought for a moment. "I bet that didn't go over well . . ."

Colbie nodded. "He offered me a fresh drink, suggesting we have one for the road before taking me back to the hotel." She glanced at Ryan. "I'll tell you one thing—after having time to think about it in the hospital, I'm convinced I'm not his first victim. I'll bet Nigel Blackwell is quite comfortable with getting rid of what he considers niggling irritants."

Colbie pictured Nigel's library as she recounted her story, her eyes signaling she was reliving every moment. She recalled asking Blackwell if she could take notes. "And," she continued, "I was shocked when he said he didn't mind—a smart move on his part." She wrinkled her forehead as she remembered a detail she hadn't previously considered. "That's not all—I dropped my pen on the floor and, as I picked it up, I noticed small stains on the rug . . ."

"Stains? What kind of stains? He doesn't seem the type to allow stains on his rug—at least, from what you told me." Brian glanced from Ryan to Colbie, trying to understand.

"Especially an expensive, hand-crafted rug . . ." Colbie agreed.

They sat, thinking about the implications of what she remembered.

"Blood?" Ryan asked.

"I'm not sure—but, I'm sure if the Metro Police send in a forensic team to Blackwell's house, they're going to have a field day. I feel it . . ."

Brian chuckled. "Then I'll put money on it . . ."

Colbie leaned over, and gave him a peck on the cheek. "I never thought I'd hear you say that," she admitted, laughing.

Ryan watched the exchange of affection, his heart a little worse for the wear. Since Brian's showing up, it was clear any affection Ryan felt toward Colbie could never be acted upon, the realization a stiff punch in the gut.

"Okay—rug stains. Got it . . . what else?" Ryan's fingers were poised on the keyboard of his laptop, ready to type everything Colbie said.

Colbie leaned forward, placing her coffee mug on the table. "And, that was about it—before he drugged me. So . . . from the time he gave me the fresh drink—my second in the library—my best guess is it took about ten minutes for the sedative to kick in . . ."

"What did you and Blackwell talk about as he waited? Did he do anything?"

"Nothing but sit across from me and admire his work— he was delighted with himself because he got the best of me. And, he was none too happy when he divulged he knew our true identities when we were still sitting in the garden." Colbie glanced at Ryan. "And, that's putting it mildly . . ."

"Was he pissed?"

"Yes—but he kept it in check. His tone, however, changed, and it was obvious he prepared for the conversation. I suspect he has a private investigator on his payroll—he baited me from the second I got there."

"It seems to me," Ryan observed, "we're going to nail him on attempted murder—if he knew your true identity, he made the decision before your arrival it would be your last day on earth . . ."

Brian shot Ryan a targeted glance. "A little harsh, don't you think?"

"Sorry—that was insensitive of me." Ryan reached in his pocket, then smeared lip balm on his lips. "I can't live without this stuff," he commented as he held up the tube for Colbie and Brian to see. A few moments later, he was ready to continue. "You know what I mean, Colbie—it speaks firmly to motive. All of us are aware how horrifically wrong a case can go if the prosecution fails to prove motive . . ."

"You're right about that—the whole purpose of my going to his home was so he would be in control. Familiarity breeds confidence, and he knew slipping me the sedative would be simple—and, it was . . ."

"That reminds me," Brian interjected. "Do you know the name of the sedative?"

Colbie shook her head. "I'll get all of my hospital records tomorrow—I want to speak with the doctors about whatever it was Blackwell gave me with respect to any adverse side effects." She paused, angered at the thought of how easy it was for her to lose control of herself—her body—at the hand of someone else.

"Good point—we should also have you checked out when we get home . . ." Brian grabbed her cup from the table. "Fill 'er up?"

"Please—and make it strong! I have a feeling the next twenty-four hours are going to be a bear . . ."

"You got it . . ." Brian disappeared into the small kitchen as Colbie and Ryan figured out their next step.

"Speaking of home . . ." Ryan began, "I'm guessing you're

traveling back with Brian?" He couldn't look at her.

"I think it's best, don't you? I hadn't told you, but when the lion was millimeters from my neck, I couldn't think of anyone, but Brian—I realized then our relationship isn't finished . . ." Colbie paused before continuing, knowing her next comment would end their friendship. "I realized, Ryan, my life with Brian is just beginning . . ."

Ryan's face blanched as he caught the full force of her words. "I know . . ."

Tears stung her eyes as she watched her friend grab his coat, and head toward the door.

"Where are you going?"

"I just need a little time . . ."

The door whooshed gently as is it closed.

****

"Nigel Blackwell?" Two Metro Police detectives as well as DCI Murray and Inspector Michaels stood at the massive front door, warrant in hand.

"Yes . . . how can I help you?" A small sweat blossomed on his forehead and temples.

"We have a warrant . . ." The Metro detective held up the tri-folded paper, handing it to Blackwell for inspection as he gestured to his officers. "Examine everything," he ordered as each descended on a different area of the house.

Nigel deftly unfolded the document, scanning its contents. "I see—may I ask why?"

"If you want to stay, I suggest you don't say anything—otherwise, my officer will escort you outside . . . " The Metro detective looked Blackwell in the eye. "But, if you think real hard, you may figure out a reason or two . . ." From the time he joined the force, the Metro detective knew Nigel Blackwell was as dirty as they come—and, he was just waiting for the right time to bring him down. Murder books existed for a string of missing women over the previous three years and, although they suspected, they couldn't connect the dots when it came to Blackwell. Then there was the rhino poaching—they came close to putting an end to it—as well as Blackwell—but, again, definitive proof was elusive. But, he knew—and he had no intention of passing up such a golden opportunity.

The forensic squad swarmed rooms on the first floor of his home, yet Nigel knew they would find nothing. *No one saw anything*, he thought as he watched a young woman examine the hand-knotted rug by the wing-backed chair. He stood casually in the foyer, an officer standing guard with the responsibility of making certain Blackwell didn't do something stupid. Nigel knew better than to attempt conversation—all he could do was watch, and listen.

And, plan.

Three hours later, computers and every other shred of possible evidence were carefully loaded into police vans. Colbie and Ryan watched from a safe distance in their car as officers made trip after trip from the house to the vehicles, each carrying something of interest. The largest item was the library rug, and Colbie felt a certain satisfaction as she watched two officers load it in their vehicle.

"That rug . . ." she commented, as she sat riveted, " . . . is going to be the nail in his coffin."

"You're pretty sure of that . . ." Ryan looked at his partner. "Why?"

"Yep—I'll bet money forensics will match DNA to someone—perhaps those missing girls . . ."

They continued to watch until the last bits of evidence made their way into boxes and Ziplock bags held by Metro Police officers. Finally, Nigel Blackwell emerged, accompanied by an officer on each side, hands cuffed behind his back. His charcoal-colored hair hung unflatteringly over one eye, the usual pomade ceasing to do its job.

"Look at him—I'll bet he has no idea I'm still alive . . ." Colbie watched as an officer placed his hand on the top of Blackwell's as he eased into the police cruiser.

"Probably—guys that arrogant and slick never seem to understand they aren't smarter than everyone else . . ."

Within minutes, a caravan of police cars left the estate, Nigel Blackwell staring out the side window of one as he made his last trip down the estate lane.

"I imagine he'll post bond," Ryan commented as he brought up the rear of the caravan.

"Probably—but, I have a feeling he knows it's over. Once we find Conrad James . . . or, once we find out what happened to him, Nigel Blackwell's days as a free man are numbered."

Neither spoke as they headed back to their hotel— things changed, and both knew it. Colbie was certain when their investigation wrapped, it would be the last time they worked together. Figuring he knew the same, she stole a look at Ryan as he focused on the road, her eyes starting to tear. *Goodbye, my friend*, she thought as they arrived on the outskirts of Cape Town.

Goodbye . . .

Chapter Twenty-six

Tammy poked her head in the door. "Hey, Boss! Long time no see!" There was no mistaking the young mom was thrilled Colbie arrived home safely.

"Hey, you!" Colbie extended her arms for a welcome-home hug. "I can't believe we're finally home!"

"When did you get back? And, why didn't you tell me you were coming?"

"Because I really wasn't sure when we would return—there was a lot to wrap up before we left Cape Town." Colbie paused for a second, completely aware of her assistant's part in their investigation. "And, if it weren't for you . . ."

"Oh, stop—I didn't do anything . . ."

"Really? The way I remember it, if you hadn't taken the initiative to stop by the house, there might well be a different ending . . ." Colbie held Tammy's gaze. "I'm certain I can never repay you . . ."

Tammy dramatically thought for a moment before answering. "Hmmm . . . how about a raise?"

Colbie laughed, hugging Tammy again, only harder. "Now—have a seat. The story I have to tell is quite the heady cocktail of intrigue . . .

****

They sat on the back patio with freshly opened bottles of beer, a basket of buffalo wings between them.

"These are impossible to eat," Colbie laughed as she grabbed a wing, snapping it apart at its joint. "Remind me never to devour these in front of people we don't know . . ."

Brian raised his bottle, chuckling at the sight of a bit of blue cheese that didn't quite make it into her mouth. "Always eat wings in the company of those who love you . . ."

Colbie met his toast, then placed the bottle on the table between the two Adirondack chairs. "It's interesting, isn't it?"

"What's that?"

"Oh, I don't know—since we got back from Cape Town, I can't remember a time when I've felt more peaceful. Happier. Back to the person I was years ago . . ."

Brian shifted in his chair so he could get a better look at

the woman he nearly lost. "Why do you think that is?"

"Well—you have to admit when I first took the gig with Ryan, you and I weren't in the best place . . ." She hesitated, unsure if her words could possibly explain how she felt. "And, until Cape Town, I had no idea much of it was my fault . . ."

"Hold on—I think you're being a little too hard on yourself. I sure as hell didn't make things easy for you . . ."

"True—but, the fact is if I hadn't been so hell bent on carving out a successful career for myself, none of this would have happened." She thought back to prior years—years when she forced her desires on Brian without regard to what was best for him.

"How about if both of us take responsibility? That's seems a fair way to go . . ." He grinned at Colbie knowing they weathered what was much more than a 'bump in the road' of their relationship. She was what he wanted.

What he needed.

They sat silently, thinking about the past months as well as how much their lives changed. Yes, they made progress, but each knew they had much work to do if they were to get past their hurt.

"So," Brian interrupted her thoughts, "when you called this afternoon, you said you heard from the gents in Cape Town . . ."

Colbie reached for another wing. "I did—it seems they have enough to put Nigel Blackwell away for a very long time."

"Seriously? That sure didn't take them much time—we left only a few months ago . . ."

"I know—it seems that way to me, too. But, according to DCI Murray, Blackwell wanted to cut a deal when he learned they figured out what happened to Conrad James . . ."

"Oh, yeah—I forgot about him . . ."

"I'm sure Nigel never saw it coming—as far as he was concerned, he was untouchable . . ."

Brian ripped open a wet nap, licked his fingers, then wiped them clean. "So—what did happen to Conrad James? From what you told me, he's kind of been the loose end in all of this . . ."

"Yep—according to his wife, he left for Australia just as we were on his tail . . ."

"And, I take it, that's not the case . . ."

"Nope—I found out today he's another victim of Nigel Blackwell . . ."

Brian paused, mid-swig. "No shit? Did they find his body?"

"Not quite—remember when you rescued me at the game reserve?"

Brian cocked an eyebrow. "Remember? Of course, I remember!"

"Well, as I understand it, when the police investigated where it went down, they found something of interest . . ." She was enjoying keeping Brian wondering—it felt good to tease him without his getting bent out of shape.

"Geez! Get on with it, already!" He swiped at his mouth with a napkin, then sat back in his chair with a good-natured smile.

"Okay, okay! I'm just giving you jazz! They found something belonging to Conrad James . . . a chunk of tweed fabric that his wife identified as the tweed of her husband's jacket."

"That's a little thin, isn't it? How are they going to prove it belonged to James?"

"Well, you're right about that—technically—the patch of tweed could belong to anyone. However, my guess is they'll lift DNA from it, and it will come back as James's . . ."

Brian was quiet for a moment as he considered Colbie's convoluted case. He was proud of her for taking the investigation to the next level—she told him of her visions, especially that of the lion and, in retrospect, all of them fell into place. He no longer doubted her intuitive abilities and, if they were to be partners in life, he had to accept her as she was—a profiler who could turn a case up on end just because she has a feeling.

"So, you're saying Nigel Blackwell disposed of Conrad James the same way he tried to dispose of you . . ."

"Exactly. And, as I suspected, after a thorough search of the area, they found items they haven't identified yet . . ."

Brian eyed his girlfriend. "What do you think they are? I can tell by looking at you there's something swimming around in that brain of yours . . ."

Colbie drew a long breath, then exhaled slowly. "Those missing girls—of course, I don't know that for sure, but it's a pretty good guess . . ."

They sat quietly, both aware the art theft investigation came to an unceremonious close. Brian reached over the chicken wings to take Colbie's hand.

"Are you ready?" he asked.

"Ready? Ready for what?"

"Us—are you ready for us?" He gripped her hand, letting her know he wouldn't let go.

Colbie smiled. "I've never been more ready . . ."

Faith Wood
CPS, Behaviorist

Faith Wood is a Behaviorist, Certified Professional Speaker, Hypnotist, and Handwriting Analyst. Her interest in Behavior Psychology blossomed during her law enforcement career when it occurred to her if she knew what people really wanted, as well as motives behind their actions, she would be more effective in work and life. So, she hung up her cuffs, trading them in for traveling the world speaking to audiences to help them better understand human behaviors as well as how they impact others. Wood speaks about how to tap into the area of the brain that controls actions which, in turn, have a tendency to adjust perceptions, thereby launching a more empowered life.

Faith Wood touches lives, leaving a lasting impression. A mother of four, she lives with her husband in Vernon, British Columbia, Canada.

To learn more about her as well as her professional services, please visit her website and Facebook fan page. Worldwide, she helps people change their lives, and she can help you.

Unleash the power of Faith!

www.faithwood.com

https://www.facebook.com/Inspiring-Minds-Consulting-82419359589/

PROFESSIONAL ACKNOWLEDGMENTS

CHRYSALIS PUBLISHING AUTHOR SERVICES

L.A. O'NEIL, Editor
chrysalispub@gmail.com

COVER ART DESIGN

JEN KRAMP
jenkramp@gmail.com

Made in the USA
Charleston, SC
21 August 2016